W9-AZV-012

"I suspect I was already developing a weakness for you, an inexplicable desire to know you better."

"Inexplicable, huh?" His icy fingers suddenly seemed to scorch Linnet's wrist. She felt her pulse throbbing under his touch. She caught herself leaning back to gaze up at him.

"I'd never met a human female I couldn't fascinate at a glance. Do you wonder that I responded to the challenge?" Max's head bent toward hers.

She watched him with wide eyes and parted lips. "Just a challenge?"

"A distraction," he muttered. "Definitely a weakness." Just before his mouth would have touched hers, he straightened. "A weakness for both of us. Remember our resolution."

Dear Reader,

Make way for spring—and room on your shelf for six must-reads from Silhouette Intimate Moments! Justine Davis bursts onto the scene with another page-turner from her miniseries REDSTONE, INCORPORATED. In *Second-Chance Hero*, a struggling single mother finds herself in danger, having to confront past demons and the man who haunts her waking dreams. Gifted storyteller Ingrid Weaver delights us with *The Angel and the Outlaw*, which begins her miniseries PAYBACK. Here, a rifle-wielding heroine does more than seek revenge—she dazzles a hot-blooded hero into joining her on her mission. Don't miss it!

Can the enemy's daughter seduce a sexy and hardened soldier? Find out in Cindy Dees's latest CHARLIE SQUAD romance, *Her Secret Agent Man*. In Frances Housden's *Stranded with a Stranger*, part of her INTERNATIONAL AFFAIRS miniseries, a determined heroine investigates her sister's murder by tackling Mount Everest and its brutal challenges. Will her charismatic guide be the key to solving this gripping mystery?

You'll get swept away by Margaret Carter's *Embracing Darkness*, about a heart-stopping vampire whose torment is falling for a woman he can't have. Will these two forbidden lovers overcome the limits of mortality—not to mention a cold-blooded killer's treachery—to be together? Newcomer Dianna Love Snell pulls no punches in *Worth Every Risk*, which features a DEA agent who discovers a beautiful stowaway on his plane. She could be trouble…or the woman he's been waiting for.

I'm thrilled to bring you six suspenseful and soul-stirring romances from these talented authors. After you enjoy this month's lineup, be sure to return for another month of unforgettable characters that face life's extraordinary odds. Only in Silhouette Intimate Moments!

Happy reading,

Patience Smith
Associate Senior Editor

Please address questions and book requests to:
Silhouette Reader Service
U.S.: 3010 Walden Ave., P.O. Box 1325, Buffalo, NY 14269
Canadian: P.O. Box 609, Fort Erie, Ont. L2A 5X3

Embracing Darkness
MARGARET CARTER

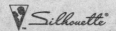

INTIMATE MOMENTS™
Published by Silhouette Books
America's Publisher of Contemporary Romance

If you purchased this book without a cover you should be aware that this book is stolen property. It was reported as "unsold and destroyed" to the publisher, and neither the author nor the publisher has received any payment for this "stripped book."

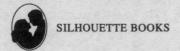 SILHOUETTE BOOKS

ISBN 0-373-27425-4

EMBRACING DARKNESS

Copyright © 2005 by Margaret L. Carter

All rights reserved. Except for use in any review, the reproduction or utilization of this work in whole or in part in any form by any electronic, mechanical or other means, now known or hereafter invented, including xerography, photocopying and recording, or in any information storage or retrieval system, is forbidden without the written permission of the editorial office, Silhouette Books, 233 Broadway, New York, NY 10279 U.S.A.

All characters in this book have no existence outside the imagination of the author and have no relation whatsoever to anyone bearing the same name or names. They are not even distantly inspired by any individual known or unknown to the author, and all incidents are pure invention.

This edition published by arrangement with Harlequin Books S.A.

® and TM are trademarks of Harlequin Books S.A., used under license. Trademarks indicated with ® are registered in the United States Patent and Trademark Office, the Canadian Trade Marks Office and in other countries.

Visit Silhouette Books at www.eHarlequin.com

Printed in U.S.A.

MARGARET CARTER

read Bram Stoker's *Dracula* when she was twelve, and it changed her life. She put pen to paper to write the vampire's side of the story, and her love for writing paranormal romances was born. She happily admits that her Ph.D. in English included a dissertation that featured a chapter on *Dracula*.

Even with a busy schedule teaching college English, working part-time as a legislative proofreader and traveling with her U.S. Navy captain husband, she miraculously found the time to publish books and articles on the supernatural in literature, including a vampire bibliography and, most recently, *Different Blood: The Vampire as Alien*. Her first novel, *Shadow of the Beast*, a werewolf tale, was followed by the Eppie Award-winning vampire novel *Dark Changeling*.

She and her husband live in Maryland, near the setting for her first Intimate Moments book, *Embracing Darkness*, and close to her four sons, five grandchildren, three cats and a Saint Bernard. You can visit her online at www.MargaretLCarter.com.

Dedicated with gratitude to Sandy, my critique partner.
I couldn't have done it without you!

Chapter 1

No sign of life stirred inside the building below. Maxwell Tremayne soared on silken wings, circling the three-story split-level. He didn't worry about chance observers, since the house sat off the road in the center of a wooded lot. The vacant driveway only confirmed the emptiness his inhuman senses detected. Had the owner left temporarily or permanently? *Permanently, if she has any discretion,* he reflected. Not that her recent behavior suggested any.

He scanned the trees around the house. The sun had barely set, and its afterglow made his head ache and his eyes sting. He knew he shouldn't have shape-shifted until full dark, but his patience had worn out. From this vantage point he would notice at once if his quarry, or anyone else, showed up. Amid random heat traces that he identified as small animals, a motionless patch of deeper red caught his eye. A human intruder. Max spiraled lower, shrouding himself in a psychic veil that rendered him invisible to human eyes. Through the summer-green leaves, he glimpsed a woman crouching near the edge of the woods. She was watching the front of the house with a pair of binoculars.

Not a casual hiker, then, but someone who, like him, took a particular interest in this place. Still veiled, Max glided toward her. He landed a few yards away and let his body melt into its wingless, fully human shape.

The female's scent and the crackling of her aura conveyed fear, frustration and tightly reined anger. Any ephemeral who knew the truth about that house would be wise to fear its owner, but the other emotions puzzled him, as did her intense watchfulness. She swatted a mosquito just below the cuff of her denim shorts without shifting her eyes from the binoculars.

His nostrils flared, savoring the salty tang of her flesh. The humidity made her T-shirt cling to her breasts. Her soft curves implied a wholesome disdain for obsessive dieting. The sweetness of her natural fragrance confirmed that sign of robust health. She had pale golden hair, a color never found in his own species. Cropped to just above her shoulders, it left her neck bare. If he had time for self-indulgence—

But I don't. He shook his head, impatient with his own woolgathering. No matter how appetizing this ephemeral might be in other circumstances, here and now she presented a threat to his mission. He had to get rid of her.

Twilight promised some relief from the June heat but meant that nightfall would soon put an end to her surveillance. Linnet Carroll wiped her damp forehead with the back of her hand. So far she hadn't accomplished anything more today than the day before. The house looked deserted. Behind her she heard an occasional car on the two-lane road that wound through this expensive neighborhood. Beyond the house, rays of sunset on the Severn River gleamed through the trees.

What do I expect to find, anyway? I'm no detective. Still, just because the police were acting like the obtuse cops in a TV mystery didn't mean she had to give up on her prime suspect. The memory of her niece Deanna's funeral, only two days past, haunted her too vividly for such easy surrender. Linnet clutched her bronze ankh necklace, a gift from Deanna and her boyfriend, Anthony.

After a sip from the water bottle hooked to the belt of her shorts, she again raised the binoculars that dangled around her neck and stared at the empty driveway with fresh determination. The woman had to come home eventually, didn't she?

Leaves rustled a few feet to Linnet's right. She cast a quick glance sideways. Nothing, not even a bird. The faint sound teased her ears again. Not quite a rustle, but a mere stirring, as if from a light breeze, though the air felt still. She shook her head. *Quit spooking yourself.*

Seconds later, a branch swayed at the edge of her vision. She thought she glimpsed a flash of red through the leaves. She dropped the binoculars and snapped her head around. A man stood there.

Holding the branch out of his way, he took a long stride closer.

Linnet rocked back on her heels. She had to gulp in air before she could speak. "Where did you come from?"

He responded only with a thin smile. Tilting her head back, she stared up at him. He loomed over her. For an instant the fading daylight sparked a glint of crimson in his eyes. Immediately the illusion vanished, though his gaze became no less formidable under the dark eyebrows. A mane of black hair curled from his high forehead to just below his ears. He wore black jeans and no shirt. Yet his bare chest was marble pale rather than tan.

"What do you want?" Her voice came out as an embarrassing squeak. *Some intrepid avenger!* She grabbed the nearest low-hanging limb to pull herself upright. The man appeared a foot taller than her own five feet five. Though lean, he surely had the strength to overpower her, in case he turned out to be a homicidal maniac. Not that he looked like one.

Well, neither did Ted Bundy, so they said.

"I want to speak with you." Gazing directly into her eyes, he took another step toward her.

Suddenly light-headed, she backed up, slipped and stumbled. He caught her by both arms. With her pulse racing, she resisted the impulse to struggle against his grip. As she'd expected, his strength far outclassed hers. His cool fingers held her steady with no apparent effort.

"Speak about what?" To Linnet's satisfaction, her voice sounded normal this time. Never mind that her eyes wandered to the inverted triangle of fine dark hairs descending from midchest to his waistband.

"I want to know what you're keeping watch for. And you needn't claim it's local songbirds, because I won't believe you." His level tone gave no indication of the emotions behind it.

Linnet swallowed a growing lump of nervousness. "What makes that any of your business?"

His thumbs traced slow circles on her bare forearms. "Because I can't have you accidentally interfering with my...business." His eyes captured hers. "It will be dark soon, anyway. You may as well give up and go home. For your own good." His voice caressed her as smoothly as his touch.

"I can't do that," she whispered. Her skin prickled as if a chill breeze had swept over her. Now he clasped her arms loosely, but she couldn't conjure up the will to break away. Her right hand, though, groped for the ankh at her throat. The pressure of the metal in her palm dissolved the mist gathering in her brain. "I need to be here. It's important."

The man's bristling eyebrows arched in apparent surprise. "Not as important as my reasons, and you're in the way. Go home. Resume your vigil tomorrow, if you must."

Though his touch remained light, she felt pressure on her mind, as if his eyes pierced and impaled her. She squeezed the pendant tighter, and the pressure receded. "No. I might miss her if she comes back."

"Nola Grant?" He let go of her arms but didn't move otherwise.

"You know her?" If this man was a friend of Nola's, Linnet definitely didn't want to stay within a mile of him.

"By reputation. Enough to know you'd be wise to keep out of her path."

The image of Deanna's pale, blank face as she'd seen it at the medical examiner's office crowded into Linnet's mind. "Too late for that."

"Why?"

The softly breathed question insinuated past her defenses. The answer leaped out before she realized she'd begun to speak. "That woman murdered my niece."

"Indeed?" He showed no surprise at that declaration. His eyes bored into hers until she could barely keep from squirming. Finally he said, "Would your niece be named Deanna?"

Linnet jerked as if he'd slapped her. "How do you…" She gaped at the man in the fading light. She'd been too flustered at first for a close examination of the satanic brows and aquiline nose, but now she realized he looked familiar. And after a few seconds' concentration, she guessed why. "You must be Anthony's—what? You're too young to be his father."

With a sardonic smile, the man said, "You think so? No, I'm not his father. Anthony was my younger brother. His latest letters were full of that irresistible girl he met at one of Nola's…soirees." The remark held a tinge of bitterness.

"Orgies, you mean? Don't bother being delicate with me."

He acknowledged the correction with a nod. "Very well. You think Nola killed your niece and my brother—"

"I know she did! The police won't listen to me." Linnet tore her eyes away from his for a glance at the house. It still looked deserted. Despite the gathering twilight, its windows stayed dark.

He turned to follow the direction of her gaze. "So you're playing detective? It won't do you any good. Nola isn't here."

Linnet's shoulders sagged. "You were spying on the place, too."

"I suspect she has relocated permanently."

"Then I'll break in. She might've left clues."

"I have to admire your determination, but not your judgment." With one hand on her shoulder, he turned her to face him again and tilted her head with his other hand. Again his touch sent cool ripples down her spine. "Give up. You're only feeding your own grief. Go away."

She pressed her open palm to her chest, feeling the outline of Deanna's pendant. "No."

"Stubborn female, do I have to—" He fell silent, turning his head as if listening.

A second later Linnet heard the sound, too, a car engine. Headlights angled into the driveway of Nola Grant's house. A dark hatchback slowed to a stop, and the lights and motor cut off. A lanky man stepped out.

Linnet raised the binoculars to peer through them. The newcomer, about Deanna's age, wore dark jeans and a black T-shirt with the sleeves chopped off. A silver earring dangled from one ear. A tiger-striped mohawk topped off the ensemble. Though Linnet didn't think she'd met this particular young man, she recognized the type.

"It's one of the purple-haired people," she said.

The man beside her gave her a perplexed frown. "His hair is orange and black."

"That's just what I call them, the crowd Deanna started running with last year, because the first guy she brought home had purple hair. I don't have anything against those Goth kids in general, but some of them dragged her into Nola's group."

"So this boy is one of the group."

"Looks like it." She continued watching through the binoculars as the tiger-haired man stalked up to the front door, knocked and rattled the knob. To Linnet's surprise, when he got no answer he extracted a key ring from his jeans and unlocked the door. "Hey, he's got a key." She lowered the binoculars and started working her way down the hillside, fuming at the need to watch out for roots and underbrush.

Anthony's brother kept pace with her. "Where are you going?"

"Where does it look like?" she whispered, though she doubted that the man inside the house could hear them. "To get a closer look. If Nola gave that guy a key, maybe he knows where she went."

"And you plan to capture him and administer the third degree, I suppose."

"You've got a better idea?" Creeping toward the side of the house, clutching branches for support, she wondered why she even bothered to talk to the man. If he did have any useful ideas, it wasn't likely he would share them. He'd done little so far except amuse himself with sarcasm at her expense.

By the time the ground leveled off, Linnet's breath came in rapid gasps, from nervousness as much as exertion. The intruder hadn't reappeared yet. She paused uncertainly in the side yard, scanning the windows. Light seeped between one pair of curtains, probably in the living room. "Wonder what he's doing there?" She kept her voice low.

Her unwanted companion responded in a barely audible

whisper, "Perhaps the same thing we're doing, searching for Nola."

They'd watched for less than a minute before the front door opened and the tiger-haired man stormed out. He got into his car, slammed the door and gunned the engine.

The man beside Linnet turned and loped through the trees toward the point where the private drive curved out of sight. Struggling in his wake, she cursed under her breath at his graceful movement over terrain that forced her to lurch and stumble. Under the trees, she could barely keep him in sight. Fortunately his unclad torso provided a light patch to follow in the thickening darkness.

When she reached the gravel-surfaced lane, the tiger-haired boy's car roared past. A second later she heard another car door open and close, then caught sight of a pale-toned compact parked at the edge of the curve. She sprinted to it and flung open the passenger door just as Anthony's brother switched on the ignition.

He glowered at her. "What the devil do you think you're doing? Get out!"

"No way!" She fastened the seat belt. "Better get moving or you'll lose him."

"Not when he'll have to wait for an opening in the Route 50 traffic." He stared at her in that intense manner she had noticed several times before, as if he expected to dislodge her by sheer force of will. "Get out of this car. I am not taking you with me."

Though his eyes felt like fingers caressing her flushed cheeks, she fought off the impulse to obey him. "What'll you do, push me out on my rear?" On second thought, Linnet didn't put it past him to do just that. "If you try it, I'll write down your license plate and sic the police on you."

With a sound remarkably like a growl, he shoved the gear-shift into first and accelerated toward the highway. "Damn it, I can't waste time on this!"

Linnet stifled a shriek when she realized he hadn't turned on the headlights. Within a couple of minutes he slowed down, and she saw the other car's taillights just ahead. Sure enough, it was idling at the junction with Route 50. When it pulled into traffic, Linnet's companion turned on his lights and followed, barely missing an oncoming van. This time she did scream, squeezing her eyes shut and clutching the armrest.

"Keep quiet," the driver snarled.

"I'm trying to catch Deanna's killer," she said. "Not get killed myself."

"So you don't trust my driving skills?" The anger had faded from his voice, replaced by an unexpected tinge of humor.

"How could I?" She ventured a peek and was relieved to see that he'd merged smoothly into the flow of traffic. Their quarry hovered two or three car lengths ahead. She removed the binoculars thumping against her chest and placed them in the back seat. "I don't know a thing about you. Not even your name."

"Max Tremayne."

"I'm Linnet Carroll. Nice to meet you, Mr. Tremayne." *Now, if that doesn't take the cake for ridiculous statements,* she thought. "Uh—I'm sorry about Anthony. He seemed to be good for Deanna." *Until staying with him got her killed, anyway.*

"Indeed?" The chill in his voice puzzled her. "You may as well call me Max, if you're going to force yourself on me."

"Look here, Mr. Max Tremayne, I have just as much right to track down that woman as you do. My niece is dead, too, remember."

"The difference is that I have the power to deal with Nola. You'll do nothing but get in the way."

Reduced to silence, Linnet folded her arms and glared out

the windshield. By the time the other car switched over to Route 2, also congested with evening traffic, her outrage had simmered down enough to let her speak again. "If you think I'm so useless, what's your great plan? What are you going to do with the guy when we catch him?"

"Make him tell me all he can about Nola's present whereabouts—and then silence him."

Chapter 2

His words hit her like a punch to the stomach. "You don't mean kill him?"

Max gave her a long stare before turning his attention back to the traffic-clogged highway. "Not if I can avoid it."

For the first time since jumping into the car, Linnet wondered whether she'd been smart to grab a ride with a man she knew nothing about. "Do you think this guy had anything to do with—" She couldn't force the words past the lump in her throat.

"The murders of my brother and your niece? If you're plotting revenge for the act, you shouldn't be too squeamish to mention it."

"Not revenge. Justice." Her chest felt so tight she had to gulp air before continuing. "And don't talk to me about squeamishness. I had to identify both of them—Deanna *and* Anthony. Where were you?"

He showed no spark of anger at her rudeness. His tone of

voice just became flatter. "I learned about his death only two days ago. An acquaintance of mine in this area read the newspaper article and notified me. I claimed Anthony's body yesterday and arranged the cremation."

"I'm sorry," Linnet whispered.

Max continued as if she hadn't spoken, "I came looking for Nola as soon as I could and found her already gone."

"So you agree with me! She killed them."

"I don't believe she did it by her own hand," he said. The tiger-haired man's car cut right through a break in traffic. Max whipped into the right lane and followed. "At the same time, I have no doubt she's responsible."

Linnet's heart jumped. She swallowed the acid that welled up in her throat. "The police wouldn't take me seriously. Oh, they questioned her once, and the detective even gave me two minutes on the phone when I made a follow-up call." She remembered the man's patronizingly soothing voice. "He said they were convinced Nola Grant had nothing to do with the crime, so I should stop bugging him about her. Oh, he used more polite language, but that's what he meant."

"I'm not surprised she managed to persuade him of her innocence. Why don't you believe it?"

"Nobody else had a motive. After Deanna broke away from Nola's gang and moved in with Anthony, they told me they were worried about Nola's reaction. That's when Deanna gave me this." Linnet clutched the ankh with one hand while wiping away the sting of tears with the other. "It was Anthony's idea. He even said I should watch out for her—Nola—and this would protect me from her."

"Protect you?" came Max's sharp response. "He used that word?"

"Yes. Protect me against Nola and anybody like her, he said."

"Did he emphasize this promise? Look into your eyes and repeat it once or twice?"

And this is important, why? Max's assurance that he agreed with her suspicions had made Linnet start to trust him, but now she veered back to the idea that he might be slightly deranged. "Well, yeah. That didn't make much sense, but I figured it proved how worried he was." She saw no reason to mention the fact that she had only a hazy memory of the whole conversation. She had the impression that Anthony had lectured her at length on the subject, yet she drew a blank trying to recall what he'd said.

"I see." After a brief silence, he said, "You identified Anthony? Then you witnessed…?"

"Not much, thank heaven." Her stomach lurched. She breathed deeply until the nausea subsided. "They didn't make me look at anything except the faces."

She flashed on a memory of that night at the medical examiner's office. The frigid room with a hospital smell that barely disguised an earthy odor in the background. The metal drawers lining the wall. She had drawn shallow breaths through her mouth, praying not to vomit or faint. The antiseptic in the air had made her nose and tongue feel numb. A middle-aged black man in a lab coat had pulled out the drawer. Above the folded-back sheet she'd seen Dee's waxpale face, the muscles slack in death, so that she had no more expression than a mannequin.

Linnet remembered the attendant gripping her elbow to steady her while she nodded and stammered, "That's her—Deanna—that's her." After he'd slid that drawer into its slot, he'd pulled out the one where Anthony lay and turned down the cover to just below the chin. She hadn't asked whether the neck under the sheet had been reattached to the torso yet. She had only confirmed the boy's identity and stumbled out, her own head feeling hardly in contact with the rest of her body.

Now the mental image of Anthony's lifeless face brought

on a surge of faintness. She leaned over to rest her forehead on her knees until the grayness cleared from her vision. When she sat up, Max gave her a quick glance but said nothing.

He ran a yellow light and whipped in and out of holes in traffic where Linnet wouldn't have suspected the car could fit. She gripped the armrest and swallowed another screech of alarm. Aside from a few blaring horns behind them, though, they continued unscathed, keeping the other car just barely in sight. Shortly it turned off the highway and drove past a shopping center into a maze of residential streets.

"Forgive my curiosity," said Max, sounding not in the least contrite, "but why are you undertaking this quest? Why not your niece's parents?"

The faintly sarcastic edge in the word "quest" made her skin prickle with annoyance. She reminded herself that people reacted to grief differently. She should make allowances for the man. "Deanna lived with me for the past two years, ever since she started college. That is, until she moved in with Anthony."

Max obviously didn't miss the accusatory tone she couldn't filter out of that last sentence. "Believe me, I was as unhappy about that situation as you must have been. If those two hadn't insisted on taking that step, they would probably be alive tonight."

Since she agreed with that judgment, Linnet didn't say anything. Instead, she wiped her eyes and breathed deeply to settle her temper. By now she couldn't see anything of the car ahead except fleeting glimpses of taillights. She could only trust that Max was still tracking the right vehicle through the darkened streets. When she'd reburied her outrage beneath the surface of her mind, she dug her glasses out of the belt pouch and put them on to peer through the windshield. The view didn't improve.

"Don't worry, I haven't lost him," said Max, as if reading her thoughts.

Linnet settled back and folded her arms, casting a sidelong look at her companion. He drove with both hands tightly clenched on the wheel, occasionally flexing his fingers before returning them to the same white-knuckled grip.

After several minutes of silence, she ventured, "I liked Anthony. Compared to the rest of that crowd, he seemed so normal."

"Really?" She couldn't interpret Max's brief smile.

"Sure, his hair was a little long, but that didn't bother me. At least it wasn't two-toned or half shaved off. And as far as I could see, he didn't have any tattoos or a single pierced body part."

"No, that wouldn't have suited him at all."

"Mainly, he distracted Deanna from Nola. Yeah, in my book your brother was a breath of fresh air."

A block ahead, the car they were following turned right at a convenience store. Unhurried, Max did the same, maintaining the same cautious distance. Their quarry slowed down to circle the parking lot of a sprawling, one-story apartment complex, divided into six-unit buildings. With no other traffic to provide cover, Max had to drop back almost out of sight. He switched off the headlights again, but this time Linnet didn't freak out. In the well-illuminated lot, she didn't worry about having an accident at this low speed.

"In our…family," he said, "it's customary to act as mentor to one's sister's children. We're unlike most Americans in that respect, though. How did you get into that situation?"

"I'm eight years younger than Robin—Deanna's mother. I was more like a big sister than an aunt to Dee. When she graduated from high school, her folks were having such a rough time with her that it made sense to let her move in with me while she went to college. Plus, I live in College Park, not too far from the University of Maryland campus, so she didn't have to choose between a long commute from Baltimore or paying a bundle for a dorm room."

"So you took her in." He slowed the car to a crawl and gestured toward the row of parking spaces just ahead. The tiger-haired boy disembarked from his car and walked, keys in hand, to an end unit, where he ducked inside after a nervous glance over his shoulder. Max sped up and drove around the curve to the back of the complex.

"She was a good kid, really. The rebellious pose was mostly a surface thing to bug her folks. Never gave me any trouble until she got sucked into Nola's entourage, less than six months ago. That's when her grades went down the tubes. I suspected drugs but never found any evidence."

"No, you wouldn't." Max pulled into a vacant space and cut off the engine. "Nola wouldn't have let any member of her 'entourage' take drugs. She wanted them healthy."

"For what? Her orgies?" Her stomach churned. That scenario sounded almost as bad as a drug ring.

"Not exactly." He turned on the dome light. "Now, Linnet, look at me." He hadn't addressed her by name before, and the syllables seemed to linger on his tongue as if he were tasting them. His voice sent a shiver through her despite the circumstances.

She automatically obeyed him. For a second she felt dizzy, about to drown in his unblinking gaze. She half-consciously fingered the ankh around her neck, and Max's face snapped back into focus. "What do we do now?"

"You sit here quietly, while I interrogate that young man."

Linnet shook her head. "Forget that. I'm sticking with you every step of the way."

"Damn it, woman, I don't need you underfoot." To her surprise, he reached up to stroke her hair with gentle fingertips. She froze. In a softer tone, he said, "Listen to me, please. You will feel much better if you relax and wait here peacefully until I'm finished."

Yes, maybe she would. She felt worn-out from an afternoon of spying on Nola's house, followed by an unexpected car chase. She did need to rest, just close her eyes for a minute—

No, I don't! Was the man trying to hypnotize her? "Not a chance. I didn't take my life in my hands riding with you so I could wait in the car. We're going in together. I have as much right to question that guy as you do."

"It's a matter of efficiency, not right. I can get answers that you cannot."

Given how she'd nearly caved in a minute earlier, Linnet almost believed he could. "Well, if we're talking about efficiency, how do you figure on getting to him? You think he'll just let a strange man into his house? You'll have to barge in and maybe attract a lot of attention from the neighbors."

"Your point?"

"I can probably persuade him to open the door. He won't feel threatened by a woman, especially when I mention that I'm Deanna's aunt. And once he lets down his guard, you can come in and do your interrogation thing." She glared at him. "If he doesn't spook the moment he sees a man with no shirt right behind me."

Max leaned back in the driver's seat, scanning her as if evaluating her fitness as a decoy. "A valid suggestion. You do look fairly harmless."

Gee, thanks. "Another point—I can still call the cops on you. The authorities wouldn't take kindly to people snooping around a suspect's house. I bet you don't want them interfering with your private investigation, either."

He let out a clearly exasperated sigh. "Very well, I accept your suggestion. But for hell's sake, don't get in my way once my...interrogation begins." He turned off the dome light and reached into the back seat for a short-sleeved shirt, which he shrugged into and partially buttoned. "Tell me one thing, though. Why do you feel you must do this personally? You aren't a detective any more than I am."

"Because it's my fault." She inhaled a steadying breath, determined not to get weepy again.

His eyebrows arched. "What is?"

"Deanna's death. Robin said having her live with me would end up as a disaster, and she was right. I can blame Anthony for not protecting Dee, but I'm the one who didn't stop her from hanging out with Nola in the first place. I'm the one who let her move in with Anthony, which got her killed."

"By that logic," he said, "I ought to blame you for Anthony's death, as well. Have you heard me say anything of the kind?" He gave her shoulder a quick, firm squeeze. "Now, if your peculiar sense of responsibility compels you to go through with this, pull yourself together. I can't have an over-emotional, scatterbrained decoy."

Her mood snapped from depression to annoyance. "My brain's no more scattered than yours. Let's get it over with."

"Yes, let's discover what really got those two killed." He got out of the car, took a couple of long strides, then paused for her to catch up.

She scanned the car for a few seconds, noting the color and memorizing the license plate, then hurried after Max. When they came within sight of their target's apartment, he faded into the shadow of a tall bush. "Go ahead," he whispered almost inaudibly. "Once you're inside, make sure he doesn't lock the door again. I'll come in immediately after you."

Linnet walked up to the front stoop feeling less confident than she had when arguing with her exasperating coconspirator. She would probably squeak like a mouse when she tried to spin some plausible excuse for her visit. But she wasn't about to back down after making bold noises to Max. No doorbell. She knocked.

The door opened to the length of the chain. The young man peered through the crack. "Yeah?"

Might as well state her mission straight-out, before he got impatient and slammed the door in her face. "Can I please talk to you for a few minutes? I'm Linnet Carroll."

He didn't look hostile, but he didn't relax, either. "Should I know you?"

"I'm Deanna's aunt."

"Oh, my God."

"You knew her, didn't you? Please let me in." Somehow she kept her voice from shaking, even though her pulse was racing.

"What do you think I can— Okay, all right, come on." His hand trembled as he unhooked the chain. Now that she saw him up close, she noticed a tattoo of some kind of bird on his forearm.

She slipped inside, watching his face as she said, "I have so many questions. I just need to talk to one of Deanna's friends."

He flushed. "I didn't know her that well. We hung with the same crowd, that's all."

"Nola Grant's crowd, right? I went to her house, but it was empty."

"Yeah. We haven't gotten together since…" His voice trailed off with a stammer that sounded almost guilty. For what, Linnet wondered? Failing to warn Deanna against Nola— or something worse?

Hovering near the door in case he suddenly remembered he hadn't refastened the chain, she surveyed the living room. An entertainment center covered an entire wall, with a couch that looked like a garage-sale bargain on the opposite wall. A leather jacket lay on the floor, and newspapers spilled off the edge of the couch. A full ashtray on the scarred coffee table accounted for the smoke in the air. "Since Dee and Anthony died?" The man flinched at the question. Linnet decided to go on the offensive. "Can you think of any reason why Nola would murder them?"

He backed away as if she'd aimed a gun at him. "Nola didn't do it."

"Then who did?"

The door behind her swung open. Linnet jumped. In the heat of the conversation, she'd forgotten about Max lurking outside. He darted around her so fast her head spun, grabbed the young man and shoved him onto the couch. "Linnet, lock the door," he growled without looking at her.

Shaking, she fumbled for the doorknob, closed and locked the door, and hooked the chain. The man didn't even try to fight off Max. Instead, he gibbered incoherent phrases that conveyed nothing but terror.

"Shut up." At Max's quiet command, the man fell silent. "You will be quiet and listen. You will not speak or move unless I order you to. Is that clear?" The man nodded. Though he was slumped with his arms limp at his sides, his eyes stayed wide-open. "Good. Now sit still."

Linnet couldn't help retreating a step when Max walked over to her. "You hypnotized him somehow." She'd never heard of any form of hypnosis that worked so fast, with no soothing chants or shiny focal objects.

"More or less." His hands skimmed up her bare arms to settle on her shoulders.

Recalling the vertigo that swept over her each time his eyes captured hers, she said, "You tried to do the same to me. But you can't."

"So I've concluded. Very intriguing." One of his hands crept from her shoulder to her neck. His cool fingers on the flushed skin made her shiver. "But I don't want you to hear my conversation with our host, so—"

She felt pressure on the side of her neck. Gray spots clustered before her eyes. *He's strangling me!* The gray thickened to black. With a sensation like a rapid fall in an elevator, she tumbled into the blackness.

Voices murmured like wavelets on a beach. Queasy and light-headed, Linnet strained until the words came into focus, like a radio being tuned.

"Don't fight me. You know it only causes pain." Max's voice. "There, that's much better. Now, I ask again. What is your name?"

The voices sounded distant, barely distinguishable. Linnet kept her eyes closed, both to hold nausea at bay and to avoid letting Max know she'd awakened. She was lying on what felt like rumpled sheets. The odor of stale sweat permeated the air. She felt no bruises. So Max had set her down easily, instead of just knocking her out.

Pins and needles prickled the arm tucked under her body. She shifted position to ease the numbness. Opening her eyes, she discovered she was on an unmade bed. The small room was littered with magazines, CD cases and dirty clothes. A couple of drawers in the bureau gaped open, and a half-packed suitcase took up part of the bed. On the opposite wall a garish poster from some Japanese horror movie hit Linnet between the eyes.

She pulled herself to her feet, tiptoed to the closed door and pushed it open a crack to hear the conversation more clearly.

Max repeated, "Your name?"

A second voice mumbled, "Falcon."

In a tone between a purr and a snarl, Max said, "Your real name."

"Okay! Fred Pulaski. Just don't hurt me."

"Answer my questions peacefully and you'll feel no discomfort at all. Fred, tell me about your relationship with Nola Grant. Did you nourish her?"

"Yeah. It was…" His voice trailed off.

"Did she enter your mind?"

Linnet's head buzzed with confusion. She wondered whether she'd heard him right.

"Yeah. We bonded. I was special to her."

"Are you linked with her at this moment?"

"No. Must be too far."

She opened the door far enough to sidle into the hall. Still woozy, leaning on the wall, she crept toward the living room.

"Listen carefully, Fred. I'm stronger than she is. My power cancels hers." Again a growl crept into Max's tone. "As of right now, that bond is severed."

"No—please—" A noise of thrashing and wheezing.

"I told you not to fight me." Silence. "That's right, relax. She can no longer invade your thoughts. You'll be much happier out of her control, won't you?"

"Uh-huh."

"Why did you enter her house this evening?"

"Looking for her. She wasn't supposed to leave without me."

"Why not? Did she make you a promise of some kind?"

"She told me to stay out of sight for a few days. But she gave me a key to the house. That's got to mean something. Trusted me—said she'd take me with her, when it was safe."

"Take you where?"

"To her other house." A resentful whine tinged Fred's voice. "She must've been lying all along. I came back when she told me to, and she was gone."

"You expected Nola to wait for you. What about the other people in her group?"

"Naw, she wouldn't trust any of them with her secrets. Just me and a few others."

"Including Deanna?"

"Yeah, she was one of Nola's favorites. Plus me and Jodie."

"Who is Jodie?"

Linnet remembered her—a skeletally thin, blue-haired girl who wore white makeup and had a dragonfly tattooed on her cheek, one of the few kids from the gang Deanna had brought home.

"One of the other girls. I'll bet Nola tricked me—used me for her dirty work and then took Jodie along instead."

"Oh, and why would she do that?"

"So I'd get blamed for what she made me do." Linnet heard Fred's labored breathing. "I didn't want to. I didn't have anything against them."

Max lowered his voice. "Against whom?"

"Anthony and Deanna." A choking sound, followed by a rapid mutter of, "Oh, God, your eyes... You're like them— Nola and Anthony! Who the hell are you?"

Still deadly quiet, Max said, "I am Anthony's brother."

"I didn't mean anything—she made me—"

"Nola didn't kill them, did she?"

"For God's sake, please don't take me!"

"Fred, who did murder Anthony and Deanna?"

"She made me!"

Linnet's breath caught in her throat. She barely kept herself from screaming. Releasing air in a long sigh, she prayed Max wouldn't notice her watching from the end of the hall. She still wore her glasses, but they were slightly crooked. She cautiously adjusted them and peered into the living room. Fred sagged on the couch, goggling up at Max, who loomed over him.

"What, exactly, did Nola force you to do? Tell me all about it."

"She said those two had to be punished. Deanna left her, and Anthony helped. They had to be punished for that."

"Did Nola specify the kind of punishment?"

"She didn't have to. I figured out what she was, what Anthony was. Most of the guys didn't have a clue. Thought it was all a game, like role-playing but with more realism. I knew better."

"Of course. No doubt Nola allowed you to remain conscious while she preyed on you. So you knew how to deal with Anthony? Tell me exactly what you did."

Fred's hands twitched. His mouth twisted as if suppressing words that fought to burst out. "No, I can't! She'll kill me!"

"Nola isn't here. I am. Continue."

"I remember Nola telling me to take care of them. She didn't want Deanna back after Anthony messed with her, but she wanted them both taught a lesson. She said after I took care of that, it would be too dangerous for us to hang around, so she was packing up to move, and she'd let me come along."

"Your reward? I see." How could Max stay so calm? Linnet felt acid burning in her throat. "Then what?"

"Things got a little fuzzy. Next thing I knew, I was in the car, driving, with a gun on the floor beside me. I guess I got it from Nola—don't remember. I spaced out again, and then I was at Anthony's place. I had a hatchet, too. Must have swung by my apartment to pick it up, because I didn't get that from Nola. I knew I'd need it for Anthony."

"How did you get in?"

"Parked a block away and walked to the house, then went around back and picked the lock. Nola must've given me the lock-picking tools and showed me how to use them. Not like I ever did that before."

"No one saw you, then?"

"Middle of the afternoon. People were at work. Anyhow, Anthony had this little house with a lot of trees and hedges around it."

"Inside, what did you do?"

Fred writhed on the sofa, tossed his head from side to side. Max grasped his temples and held him still. "Tell me."

No, I don't want to hear that! Linnet silently cried.

"Sneaked into the bedroom." Fred's breath came in spasmodic gasps. "They were both asleep. I wrapped the gun in a towel and shot them in the chest, him first, then her. She died fast. But Anthony—I knew a bullet wouldn't be enough. I cut off his head so he couldn't come back." A long moan, almost a sob. "The blood—I didn't want to—Nola forced me—"

"Yes, I know. What did you do with the weapons?"

Linnet's chest felt crushed by an invisible weight. She drew a labored breath and squeezed her eyes shut for an instant, praying for the image spawned by Fred's words to fade.

"I dumped them in the river, everything separately, like Nola ordered. Then I guess I drove home and passed out. The rest of the day is a blank."

"After which you waited a suitable time, as Nola commanded."

"Yeah. I slept most of the week, didn't dare leave the apartment. All I remember thinking was that the police would show up any day and haul me off to jail. But they never did."

"Nola would have persuaded them to ignore anyone associated with her. You obediently waited for a summons from her that never came. Today you became impatient enough to return to her home, and you found she'd vanished."

"Yeah. With Jodie—I just know it."

"I wouldn't be surprised. Nola isn't the type to leave all her pets behind. Do you know where she went?"

"Somewhere in California. Promised she'd take me, too. Liar. I have to go look for her."

Max sighed aloud. "You're obviously not responsible. You acted under Nola's compulsion."

His eyes widened in desperate hope. "You mean you're not going to, like, rip out my throat?"

"Why would I do such a thing?" Max's gentle tone didn't reassure Linnet. If tigers purred, they would sound that way. "You aren't worth the trouble. I have a better idea." He leaned closer to Fred.

With Max's back to her, Linnet couldn't see his face, but whatever the young man saw there threw him into a frenzy of high-pitched babbling. Max seized his flailing arms. "Quiet! Be still!"

Fred fell silent and went limp in Max's grip. Only his wide-eyed stare conveyed his panic.

"Relax. I won't hurt you. No more than Nola hurt my brother and his lover. Not personally." After a long silence, Fred's face went slack, his eyelids drooping. "That's fine. Now, this is what you will do. After I leave, you will sit here for half an hour, resting in perfect tranquillity. You will not be afraid. Understand?"

Fred nodded.

"Do you have any liquor in the house?"

"Scotch," he mumbled.

"Good. After the half hour has passed, you will drink as much of the bottle as you can manage without losing consciousness. Then you'll go into the bathroom and get a sharp razor blade. You will fill the bathtub with very hot water, strip and get in. You will slit your wrists with the blade. Make long, deep vertical cuts. This will not hurt. Continue cutting until you become unconscious."

The young man murmured something incomprehensible.

"No, I assure you that you'll feel nothing. Do you believe me?"

Another nod.

"You want to do this, Fred. You're sorry for murdering your two friends. You want to atone, don't you?"

"Yeah."

The glazed stare and calm affirmation shocked Linnet out of her paralysis. "No—stop it!" She let go of the wall and staggered toward him. She had to grab the back of a chair to keep herself from toppling over.

Max spun around. "How long have you been listening?"

She took a shuddering breath and swallowed bile. "Long enough. You can't—"

"Blasted female, I should have knocked you out." He turned to his victim, who'd begun to stir and mumble. "Fred, you had better rest now. You cannot see or hear anything until I speak directly to you again." Fred's eyes closed, and he slumped sideways.

Linnet's legs trembled. She sat down on the coffee table, staring at the entranced victim. "How did you do that? I've never heard of anything like it."

"I don't have time to explain things to you. Just accept that our young hit man is extraordinarily suggestible."

Linnet didn't buy that premise for a second, but she had more important things to worry about. "No matter what he's done, you can't make him commit suicide. You said yourself it was really Nola's fault, not his. He belongs in a mental hospital."

"What right do you have to interfere?"

"Right?" She clenched her fists, her head pounding as she fought the urge to shriek at him. "He shot my niece!"

"Yes, and for that reason I let you participate thus far. But I won't allow you to interfere with my revenge. Which is yours, too, for that matter."

"I told you, I don't want revenge just for the sake of it. Killing some poor kid Nola used like a robot is going too far."

Max glowered at her, his eyebrows drawn together in a satanic V. "Anthony and Deanna died. Their killer will die, much less painfully than they did. That is my idea of justice."

"Well, it's not mine." She clutched her necklace and glared back at him. "I won't let you."

Chapter 3

"Do you seriously think you can stop me?"

She sprang to her feet and slammed both fists into his chest. "If I don't, I'm as bad as *she* is!"

Max grabbed her wrists just as her knees buckled. Holding her upright, he said with a thin smile, "Yes, I had certainly better ask your permission."

When her head stopped swimming, she said, "What did you do to me a few minutes ago?"

"Simply applied arterial pressure to cut the flow of oxygen to the brain. No permanent damage. I wish I'd knocked you unconscious instead. Then I wouldn't have to waste energy on this ridiculous argument."

"Ridiculous?" Panting, she strained against his effortless strength.

"Come in here and sit down before you fall." He led her into the adjoining bedroom and steered her to the unmade bed. She cooperated, afraid she really would embarrass herself by collapsing. Max pushed aside the open suitcase, sat next to her and cupped her chin to make her face him. "Have you considered that I don't need to listen to you at all? I can't hypnotize you, but I could certainly use more direct methods."

"Yeah, like decking me. That's just a temporary solution."

"You don't believe I'd resort to a permanent one?"

Recalling the cold voice in which he'd ordered Fred to commit suicide, Linnet felt her stomach clench. "I don't believe it." Sourness filled her mouth. She swallowed and said, "If you wouldn't kill a murderer outright, you sure won't do it to me. Too messy."

His fingers tightened on her jaw, not hard enough to hurt, but enough to make her pulse race. "If you become an intolerable nuisance…"

Linnet shook her head. Relaxing his grip, he rested his hand lightly on her shoulder. "You don't know me at all."

"No, but Anthony seemed like a nice guy."

His eyebrows arched. "Far nicer than I, you mean."

"I didn't say that." Not that she hadn't thought it. "He must have gotten his character from somewhere. You're his brother."

"I'm much older. We had little contact during his adolescent years, so you can't predict my behavior by his."

"You're right, I don't know you. All I can go by is what I saw in him."

Max's thumb idly caressed her collarbone under the neck of the T-shirt. Again his touch felt refreshingly cool.

For a second the tension trickled out of her, and she leaned toward him. When she realized what she was doing, she snapped herself to attention. "What the hell do you think you're doing?"

With a faintly puzzled look, he removed his hand. "I don't understand you at all. That man in the other room committed a loathsome crime. You share my anger. I sense the bitterness in you."

"Yeah, sure. But if you can hypnotize him into slitting his wrists, I believe Nola could hypnotize him into killing. I've always heard hypnosis can't make people do things against their will, but this is different."

"Yes, it is."

"He was really scared out of his mind—I saw. I believe Nola's the one responsible, not him."

"Yet he pulled the trigger. Shouldn't he die?" Max spoke as dispassionately as if they were debating over coffee, not deciding the fate of a man who sat a few yards away in a trance. "Surely you want your vengeance."

"Doesn't matter how I feel. It wouldn't be right." She stood up and paced around the cluttered room.

"Right!" He shook his head and said in the tone of an adult humoring a child, "Very well, tell me what you would do with him."

"Make him confess to the police, turn himself in."

"With what result? A few years in an institution for the criminally insane, then set free to live out his life?"

She couldn't bring herself to deny that all-too-probable scenario. "That's not our decision. The law should deal with him, not us."

"Your law wasn't written for cases like this."

My law? What is the man talking about? She decided that either she'd heard him wrong or he was referring to the laws of Maryland, as opposed to wherever he lived. Or maybe he was some kind of anarchist, a militant survivalist or something. "I have another reason, too. Robin."

"Your sister? What about her?"

"She needs to know the truth, needs to see someone convicted of the crime. I hate to use the word 'closure' like some radio phone-in psychologist, but that's what I'm talking about. I owe that to Robin and her husband."

"Owe? What's this, more guilt?"

"They trusted me with their daughter, and I failed. This is the least I can do, make sure they see her killer put on trial. If he just drops dead, they'll never—" Linnet's chest heaved with ragged gasps. She slumped onto the bed again.

"Hush. Calm down, breathe slowly." He massaged her shoulders, sending alternate waves of warmth and cold down her back. "Surely you don't believe delivering your niece's murderer to what you call justice is your responsibility?"

"Yes, I do." Moisture stung her eyes. "I got the first call from the cops and went down to the medical examiner's office to identify the—the victims. I made most of the arrangements for Deanna's funeral. But it's not enough. Robin still wouldn't speak to me at the service." To her dismay, she felt hot tears trickling down her cheeks. Taking off her glasses, she wiped her face with the back of her hand.

"Oh, damn. Don't do that." Max's fingertips brushed lightly at the stray drops.

Her skin quivered under his touch. His eyes captured hers. Silver-gray, she noticed, with a tinge of violet. She imagined a swirl of smoke in their depths. When he leaned closer, she gazed at him, immobilized. His lips alighted on her cheek, and she felt the flicker of his tongue. She inhaled his scent, a chill, metallic aroma. Her breath caught in her throat. Drawing back, she reached up to close her fingers around his. He allowed her to remove his hand from her face, and an involuntary sigh escaped her.

Max gave her a fierce glare. "No doubt Anthony would have let a female's weeping influence him."

Linnet sat up straight, appalled at her own reaction. What was wrong with her, letting a strange man kiss her at a time like this? *He doesn't need hypnosis to turn my brain to mush.* "I bet he would," she said as tartly as she could manage. "Because he had some human emotions. How would he feel

about what you're doing? Do you think he'd want you to condemn Fred to death this way?"

"Do you expect me to base my conduct on hypothetical
assumptions about what my brother would have wanted?"

She pounded a fist into the mattress. "You're avoiding the
question."

Max ran his fingers through his hair as if he felt like tear-
ing it out. "Very well, I concede that Anthony might have
agreed with you. He was devoted to *causes*." He spoke the
word like the name of a plague. "I can see him insisting on
turning this deranged boy over to the authorities." Standing
up, he took her hand and pulled her to her feet. "All right, I'll
do as you suggest. Now, shall we get it over with?"

Caught off guard, Linnet stumbled. Max clasped her arm
to steady her. Half turning, she unthinkingly placed her hand
on his chest. Her knuckles grazed his chest. Touching the
silken hair, finer than the coarse curls typical of most men,
sent a shock up her arm. With a smothered gasp, she tilted
her head to meet his eyes. He stared down at her, his lips
parted. He leaned toward her. She held her breath.

Oh, Lord, I'm doing it again! "No." She detached her hand
from his shirt. Taking a step back, he released her.

"I don't have time for this." He stalked into the living room.
Shaking her head to dispel the dizziness, Linnet followed.

Fred sat like a stringless puppet, just as they had left him.
Max sat on the coffee table and tapped the young man's
shoulder to get his attention. "Listen carefully. You have
changed your mind. You still feel remorse for your crime, but
you don't want to kill yourself."

"I don't?" His voice was slurred, like a sleepwalker's.

Linnet still couldn't fathom what had put him in this condition. From what she'd read about hypnosis, it didn't work
this powerfully. Maybe while she'd lain unconscious in the
bedroom Max had injected Fred with a psychotropic drug.

"No, there's a better way to atone," said Max. "You want to confess. You want to pay for what you did."

"Yeah."

"After visiting Nola's house and finding her gone, you decided to turn yourself in. Why?" After a pause, Max said, "Obviously, because her disappearance made you realize how wrongheaded and futile the crime was. You killed those two people for nothing."

"Nothing."

"One half hour after I leave here, you will get into your car and drive to the nearest police station. You will confess to the murders of Anthony and Deanna. The authorities may not believe you at first. You must persist until they do."

Fred nodded.

"Describe the act in detail. Tell the officers exactly how and when you killed your friends. Tell them where you dropped the weapons, so the investigators can search for them."

Another nod.

"Now, this is important. When they ask why you committed the murders, you will not say Nola ordered you."

Linnet almost yelled in protest, but a frown from Max warned her not to interfere.

"You won't involve her directly at all. Instead, admit that you resented Anthony and Deanna's being Nola's favorites. You wanted to eliminate them because they distracted her attention from you."

"Uh-huh."

"Feel free to tell the police about Nola's blood rituals. That will help them understand why you became so deranged that you would kill two people for such a tenuous motive. But don't reveal Nola's true nature. Understand?"

Fred's brow furrowed in obvious confusion.

"In fact, you will forget all about that dimension of her character."

What dimension? Linnet wondered. That command might make sense to the entranced killer, but it baffled her.

"As far as you know, she was an ordinary woman," Max continued. "Merely a devotee of a bizarre fetish—strange, perverted, but otherwise normal. Yes?"

"Right," Fred mumbled.

"There's no telepathic link between the two of you. There never was. That was a delusion on your part."

Telepathic? How could that be anything but a delusion? Linnet wondered.

"Now, to review. In half an hour, you will drive to the police station. You will turn yourself in." The man flinched as if each word lashed him like a whip. "You will give a full account of your crime. You will explain why you committed the murders. Tell me why, Fred."

"Nola ignored me. Broke her promises. I had to get rid of Deanna and Anthony to make Nola pay attention to me." He recited his answer in a barely audible monotone.

"And what is Nola?"

"Crazy lady who ran a blood cult."

"Is she anything more than that?"

"No, just a rich weirdo."

"Exactly right." Max leaned toward the couch, his hands on either side of Fred without touching him. "Nola is only a rich, eccentric woman with decadent tastes. Anthony was an ordinary young man, not so different from you. You decapitated him because you disliked him more than Deanna. No other reason. Understand?"

"Yeah."

Linnet listened in growing confusion. Why did these details matter? And how could Max discuss his own brother's mutilation so coldly?

"One more thing, Fred. As soon as I leave this room, you will forget my visit. You were completely alone from the time you visited Nola's house until you decided to confess. You've seen nobody else this evening."

"Huh?"

"Nobody else has been here. You've been alone the whole time." Max rapped out the words like hammer blows.

Slack jawed, Fred only groaned in response. Linnet's chest constricted, and ice water seemed to trickle down her spine.

"Now I'm leaving. You will obey my instructions, but you will not remember this conversation. We never met. The moment the door shuts behind me, you'll forget you talked to anyone tonight."

This time the young man made no sound at all. Max stepped back, glowering down at him.

Linnet scanned his slumped posture, sagging facial muscles and blank stare. "What did you—"

"Quiet," Max whispered. He grasped her arm and steered her to the door. "We're leaving."

Fred didn't stir as they walked out the door and shut it behind them. His glassy-eyed trance made Linnet queasy. "Oh, God, you've turned him into some kind of zombie."

"You didn't want him to remember meeting you, I'm sure."

She scurried to keep up with Max's long strides. "But he looks brain damaged."

"May very well be." At the car, he whirled to face her. For a second she thought crimson sparks glinted in his eyes. "Look here, you asked me not to kill that boy. In fact, having him confess to the police was your idea, wasn't it?"

"Well—"

"Did you expect me to concoct that particular omelette without breaking an egg or two?"

She swallowed, wrapping her arms around herself despite the humid air. "I just didn't realize the egg would be totally smashed, so to speak."

"Doubtless it already had a few cracks." He unlocked the car. "Feel sorry for him if you must, but don't whine about the justice *you* asked for."

"Now wait a minute! It's not as if you told me your whole plan in advance!" Fuming at the way Max had twisted the argument to make Fred's condition her fault, Linnet silently got in the car and buckled her seat belt. As he started the engine, she said, "What will the cops think when he shambles in practically drooling? Won't they be suspicious of anything he says?"

"They'll probably attribute his condition to long-term drug use."

"Which he might've really done at some time, even if he's clean at the moment." Now that she'd calmed down a little, she remembered another problem. "All right, why did you order him not to mention that Nola goaded him into the murders?"

"I don't want her implicated, obviously." He waited until exiting the parking lot before switching on the headlights. "Did you leave a car at her place?"

"No, I took a cab. Seemed safer. If the police came back, they might've recognized my car."

"Very well, I'll drive you home. College Park, you said? Where, exactly?"

She gave him directions. "Why don't you want Nola implicated? Morally, she's the real killer. We agreed on that."

"And what would happen if our young friend tried to convince the police of that? Besides clouding the issue."

"But she can't just get away with it."

At a traffic light, Max turned his cold stare upon her. "Think! Homicide detectives questioned Nola once and got nowhere. Suppose they did bother to trace her and actually succeeded in finding her. Then what? Do you think the result would be any different?"

Linnet realized the truth of this prediction, though she wasn't about to admit it aloud. "So you're just going to let it go?"

"Certainly not. The police can't deal with her, but I have other methods."

"Talk about me going overboard with responsibility— what makes this your job?"

Another sidelong glance, this time with a rueful smile. "Much as I dislike admitting it, Nola Grant is a distant cousin of ours. That may explain why Anthony started attending her parties. He probably felt obligated to protect oblivious young people from her. That would be like him."

A bitter taste welled up in Linnet's mouth. "Well, he didn't do a great job of protecting Dee!"

"He endangered himself for her. If he hadn't meddled with one of Nola's favorites, he would still be alive."

Linnet's pulse pounded in her ears. "Don't you dare blame her!"

"I don't blame anyone except Nola. It's nevertheless a fact. And you seem to think my brother was at fault."

She unclenched her fists and expelled a long breath. "Okay, forget about throwing the first stone. What now?"

"Now I take you home and begin searching for Nola."

Ignoring that "I" for the moment, Linnet said, "You don't even know where she went, just someplace in California."

"I have contacts who can help me with that. I'll find her."

"Fine. Except it's *we* who'll find her." She braced herself for an explosion.

"Damn it, woman—" Max's hands flexed on the wheel, as he visibly scaled back his reaction to a slow boil. "How bluntly must I tell you that you're a liability I don't want? You'll only slow me down."

She gazed out the window at the freeway lights, trying to suppress her awareness of the anger radiating from him like heat from a furnace. "I helped you get into Fred's house."

"This isn't the same. You don't know what you're dealing with."

"Yeah? So explain it."

He shook his head. "I can't. Just keep in mind that if apprehending her were a matter of routine, your police would have done it."

"And what are you, Secret Agent Man?"

"I'm familiar with her kind."

Which isn't much of an answer, Linnet grumbled to herself. She stared out the window a while longer, mentally sifting her options. After they merged from Route 50 onto the Washington beltway, she said, "I won't let you leave me out of this."

He gunned the engine, whipping from lane to lane as if he couldn't wait to get rid of her. She gritted her teeth and clung to the armrest. Finally he said, "Now that we've finished with that boy, I don't need your help, and you have no way to force the issue."

"I can still call the cops on you. I'll make something up." The words tumbled out before she stopped to think. "If I report you for assault, say, or—"

"No marks on your admittedly tempting flesh."

Tempting? Now where did that come from? She forced herself to ignore the heat flooding her cheeks. "Okay, that was far-fetched anyway. What if I claimed I saw you trying to break into Nola's house? That might make you a credible suspect or at least a material witness. Credible enough to get them to put out a bulletin for you."

"When I'm already on my way to the West Coast?" He glanced at her with a Mr. Spock eyebrow arch and a fleeting smile.

"I memorized the description and plate number of this car. It's a rental, right? So you had to give your name—*a* name, anyway—and a credit card number. Not to mention that I could identify you as Anthony's brother and make up some story about why I recognized you. That should intrigue them. They'll catch up with you, at least long enough to interfere with your vigilante project." Trembling at her own audacity, she added, "I'll make them listen to me, even if I do get labeled a nutcase or arrested for filing a false crime report."

This time the glare he aimed at her held no hint of humor. "Damn it, you really mean that."

A roaring sounded in her ears. "I'll do anything to track down Deanna's real killer."

After a prolonged silence, during which she breathed deeply until her head stopped buzzing, he said, "Even if she can never be hauled into court for it? Because I assure you, she can't."

"I don't understand why not. And obviously you're not about to explain. But yes, even then. Robin doesn't need to know about it. Fred's confession will be enough for her. But I have to find out the full truth."

"We'll discuss it at your home." The anger had faded from his voice. Maybe he'd finally accepted her determination.

Drained of emotion for the moment, she felt woozy with fatigue by the time they pulled off the freeway into College Park. She expected to have to repeat the directions to her place. Max, though, negotiated the suburban streets as if he'd driven the route a dozen times.

After parking in her driveway, he reached into the back seat and snagged a carry-on bag. Linnet didn't quite register its significance until he locked the car and started up the sidewalk with her.

"What the heck is that for?" she sputtered, rummaging in her belt pouch for her keys.

"What did you expect me to do, after you badgered me with wild threats?" He plucked the key ring from her fingers and unlocked the door. "I'm not letting you out of my sight until we get this matter settled. I'm staying here."

Chapter 4

The rainbow of conflicting emotions that rippled in the woman's aura tempted Max to linger, feasting on her energy if nothing else. Perhaps it was a good thing she'd proved immune to his mesmerism, for that immunity gave him no choice but to stay focused on his goal.

"What makes you think I'd let you spend the night?" Her shrill tone felt like a needle piercing his skull.

With a firm grasp on her arm, he stepped inside. "Did I ask permission?" The front door opened directly into the living room of the small, ranch-style house. The artificially cooled air smelled clean, neutral except for a faint coffee aroma left from earlier in the day, a welcome change from the smoky atmosphere of Fred Pulaski's apartment and the gasoline fumes on the freeway. Traces of Linnet's healthy scent also lingered in the house.

"Do you always get your own way?" Jerking free of his hold, Linnet paused to lock the door before flicking on the overhead light. He closed his eyes briefly against the unwelcome brightness.

"Usually. This is in your best interests, too. You don't want me to disappear, do you?"

"Come to think of it, you have a point."

He dropped his airline bag onto the claw-footed, wing-backed couch. "I assume there's no one to object? You don't share the house?"

He couldn't help smiling to himself at the spike of fear she emitted. Did she imagine he had asked the question in preparation for murdering her and hiding the corpse? "Not anymore." She closed her eyes momentarily. "'A poor thing but my own,'" she misquoted. Fast, shallow breathing underscored her nervousness, and he heard her pulse accelerate. "Make yourself at home. I'll be back in a few minutes. The hall bathroom is that way." She pointed, then fled into a bedroom and slammed the door.

Splashing cold water on his face in the unlit bathroom, Max glimpsed sparks of red in his own eyes when he glanced at the mirror. Had Linnet noticed that dark-induced anomaly? If so, she'd probably dismissed it as illusion. Ephemerals had a talent for dealing with the "impossible" that way. Thanks to that tendency, spending a night under her roof didn't worry him much. It helped that most people believed the ludicrous superstitions found in horror movies, such as the notion that the sun made his kind burst into flames. Seeing him walk in daylight, even if uncomfortably, would cancel any wild notions Linnet might entertain about his not being human.

Still, he would have felt more confident if he'd been able to wipe any such ideas from her mind. Ironic, that his own brother had put him in this position. How like Anthony, to insist on using his hypnotic power to protect a human female simply because he happened to be infatuated with a relative of hers.

Max considered ripping the necklace off Linnet. He

wouldn't even have to resort to violence; he could easily remove it while she slept. But would the loss of the ankh's
"magic" destroy her immunity to his influence? Perhaps not,
now that she had fixed in her mind the belief that he couldn't
mesmerize her. And the absence of her talisman might make
her vulnerable to Nola, if they should meet. The last thing
Max needed was a human fellow-traveler whom Nola could
interrogate about him. He imagined the worst possible scenario, that without the ankh Linnet would still be able to resist him, because she'd already proved to herself *and* to him
that she could, but unable to fight off Nola's doubtless more
brutal assault on her mind. Another potential problem occurred to him. Suppose Anthony had also given Linnet a
posthypnotic suggestion to fight the loss of the thing, even
wake instantly if anyone tried to separate her from it while
she lay asleep? If Max himself had devised a similar plan, he
would certainly have included that precaution. And the more
importance his actions placed on the ankh, the more suspicious of him Linnet would become. He decided to leave her
the comfort of Anthony and Deanna's gift. He smiled to himself again. If he couldn't handle a young human female
through superior intelligence and experience alone, he deserved whatever she managed to get away with.

He dried his face and put on the clean shirt he'd grabbed
from his carry-on bag. Better not leave room for further ac-
cidental skin-to-skin contact. His throat burned at the memory of Linnet's fingers on his chest. Not to mention the
tantalizingly salty flavor of her tears. If he could have hypnotized her, he might have yielded to temptation.

That damnable immunity was the most important reason
for keeping watch on her. An ephemeral who couldn't be
made to forget about him was too dangerous to run loose. He
resigned himself to dragging her along, at least for the present, although he distrusted her effect on him. He could hardly

believe she had persuaded him with that sentimental argument about what Anthony would have wanted done to the murderer. *I must have gone temporarily insane.* Especially galling was the awareness that Anthony would have agreed with her. He would have respected human law.

Through the wall, Max heard water running in the master bath. Yielding to curiosity, he took advantage of the chance to make a quick survey of the house. In addition to Linnet's room, it had two small bedrooms, one furnished as an office. Bookshelves lined this room, as well as the living room. A small alcove off the compact kitchen served as a dining nook, completing the floor plan. She'd clearly told the truth about living alone. He extracted his cell phone from his bag and prowled the living room, scanning the shelves, while entering a California number. Science textbooks and paperback mysteries dominated Linnet's collection. Agatha Christie occupied an entire shelf.

After four rings, a recording began. "Professor Valpa here. If you are a student…"

Max fumed through a menu of alternatives until the beep. "Pick up, Valpa."

"Yes, is that you, Maxwell?" said a richly resonant voice that had doubtless enthralled hundreds of female graduate assistants over the years. Max visualized the speaker, with his mane of white hair and deceptively benevolent features.

"I need information." Max flung himself onto the couch. "Nola Grant was living in Maryland, and she's bolted. I need to find her."

"Why? Not from friendly motives, I suspect."

"The other day I got a call from Roger Darvell, who'd noticed a report of my brother's death in the local newspaper," said Max. He summarized the events surrounding the murders. Valpa listened without comment, except for occasional murmurs of dismay. Though the old man could behave as ruthlessly as any other predator when conditions demanded, Max regarded him as soft on ephemerals. Valpa seemed to regard Deanna's death as no less appalling than Anthony's.

"What do you want of me, dear boy?"

"Damn it, when are you going to stop calling me that?" Though Max knew that Valpa, older than most living members of their species, addressed almost everyone that way, the phrase remained annoying.

"When your age equals mine. As for Nola, all I'm certain of is that she has a house in Pacific Grove. I don't know the address." Valpa's tone cooled a degree or two. "What do you plan to do when you catch her?"

"Execute her, of course. She destroyed one of our own kind."

"According to your story, an ephemeral did that."

"As her tool. Confound it, Valpa, you can't deny her guilt."

"I'm inclined to believe your version—"

"Profoundest thanks, venerable one."

With no acknowledgment of the interruption, Valpa continued. "Some of the other elders may not, especially those less than sympathetic to the notion that ephemerals have rights. After all, Anthony poached on Nola's territory, and there's no proof that the young man killed him on her command. If you retaliate in kind, a few of my peers might condemn *you*, instead, for murdering her."

"If I open my mind to them, they can read the truth in my emotions."

"What you *believe* to be the truth. If they consider you deluded, your belief wouldn't justify murder."

"When did my word cease to be enough?"

"When it concerns your closest kin."

"Well, what do you suggest I do? Haul her in front of the elders' council for trial? How?"

"To belabor the obvious, killing her wouldn't resurrect

your brother. Revenge is a game for the short-lifers. Would it be worth getting ostracized, possibly condemned to death yourself?"

Max shot a glance toward the hallway and the closed door of the master bedroom, where the shower had stopped running. "Can't you offer me any help?"

"If she gives you any grounds for killing her in self-defense, I'll back you up," said Valpa. "That's as far as I can go."

Max lowered his voice. "But that would rest on my unsupported word, too, wouldn't it?"

"With the difference that you'd have firsthand knowledge of her behavior, which the elders could read in your aura. Provided you're fully open to the probe, of course."

"Of course." He resisted the urge to lash out again, a futile exercise on the telephone.

"You do have one possible ally there in the local area. Roger Darvell has worked with the police as an expert witness. He could probably arrange to interview Nola's minion. If the others on the council distrust your version of events, he could support you."

"That half-breed? I owe him thanks for notifying me of Anthony's death, but otherwise, I don't want to associate with him. I certainly would not ask for his help." Max forced his indignation under control. The existence of a human-vampire hybrid revolted him, and the idea of one of his kind, even a mixed-blood, practicing the witch-doctor vocation of psychiatry struck him as ridiculous.

"Have it your way, then. As to Nola's whereabouts—Pacific Grove, probably directly on the waterfront, which seems to be her usual preference. From what I know of her, she wouldn't bother using different aliases in her various residences, so you may be able to find her easily enough."

After a mutter of grudging thanks, Max cut the connection.

He had just turned off the phone when he heard Linnet step out of the bedroom. Her clean fragrance, embellished by soap and powder—but, he thankfully noticed, no perfume— drifted to him. Her scent stirred hunger pangs. Since arriving in Maryland, he'd had time for only a rabbit and a couple of squirrels. The true satisfaction possible only with a human donor would have to wait. Linnet, whom he couldn't mesmerize, certainly didn't offer any relief for the craving.

But there are ways, even without hypnotism, his appetite whispered. With care, the target wouldn't even notice a discreet nip in the midst of a passionate embrace, much less recognize the feeding for what it was. *Shut up!* he ordered the seductive voice. He would be a fool to risk his mission for a few minutes of self-indulgence.

Yet he couldn't deny he found her appealing, partly because of her fervent determination to avenge her niece. Her boldness alternately amused and exasperated him. *A kitten that hisses at a German shepherd might be appealing, too,* he reminded himself, *but would I trust my life to it?*

Linnet slammed the bedroom door and locked it, her hands shaking. She could hardly believe she had let a stranger into her house, one who could turn people into suicidal zombies. Feeble protection that flimsy doorknob lock would provide if Max chose to break in. Not that he would have any reason to. A more realistic worry was that he might disappear while her back was turned. She hoped he believed her threat to accuse him to the police. She wasn't sure herself whether she could go through with such lies, but Max didn't know her well enough to guess her uncertainty.

Stripping off her clothes, she plunged into the shower, first running cold water to quell the hot flush on her skin. When she'd cooled off and her breathing had steadied, she turned the dial to warm, then soaped and rinsed, her thoughts still revolving on Max Tremayne. Much as she hated admitting it, she didn't mind the prospect of spending several days with him. Assuring herself that she only wanted to know more about the family of her niece's lover only half convinced her.

She scrambled into a fresh pair of shorts and a T-shirt, ignoring the impulse to choose a more flattering outfit. *This is business, not pleasure, and I should be thinking of Deanna, not how I look to a man I've just met.* She didn't bother with her glasses, since she needed them mainly for reading. While running a brush through her hair, she wondered what she would do if Max had left.

When she entered the living room, though, he was standing near the couch, examining the bookshelves. He instantly turned toward her, his eyes raking her up and down. She felt herself blush. To cover her confusion, she plunged ahead with, "Well, do we have to go for another round?"

"I beg your pardon?"

"I mean, are we going to fight about you tracking Nola by yourself?"

"No, we don't have to fight. If you insist on accompanying me, I'm resigned to it. I just talked to a friend on the West Coast." He held up a cell phone "He gave me a general idea of where to look for her. I'll need your telephone directory to arrange a flight, though."

Taken aback by his sudden change of heart, she floundered for a minute before she could conjure up an answer. "Oh, right, phone book. Kitchen." She led the way, pulled the book out of a cabinet and handed it to him. "Or you could use my computer to order tickets on the Internet."

"No, thank you, I prefer to deal with live individuals, or a facsimile thereof." He sat down at the table in the dining nook, while she watered the fern hanging over the sink and thought about food. Now that she had a second to catch her breath, her stomach reminded her that she hadn't eaten since noon.

"I'm going to throw together a meal," she said. "Would you like something?"

"Only a glass of milk. I've eaten already."

While he flipped through the yellow pages, Linnet whipped up a cheese omelette. Since receiving the news of Deanna's death, she hadn't bothered to shop. When she dished up the finished product and poured Max's milk, she found him muttering curses into an unresponsive phone. "On hold?"

He glanced up at her with a nod. Moving the phone away from his ear, he sipped from the glass and said, "Don't you have any obligations to prevent you from flying to California on a moment's notice?"

"Nice try. No, I teach high school biology, so I'm free for the summer."

"Ah, that explains the books." He resumed listening to the on-hold music.

A moment later he started negotiating with an airline salesperson, while Linnet ate. Max recited his American Express number without consulting the card, she noticed. She decided the man must have either a phenomenal memory or more frequent-flyer miles than a space-shuttle pilot. Finally he switched off the phone and said, "The earliest flight to San Francisco with two seats open leaves tomorrow afternoon from Baltimore-Washington International."

"I'll pay you back for the ticket, of course."

"Not necessary."

"Come on, I can't let you…" Faced with his cool gaze, her protest wound down. "We'll talk about it later."

"I'll stay here until we leave for the airport, so neither of us needs to worry about the other one absconding." He obviously guessed that she'd considered that possibility.

Linnet's mouth felt dry with renewed nervousness. She soothed it with a sip of orange juice. "Then you can sleep in the spare room. It used to be Deanna's."

"If you'd rather I didn't…"

How about that? He has a grain or two of sensitivity after all. "No, that's okay. Why let it go to waste?" She washed down the lump in her throat with another drink. "So what about you? You can run around chasing murder suspects, too? No job?"

"I work at home, freelance. I write the text for folio-size volumes of photographs people like to display in their living rooms. Mostly architecture and fine arts."

"You must travel a lot." Somehow one repair or replacement after another kept her savings pared down and prevented her from taking as many trips as she would like. Owning a house without a mate to share expenses meant a constant strain on the budget.

"Not so often as you might suppose. I find it overrated. At my age, I prefer the comforts of home."

"Yeah, I'm sure you're ready for the rocking chair." She squelched the impulse to giggle, as if she were Dee's age instead of a respectable thirty-four. "You can't be much over forty. Where's home?"

"A small town in Colorado. It's something of an artists' colony, so the locals tolerate eccentrics like myself."

"Eccentric? You? I'd never have believed it."

As if oblivious to her sarcasm, he said, "Since I like solitude and follow a mainly nocturnal routine, the bohemian atmosphere suits me. I like the dry climate and cool nights, too. The view of the stars is…extraordinary. As for those blindingly bright Western days, being self-employed, I don't have to go out."

"Oh, you estivate all day."

He did the Spock-eyebrow trick again, this time apparently

signaling surprise that she knew the word. *Good,* she thought. *That'll teach him I'm more than a ditzy Miss Marple wannabe.*

"What about Anthony? He never mentioned whether he was working, in grad school, or what."

For a minute Max drank his milk in silence. She wondered whether he would refuse to talk about his brother. But at last he answered calmly enough, "Our family is financially comfortable. Anthony chose not to work. Instead he devoted his energy to various charitable projects—such as saving victims from predators like Nola."

She silently bristled at the scornful tone of the word "charitable." To think she had almost started liking the guy. "Excuse me." Linnet shoved her chair back from the table and carried her dishes to the sink, where she rinsed the plate and omelette pan, rattled silverware and banged the dishwasher door until her temper cooled. Suddenly Max popped up beside her, holding out his empty glass. She jumped, knocked her elbow on the counter and bit off a curse. "Say something before you sneak up on me!" She put the glass in the dishwasher and slammed it shut again. "Come on, I'll get you settled in Deanna's—in the guest room."

She escorted him, with his bag, to the spare bedroom. "I cleaned it out the day after—" She couldn't make herself finish that sentence. "So the bed's all remade and everything. I took Dee's stuff to Robin, except for a few things I wanted to keep. A few of her drawings, mainly."

"She was an artist?"

"Art major. I'm not sure what she planned to do with it. Hard to imagine her in commercial art, like advertising, except that she talked about wanting to do book and CD covers. She worked at a music store, where they didn't mind the weird clothes and inch-long silver fingernails."

Max dropped his bag on the bed and walked over to the

bookcase, where Linnet had arranged some of Deanna's work. "She did this?" He picked up a framed black-and-white sketch of Anthony.

"Oh, yeah, quite an imagination, huh?" The portrait showed Max's brother bare chested, in snakeskin-tight pants, with pointed ears and a pair of pale wings that flared behind him like a pearl-gray cape.

"Indeed." He set down the picture and pointed to another. "And this is a self-portrait, I suppose." Deanna had drawn herself standing on a cliff in a high wind in a Morticia Addams-style black dress, low necked to display the spiderweb tattooed on her shoulder. With her head thrown back and arms wide, she appeared to embrace the storm.

"She didn't look that way until the middle of high school." Linnet showed him a photo on the dresser of Deanna, at fourteen, on a beach at Ocean City with Robin. Back then, Dee's hair had been long and closer to platinum than Linnet's own. "I didn't think it was an improvement when she chopped off that beautiful hair and dyed the curls on top black. Made her head look like a vanilla ice-cream cone with licorice sprinkles. But I knew better than to freak over it the way her parents did."

Max turned to the other framed snapshot on the dresser. "And this must be you with your sister, yes?"

"Oh, that." Linnet couldn't help blushing. Why hadn't she thought to hide that picture of herself as a teenybopper in bell-bottoms? She and Robin were posed together in front of the family Christmas tree, with her older sister looking cool and graceful, as usual. "That was a long time ago." Robin's tolerantly affectionate expression in the photo made a bleak contrast with her present coldness. Linnet turned toward the door. "I'll set out towels for you in the bathroom. You probably want to get settled."

"Actually, I won't go to sleep until near morning. I hope my staying up won't disturb you?"

"No, that's fine." Yielding to a reckless impulse, she said, "I'm pretty wired, too. How about a drink? I could open some wine."

While uncorking a bottle of Chablis, she wondered what had come over her. With this man around, the last thing she needed was alcohol in her bloodstream. *Don't be silly, I won't get looped from a couple of glasses of wine. I just have to keep my guard up.* Maybe a drink or two would loosen up Max enough to help her get straight answers out of him. She had to find out exactly what he planned to do about Nola Grant.

Max lounged on the sofa, watching her as she walked in. Avoiding his eyes while handing him a half-filled goblet, she said, "What happens after we get to San Francisco? Your friend told you where Nola went?"

"Approximately. If she isn't listed in the local telephone book under her own name, I may be able to get more precise information from one of my other contacts. In San Francisco we'll rent a car and drive to Pacific Grove."

"Where's that?" Linnet sat at the other end of the couch with her drink, glad for the excuse to focus on the glass instead of looking at him.

"Near Monterey, not far from the famous Cannery Row. There's a small airport, but driving will probably be more efficient."

"Okay, we get to Pacific Grove and find Nola. Then what? You claimed we can't report her to the authorities."

"I'd rather not think in terms of 'we.' Do I have any hope of persuading you to let me handle her from that point?"

"Not a chance."

He sighed. "Very well. The police would be useless. You know she hypnotized your local homicide detectives into believing she was uninvolved. She would only do the same thing over again."

"Fine, no police." Linnet caught herself clenching the stem

of the wineglass. She took a swallow and put the glass down. "So what's your plan? I'm guessing you can't zombify her the way you did Fred." Would the murderer actually have gone through with suicide if Max hadn't revised the command, or would self-preservation have kicked in at the last minute? Either way, Linnet's stomach still churned at the memory of Fred's vacant eyes.

"No." Max bared his teeth in a smile that showed no trace of humor. "I'll have to deal with Nola more...directly."

"If you mean violence, I can't go along with that."

"You keep jumping to that conclusion about me. Do I look so murderous?"

Her eyes flickered over him. Tall, strikingly pale in contrast to the black hair, with the build of a greyhound, he didn't resemble her idea of a desperado. But she'd already seen evidence of his casual attitude toward the law. "There must be some other way. For one thing, I don't want to end up sentenced to life in prison as your accomplice."

"Blast it, what do you expect me to do? If we can't have her arrested and you don't want her killed, what's the alternative?"

"I don't know. I just don't know. But I have to see her— face her with what she did." With her hands trembling, Linnet gulped the rest of her wine and refilled the glass. Topping off Max's, she said, "Tell me straight. Why didn't you just throw me out of the car in the first place? Because your Svengali act wouldn't work on me?"

He nodded. "You were a wildcard. Since I couldn't predict what you might do, I thought it best to keep watch on you."

"Or maybe, partly, because you agree I have a right to the truth about my niece's murderer?"

He flinched as if she'd slapped him. "I didn't say that."

"No, you think you're the only one who should run around chasing killers instead of minding your own business with your latest book. What are you working on right now?"

"A guide to the great theaters and opera houses of Europe and Great Britain." He leaned back, stretching his legs out.

"You couldn't do all that just from photos and library research, could you?"

"I've visited most of them, if that's what you're asking, but that was years ago. I don't run around, as you put it, the way I did when I was younger."

"Right, I forgot, you're over the hill." She emptied and refilled her glass, vaguely aware that Max had consumed less of the bottle than she had. "Have you seen the Globe in London?"

"Several times," he said with a fleeting smile.

She sighed, gazing into her wine. "That must be great. I got into drama for a couple of years in college. Not acting, of course, just helping with the sets. I was still trying to measure up to Robin."

"Was she an actress?"

"No, but she tried almost every other extracurricular activity you could imagine. The family always thought of her as the creative, artistic one. As opposed to the studious, dull sister."

"You? Not the label I would have assigned."

"What you've seen isn't typical. Reading mysteries is more my speed, not trying to solve them. I got on the honor roll every semester in high school, but Robin's grades were okay most of the time, and she did all the exciting stuff, too. I tagged along like the typical adoring little sister until she wouldn't put up with me anymore. Tried to act like her, but I didn't have a prayer."

"Exciting stuff? Such as?" He stared intently at her, as if sincerely interested.

"Robin lettered in gymnastics in high school. When I was about nine, I went to the playground alone and tried to imitate some of her moves. Fell off the monkey bars and broke an arm. Needless to say, Mom and Dad were not pleased."

Max chuckled. Linnet felt a reluctant smile steal over her face. She had to admit the incident had its funny side, with the pain no more than a ghost of a memory.

"That added to my reputation as the sister with brains but no common sense. On second thought, my folks might say this amateur detective stuff is right in character. Mom always accused me of leaping before looking." Tucking her feet under her, she half turned to face Max. The warmth of the alcohol percolated through her veins. A pleasantly fuzzy sensation replaced her earlier nervousness. "And here we are in the same position after all these years, the overachieving big sister and the little sister scrambling to catch up. Robin's a loan officer at a bank and married to a doctor. I'm teaching science in an overcrowded, underfunded high school. She's still the slender, elegant one, and I'm the not-so-slender, clunky one."

"Why do you judge yourself by that standard? The fashion for undernourished women is a recent, even local, aberration."

Sure, men often said that kind of thing, Linnet thought, *but look at the women they dated.* It crossed her mind, though, that whining about how her parents always liked Robin best wouldn't enhance Max's image of her. She shifted the conversation toward him. "How did you and Anthony get along? Did he idolize you the way kid brothers usually do?"

"Hardly." Max swirled his glass. "As I mentioned, we didn't have much contact in his childhood, not past the age of five, at any rate. And we were very different. He was an idealist, an attitude that baffled me."

"Yeah, you said something about charitable projects. Such as?"

"A homeless shelter, for instance. I could accept the large donations he made. It was his money, after all, even if I couldn't fathom the way he chose to spend it. But he went a step further and worked on the spot with the volunteers."

"What's wrong with that? Lots of rich people devote their time to charity, don't they?"

"Nothing wrong with it, except when he risked his own life for his projects." He took a drink and set the glass on the coffee table. When he spoke again, the coldness had faded from his voice. "Let's not go into that again. My point is, Anthony was altogether more earnest than I. Unlike him, I devote myself to my own comfort. If we got better acquainted, you would doubtless consider me very selfish."

Linnet shrugged. "As long as we can work together for now, that doesn't matter. I'll bet you didn't treat him like an idiot, though."

"Not unless I thought he was acting like one, which didn't happen often."

"Robin thought I couldn't do anything right. Like when I let Dee borrow my car the week after she got her license."

"Your sister disapproved?"

"She thought her kid wasn't responsible enough to drive to D.C. for a concert. Worst of it was, Deanna got into an accident in downtown Washington."

"Not your fault, surely."

Linnet heard herself giggling and swallowed the sound. *Am I getting drunk?* She decided she should have consumed more dinner or less wine. "Tell that to Robin. She thought I spoiled Dee anyway, but that's what aunts are for, right? She didn't let me hear the end of the car thing for the next six months."

"She allowed the girl to live with you, though."

"She didn't like the idea very much, but it was either that or keep up the daily screaming matches with a rebellious teenager. Deanna behaved for me—usually. I think it drove Robin crazy that I got along better with her daughter than she did."

"Not uncommon, surely, for someone with a bit of distance to have a better relationship with a young person."

"Mom agreed with that. She backed up my offer, or Robin might not have given in."

"And your father?"

"He'd died the year before. Heart." She picked up the bottle and found it empty. "What about your parents? They didn't come with you to—take care of things?"

"Our mother died when Anthony was less than a year old. She never married."

Linnet was struck speechless for a second by Max's casual tone. Well, maybe bohemian lifestyles ran in his family, as well as a talent for hypnosis. "So unearthing the facts is all up to you. Then you have to understand how I feel about the situation. Come on, you've got to have a plan in mind for Nola. Let me in on it."

"In all honesty, I don't know what I'll do when I confront her. My only plan so far is to follow my instincts. While I believe she deserves death, I have no more desire to be punished for her murder than you have." Spoken in a voice as chill and smooth as the wine, his answer left her unconvinced.

She drained her glass and put it down. When she turned to face Max again, she had to blink to bring him into focus. Plying him with Chablis to uncover his true intentions wasn't working the way she'd hoped. "Don't you understand? I have to fix this."

"Fix it?" His fingertips brushed the back of her hand. Softly, so that she had to lean over to catch the words, he said, "Death is not something you can repair."

"I can find out the whole truth. And I can make that woman pay. I don't know how, but I will. Somehow." Tears blurred her vision. She rubbed her eyes, but Max's face still shimmered in the lamplight. "It's my fault. Robin didn't trust me to take care of her daughter, and she was right."

"You can't seriously believe you're to blame. Could you have stopped Deanna from joining Nola's group? Or becoming Anthony's lover?"

"Maybe not. She was a nineteen-year-old college sophomore. But I should've found a way. I should've known she was in danger, at least." Swallowing a sob that threatened to choke her, she said, "Dee and Anthony told me they had to get away from Nola. They were planning to move out of state right before—"

"Yes, I know, Anthony wrote the same thing to me. But as you say, your niece was of legal age. You couldn't lock her up like the heroine in a Gothic novel."

"Then I should've reported Nola to the police."

"On what grounds? It's a waste of energy to torment yourself with hindsight."

Linnet pounded the couch with a clenched fist, raising a puff of dust. "What are you trying to reassure me for? You think it's my fault, too. You said so—if Anthony hadn't run off with Deanna, he'd still be alive."

He stared at her as if she'd punched him between the eyes. "My dear, I didn't mean to blame you."

"Sure sounded that way." To her exasperation, tears spilled over. "And don't call me your dear."

"I lashed out in anger. Yes, if they hadn't become lovers, they wouldn't have died. But that is not your fault."

"Don't try to weasel out of it. You were right the first time." The words caught in her throat. She drew a quivering breath and started over. "I let her get killed. I have to make up for it—have to fix it—"

"Linnet, please." Before she realized he'd moved, his arm curled around her. "You know better. This isn't rational."

"Rational?" she wailed. She pounded on his chest. "Don't talk to me about rational! This whole thing is insane!"

She felt his lips graze her cheek. "I don't believe I'm doing this," he murmured.

She didn't believe she was allowing it, either. Her body shook with stifled sobs, while he rubbed her back in expanding circles. Warmth radiated from her shoulder blades down her spine and along her limbs to the tips of her fingers and toes. His lips, cool against her flushed skin, explored her face, with a butterfly-wing flicker of tongue every few seconds.

He smoothed back her hair and nipped her right earlobe. "Hush," he whispered. "Don't waste your energy this way." The tickle of his breath made her blush all over again.

I shouldn't be doing this. I should be thinking about Deanna. When his lips wandered along her jawline, though, guilt faded into the background. Delicately, his tongue explored the corners of her mouth until it parted. He skimmed her teeth, traced circles around her lips. With a long sigh, she yielded to the invitation and met his tongue with her own.

The hand massaging her back crept lower, lingering at her waistline. The kiss deepened, drawing a moan from Linnet's throat. Max's lips no longer felt cool, but searing hot. The heat rippled through her, gathering in the pit of her stomach.

Leaning into his embrace, she rose onto her knees. He abandoned her lips, evoking a whimper of frustration, and nibbled his way to her throat. With a gasp, she arched her neck, inviting him to graze there. His lips and tongue generated fresh waves of heat, while his hand moved still lower, cupping her derriere. She felt as if that hand scorched her flesh.

Her fingers curled to dig into his shoulders. Alternately nipping, licking and sucking, he teased the curve of her neck. All thought melted away, replaced by pure sensation flowing and swirling from his mouth and hands through every nerve and vein of her body. Her thighs involuntarily clenched. She found that her eyes had closed, and sparks flashed behind the lids. A cry burst from her as the heat spiraled to unbearable intensity, and her secret places pulsed to the rhythm of his lapping tongue.

Max gasped and tightened both arms around her. For an instant she couldn't breathe. Her nails gouged his shoulders through the thin cloth. Then the storm ebbed. Releasing a long, shuddering breath, she let her head droop onto his shoulder. His shirt, she noticed, was damp from her tears.

He resumed stroking her back in slow circles. She submitted to the caress, ashamed to look him in the face. *Oh, God, how did I let that happen?*

Chapter 5

Max's fingers explored her neck with gentle pressure, while his other hand moved up to stroke her hair. She squirmed out of his embrace and retreated to the other end of the couch. Her chest ached from crying. She had to struggle for breath before she could force out a sentence. "What do you think you're doing?"

"Nothing you didn't allow." His breathing, too, sounded labored. "But I shouldn't have done it. Don't worry, this won't happen again."

"You bet it won't! You caught me off guard—took advantage—" Aware of the hot flush on her cheeks, she wanted to hide from his heavy-lidded gaze. "You're trying to manipulate me."

"Really? To do what?"

"How should I know? I don't know you, and I don't have the slightest idea what you're up to. Except you seem to think you can get around me with a few kisses and string me along with whatever plot you're hatching."

"What would I get out of that, when we've already agreed to work together?"

"Maybe you're planning to dump me someplace and take on Nola by yourself, and you think you can soften me up to accept it quietly." Max's politely blank stare implied that her rant was too far-fetched to bother answering. "Well, you don't expect me to believe you were swept away with irresistible passion, do you?"

"Is that so hard to believe?"

Using the couch as a support, Linnet pulled herself to her feet. "Come on, do you think I'm that dumb? Or that desperate for male attention?" Her head swam.

"Neither assumption ever crossed my mind." He caught her elbow as she stumbled.

"Leave me alone." The room whirled when she took a step. Groping, she clutched Max's arm. "Okay, give me a second."

"Shall I carry you?"

"No!" She couldn't face one more humiliation. After several deep breaths, she unfastened her grip from his sleeve. By advancing one pace at a time, her arms outspread for balance, she made it to the hall, where she could use the wall as a guide. After a stop in her bathroom, for a drink of cool water and some of it splashed on her face, she managed to peel off her clothes and shuffle into a nightgown before crawling between the sheets. She gritted her teeth until the bed stopped rocking like a rowboat on a stream.

Had she actually climaxed from a few minutes of kissing? Granted, she had lived celibate ever since a disastrous breakup right before finishing her master's degree. But she'd been kissed plenty of times in the years since, occasionally by experts. What magic did Max Tremayne wield? Her head still spinning, she skimmed her hands down the front of her gown and felt her body tingle to life. Sighing, she reached up to rub the place where he'd nuzzled her neck.

Had he realized his effect on her? How could he have failed to notice, when she'd barely restrained herself from moaning aloud? Aftershocks of pleasure vanished with a renewed flood of embarrassment. She gratefully sank into oblivion.

She floated in a warm pool, fragrant bubbles frothing on the surface of the water. A rosy mist enveloped her. Hands played over her breasts, teasing the nipples to peaks. Lips nibbled at the corners of her mouth, her ears, her throat. Tantalizing fingers tickled her most sensitive spots, until the heat in her depths expanded and hovered on the verge of explosion. A painless sting between her breasts sent her into ecstatic convulsions.

A face drifted into focus above her. Max. "Sleep," he whispered.

Oh, Lord, what a dream! What had the man done to her? Dry mouthed, Linnet staggered to the bathroom in the dark and chugged about a pint of water. Though her head felt clogged, at least she wasn't nauseated. Dragging herself back to bed, she slept fitfully for the rest of the night. At one point she half awoke to hear the shower running in the hall bath. With the muzzy thought that Max had probably managed to find the towels on his own, she faded out again.

Now I remember, she thought when she woke up at almost nine. *This is why I don't drink at home very often.* That much wine needed the ballast of a big meal to counteract the effect. On top of the fuzziness in her head, her throat felt parched. After a glass of water followed by a shower to dispel the mild headache and overall sluggish feeling, she put on jeans and a blouse, then stood in front of the dresser brushing her hair. In the mirror, her eyes appeared glazed. The spot

where Max had kissed her neck felt sore. Peering at her re-
flection, she noticed a tiny scratch. A small price to pay for
those incredible few minutes. Her skin turned deep pink.

No, I will not think that way! She ought to be ashamed of
herself, not savoring the memory. How could she face Max
after last night? She didn't have any realistic hope that he
wouldn't remember every second. And she had to sit next to
him on a plane for hours.

Trudging into the kitchen, she found a note on the counter:
"I've set the alarm, but I tend to sleep heavily. Please get me
up at noon if the alarm fails to wake me."

Just what she needed, images of a heavily sleeping Max
Tremayne. Well, at least he hadn't abandoned her in the night
and flown off to California without her.

Or had he? The question leaped into her mind like a pounc-
ing tiger. The note could be a ruse to give him a head start. His
yielding to her threats could have been an act. Without him,
she wouldn't have the least idea where in Pacific Grove to start
searching for Nola. Fighting a surge of panic, she scurried into
the living room and checked the driveway through the front
window. The rented car still sat there. She sagged with relief.

He could've phoned a cab before I woke up, though. Feeling a little silly by now, but still compelled to make sure, she
tiptoed down the hall and turned the knob of the closed bedroom door, inch by inch. She opened it a crack and peered
into the shadows. A shape, unmistakably a human form, occupied the bed. She shut the door, relieved that he hadn't
awakened. Her cheeks grew hot at the thought of having to
explain why she'd peeked at him.

Back in the kitchen, she crumpled the note and tossed it
in the trash. She forced down juice, toast and yogurt, mulling over the trip ahead. What would Max do when they
found Nola, would Linnet feel able to support his plan, and
if not, what could she do to stop him?

After packing a carry-on bag for the flight, she filled the empty time until noon with a cleaning frenzy. Aside from clearing out Deanna's stuff, she hadn't touched the house in a week. She hoped the noise of the vacuum cleaner on the hall carpet might spare her the task of waking her unwanted guest, but no such luck. How could he possibly doze through the roar of the machine less than twenty feet from his bed? Maybe he'd taken a sedative. How dare he turn her inside out, set her up for a hectic night and then sleep like a hibernating bear? Or, rather, an estivating snake.

When the alarm finally buzzed, Linnet pressed her ear to the door, listening for any movement. She heard no sign of life, just the racket of the clock going on and on. After about two minutes of it, she had to admit Max wasn't going to switch it off himself. She eased the door open.

He lay on his back, covered with the sheet up to his waist. The visible half of his body was bare. Ordering herself not to speculate about the hidden half, she tiptoed to the bedside and hit the off button. In the abrupt silence, she waited for him to open his eyes. Nothing. He hadn't lied about his sleeping habits.

Okay, that means I have to get him up so we don't miss the plane. With her eyes adjusting to the dimness of the heavily curtained room, she glanced around, postponing the moment when she would have to face him. Aside from the man in the bed, the room showed few traces of occupancy. He hadn't disturbed a thing, just folded his clothes over the back of the desk chair instead of letting them lie where they fell like the average male. Next to the chair, his bag sat on the floor.

Linnet's eyes circled the room and veered back to that bag. With Max dead to the world, she had a chance to find out a little more about him. She slunk over to the bag and unzipped it, wincing at the loud rasp. A quick look at Max showed that he hadn't stirred, though. She fumbled through the contents. Underwear, socks, shirts, a pair of slacks, and a small travel kit that contained the standard toiletries, plus a bottle of factor-thirty sunscreen lotion. Sunglasses. A soft-brimmed, khaki hat such as a man might wear for golf or fishing. A paperback spy novel. A couple of crossword puzzle magazines and a ballpoint pen. He *would* be the type to work puzzles in pen, she reflected. A bill from a Washington hotel, indicating that he had checked out the day before. He'd apparently told the truth about the uncertainty of his plans. A side pocket held a few letters with Anthony's return address. For a second her eyes stung with tears.

She wiped them with the back of her hand and closed the zipper, mentally scolding herself for snooping through his personal things. Still, he hadn't made a move yet, and she might as well get the full benefit of her rudeness while he lay there oblivious to her intrusion. She dug into a pocket of his black jeans and pulled out his wallet. To read the contents, she had to move over to the window and part the curtains an inch.

Credit cards, about a hundred dollars in cash, and a Colorado driver's license in the name of Maxwell Tremayne. The photo matched the face of the man she knew as Anthony's brother. No pictures, though, not even a single snapshot of Anthony. So what had she expected to find? A secret identity? If he had one, he wouldn't be stupid enough to carry around evidence of it. Her face burned as she stuffed the wallet back into the pocket and straightened the clothes the way she'd found them.

Time's flying, she reminded herself. If Max wouldn't wake on his own, she had to get him moving. Maybe she could accomplish that goal without touching him. She drew the curtains.

When the sun poured in, his eyelids twitched, but he didn't

open his eyes or make a sound. She wondered if he really was drugged. Approaching the bed, she examined his motionless body in the improved light. The glossy black of his hair made a striking contrast with the pale skin, further accentuated by the thick brows and long lashes of the same shade. On his chest the fine, dark hair grew in an inverted triangle whose point vanished under the sheet.

Linnet touched his shoulder with her fingertips. "Max? Time to get up." No response. Even with that slight contact, she noticed how cool his skin felt. Maybe he suffered from some chronic illness? No, that theory didn't match the energy he'd displayed chasing Fred through the woods. And although thin, Max looked far from weak.

As if moving under its own power, her hand skimmed along his collarbone and down his chest. She couldn't resist stroking the hair, like a cat's fur under her palm.

His eyes opened.

With a gasp, she snatched her hand back. His eyes, violet highlighted by gleams of silver, captured hers. Did they actually shine? No, that part had to be her imagination.

Rolling over, he pulled the sheet up to his ears. "Close the curtains!"

She had to suck air into her lungs before she could speak. "We have to leave soon, and I don't want you going back to sleep."

"I won't," came the muffled reply. "Close them, damn it!"

She obeyed. When she turned toward the bed again, Max flung off the sheet and sat up. Linnet didn't look away quickly enough. She wasn't sure whether to be disappointed or relieved when she saw the navy blue running shorts he'd slept in. They revealed more than enough—lean hips, muscular legs that went on forever, and a discreet bulge under the cloth.

Her nipples tingled. Painfully aware of her reaction, she blushed hotly and fled from the room. She caught the sound of soft laughter as she scurried down the hall.

A few minutes later Max appeared in the kitchen, fully dressed, as she ate a sandwich. Along with it she gulped a tall glass of orange juice. She couldn't account for her unusual thirst, unless it had been caused by overimbibing the night before. Alcohol led to dehydration, of course, but should a few glasses of wine have such an effect?

Avoiding Max's eyes, she offered to fix him a quick breakfast.

"Just milk." Apparently noticing her quizzical look, he said, "I suffer from a wide range of food allergies. When I'm away from home, I keep my diet simple."

When she handed him the glass, she blurted out, "Thanks for staying."

He frowned. "Pardon?"

"Staying here instead of leaving without me. You probably could have."

He flashed her a brief smile. "What, and risk your having me arrested?" His sardonic tone left her uncertain whether he meant the remark seriously.

So that's the only reason? Well, what did she think? That he'd undergone a sudden change of heart about her right to help him pursue her niece's murderer? That the kiss he had treated as a mistake had actually meant something to him? Not that she wanted it to, of course. To her relief, he didn't try to converse while she finished her lunch and cleared the table. She called her mother's house and left a vague message on the answering machine to forestall curiosity about why she wasn't home. Finally she scooped up her bag and headed to the door. Before twelve-thirty she and Max got on the road to BWI Airport. He slathered sunblock on his face and hands, put on sunglasses and his hat, and slumped down in the passenger seat of the rental car as if hiding. He gave her the keys. "You drive."

"Okay, if you insist." She glanced at his face, half-hidden

under the hat brim and dark glasses. "Are you allergic to the sun, too?"

"Astute observation." He flashed her a smile. "Driving in daylight gives me a blinding headache. Besides, you're familiar with the area, and I'm not."

He pulled the hat farther down over his eyes, apparently prepared to doze off during the drive, but she didn't intend to let him get away with that. Since he couldn't escape from her in the car, she could worm some more answers out of him.

As soon as she pulled onto the freeway, she said, "Okay, tell me what you know about Nola Grant."

"I beg your pardon?"

"Don't play dumb. You obviously know a lot more about her than I do. You said she's a distant relative of yours. What did she really collect all those teenage followers for, if she wasn't selling them drugs? From what you said, it was more than sex."

Max emitted a long sigh from under the hat brim. "Very well, but you won't like it. She led a blood cult."

"Yeah, I remember you said something about that to Fred, but what exactly does it mean?"

"She's a blood fetishist. They allowed her to cut them and taste their blood."

Linnet's stomach churned. "Then Deanna—" She swallowed a couple of times and turned up the air conditioner.

"I warned you. But it isn't as bad as you think."

"How much worse could it be?" She caught herself bearing down on the accelerator and eased off to the legal sixty-five.

"She didn't take any significant amount from each donor. Her habits may have been unsavory, but they weren't dangerous."

"What are you talking about? What about AIDS?"

"There's no evidence of its being transmissible in that way."

"Then who knows what other horrible diseases—"

"Nola wouldn't have tolerated disciples who weren't disease free, any more than she would have accepted those who took drugs."

Max's calm tone made Linnet want to slap him. "How would she know?"

"She had ways of evaluating them."

"Why can't you give me a straight answer?" She heaved several deep breaths, still fighting queasiness. Succumbing to hysterics wouldn't get them to the airport any faster or safer. "Okay, she was rich. She could've hired detectives to check out those kids. But she still couldn't be sure. If I'd known about that, I would've done anything to get Dee out of that woman's clutches. It's my fault, everything that happened to her."

Max reached across to pat her shoulder. She flinched at the touch and had to make a sharp correction with the steering wheel. "We've already been over this," he said. "Deanna was an adult. You couldn't have stopped her, any more than I could have controlled my brother."

"I could have paid more attention. Maybe Robin was right. I let her daughter run wild. If I had just taken the time to talk more with the few friends from Nola's gang Dee brought home, like that girl Jodie—"

"The one Fred mentioned?"

"He said Nola took Jodie with her. What for, I wonder?"

"Doubtless Nola had her favorites, and this Jodie was one of them, along with Deanna and Fred. When the murders forced Nola to abandon her harem, so to speak, she must have taken her remaining favorite along. She wouldn't want to cut her losses and have to start over completely."

"I don't understand how any human being can be so warped!" Linnet shook her head. "We have to make her pay somehow."

"I am open to suggestions."

"First we have to get close to her, right? I have an idea about that."

"Another idea? Pray enlighten me."

She gritted her teeth until her flare of anger at his sarcasm died down. "Have you and Nola ever met?"

"No."

"But I bet she'd recognize you right on sight anyway. You look a lot like Anthony. It didn't take me long to guess who you were."

"Your point?"

"One look at you might spook her. But if I go to her first, after we find her address, that might catch her off guard, the way we did with Fred."

"Nola wouldn't recognize you?"

"I don't see how. I picked up Deanna at her house once and saw her from a distance, but we've never met face-to-face. And I know what she looks like, because Dee sketched a few drawings of her."

"And when you make contact, what do you propose to do with her? I thought you accepted the fact that we have no way to deliver her to the authorities?"

"I want her to admit what she did, that she murdered my niece and your brother. And I want her to tell me why." Her chest constricted at the thought of facing a woman who could order two people slaughtered.

Max sat up, pushed back the hat and stared at her. "You expect a confession?"

"There has to be a way to get that much out of her. If only in private, even if I can never use it against her. At least *I* will know why this happened." She accelerated above seventy to pass a van, then steered into the exit lane.

"Very well. That is what I want, too."

Though Linnet didn't quite believe his suddenly cooperative attitude, she didn't have the energy to probe further at the moment. The traffic approaching the airport demanded all her attention.

After returning the rental car, they rode the shuttle to the terminal and hurried to the gate. Max's stride lengthened with renewed energy as soon as they got inside, out of the sun. He set a rapid pace through the main concourse and past the giant stained-glass crab, which he gave an incredulous glance before hurrying on. He insisted on carrying Linnet's bag as well as his own, so they wouldn't be slowed down. She was panting by the time they reached the check-in counter.

She got a fresh surprise when they boarded the plane. They had first-class tickets. Linnet suppressed a groan. Still determined to repay Max for the flight, she hated to imagine the months of scrimping she would need to cover the price of her seat.

Shoving that worry under the stack of more immediate ones, she tried to relax and enjoy the new experience. Two seats abreast instead of three, plenty of legroom—she could see why Max, with his height, had expended the extra money. Free drinks, with a midafternoon snack that, although not quite gourmet fare, tasted as if it had come from a restaurant menu rather than a supermarket's frozen-diet-entrée shelf.

I could get used to this. Sitting next to the window, since Max had claimed the aisle seat, she watched the landscape below until it disappeared under the clouds. Max refused the food in favor of a Scotch on the rocks. She couldn't help getting annoyed with him for reading his paperback with such apparent calm. Her mind wouldn't fix on the pages of her own novel for more than two minutes straight.

"Hey, talk to me," she finally whispered.

"About what?" He frowned in her direction. "Would you please close that blind?"

She pulled down the window shade. "Okay, there. I've

been thinking about why Deanna would get involved with Nola." She lowered her voice, not wanting the flight attendants to mistake her for a dangerous maniac. "What possessed those kids to let that woman drink their blood?"

"Besides the common youthful rebelliousness that delights in outrageous acts? Or the equally common desire to look daring in the eyes of their peers?"

"Besides those," Linnet hissed.

"The image of the vampire holds a certain glamour for many young Americans. Surely you've noticed that?"

"Yeah, but I've never understood it."

"From what little I saw of her drawings, your niece understood that allure."

"I guess so." Linnet smiled at a memory from Halloween two years past, before Deanna had joined Nola's clique. "One time she hauled a bag of vampire videos into my living room and made me stay up into the wee hours watching them with her. I have to admit, some of those guys in capes are pretty sexy." She blushed, reminded of her dream the night before. Thank goodness Max couldn't read her mind. "But those are just movies. If vampires existed, they wouldn't be like that."

"Ah, but how do you know? Many people imagine that the vampire's embrace would be quite…erotic."

The purr-growl of his voice made her skin prickle. "Movies are a long way from actually drinking—" She remembered to whisper again. "From what they were doing."

"In a few especially privileged cases," he said, "it was probably mutual. Fred certainly tasted Nola's in return."

"Blood. I'm surprised they didn't get sick to their stomachs and swear off the 'thrill' forever. The human digestive system isn't designed for that." She glanced around to make sure nobody was listening to the peculiar discussion.

"The quantity would have been too small to cause such problems."

She stared at him, wondering how he knew so much about Nola's bizarre habits. He only gazed back at her with a faint smile playing on his lips, holding the book open in his lap with an air of patient indulgence.

"You don't think any of them believed she was really a vampire, do you?" she asked.

"Probably not, however much they might have wished to believe it."

Linnet shook her head. "Wish? No way. Not Dee, anyhow. She was a little wild, but she wasn't that unbalanced."

Max shrugged and pointedly returned to his spy novel. With a sigh, Linnet gave up on conversation and forced her attention back to her own book.

They landed in San Francisco around three-thirty California time. Still not quite recovered from the night before, she braced herself to slog through the weary hours until local bedtime. "Now what?" she asked, trotting down the concourse in Max's wake. "We rent a car and drive to Monterey?"

"We'll get a car, yes, but I don't plan to travel any farther until nightfall. I can't face two hours of daylight driving, and we both need rest. We'll check into a hotel."

Though impatient to get on with their search, Linnet couldn't help feeling relieved at the mention of rest. While Max arranged for a car, she stopped into a ladies' room. Washing her face and combing her hair restored a little of her energy. Upon emerging, she headed for the car-rental outlet. When she came within sight of it, she saw Max, his back toward her, talking with a woman behind the counter. Linnet threaded a path in that direction among the travelers scurrying up and down the concourse.

Along the way, one figure that didn't fit the overall pattern caught her eye. Instead of rushing to or from a gate, this person, a thin girl in a black leather jacket, cut diagonally across the stream of foot traffic, then ducked into the archway leading to a coffee shop. There she leaned against the wall, facing toward the car-rental counter but half concealed in the shop's entryway. When she stopped, Linnet got a good look at her mop of pale blue hair.

Jodie? From fifty feet away, Linnet couldn't be sure, but this girl bore a close resemblance to the friend Deanna had brought home a couple of times.

Yet it didn't seem likely. How would Nola's "disciple," who was supposed to be in Monterey, know where to find Max and Linnet in San Francisco? There could be plenty of blue-haired young women in a huge city like this. On the other hand, surely this couldn't be a coincidence. But how could this girl possibly be Jodie? Linnet veered toward her anyway. A closer look would confirm whether she bore the dragonfly tattoo Linnet remembered. But before she got near enough to see the girl's face clearly, the watcher straightened up from her slouched position and retreated at a brisk walk. When Linnet increased her own pace, the girl broke into a trot.

"Jodie, is that you? Wait a minute!" The girl didn't slow down, of course. Linnet clenched her teeth in frustration at making a spectacle of herself for nothing. She sped up to keep from losing the girl.

She wove in and out of the clumps of pedestrians, her purse and carry-on bag thumping her side. Her quarry didn't look back or slow down. Linnet bumped into a middle-aged man with a cell phone at his ear, gasped an apology and hurried on. The girl was about to turn a corner just ahead. An electric cart loomed in the middle of the corridor, beeping insistently, blocking both Linnet's path and her view.

After dodging around the cart, she dashed to the corner where she'd last seen the girl, then stood still, panting, glancing wildly around. The blue-haired girl had vanished.

Chapter 6

Aware that she had little hope of finding one person who'd faded into the crowd in the terminal, Linnet hurried back to the car-rental counter. She debated whether to tell Max about the futile chase. She decided not to mention the incident, at least for now. After all, she wasn't sure of the girl's identity. The panicked flight didn't mean much. Who wouldn't run if a strange woman started chasing her? Linnet irritably squelched a voice in the back of her mind that hinted she was withholding information from Max only because his own secretiveness annoyed her.

When she caught up with him, his brusque manner confirmed her decision to keep quiet. He dangled car keys and said with a frown, "What took you so long? Come on, I've reserved a room in a motel less than five minutes away."

Halfway to the parking lot, she processed that sentence. "Room? Singular?"

"They're hosting some sort of convention and had only one

nonsmoking room available." He flashed her a wry smile. "Don't worry, your virtue is safe."

Again he left the driving to her. With sunglasses on, he leaned back in the passenger seat and recited the directions he'd received from the motel operator. When Linnet pulled the compact car into the parking lot, she noticed Welcome California Wing, Civil Air Patrol on the marquee. People in dark blue uniforms milled around the lobby. So Max probably hadn't made up the excuse about a shortage of rooms. Come to think of it, sharing a room had one advantage. She could keep an eye on him to guard against his sneaking away without her.

Wilting, she sank onto a couch beside a potted palm while he stood in line to check in. Her head drooped. She hadn't managed nearly enough sleep the night before. Max's voice snapped her out of a daze.

"Shall we go upstairs?" Tossing her one of the two key cards, he grabbed her bag along with his own stuff and headed for the elevator.

The prospect of stretching out in air-conditioned comfort sounded so appealing that she didn't bother to resent his high-handed behavior. She felt almost content until Max unlocked the room door and waved her inside.

"Wait a minute! There's only one bed!" King-size, it sprawled over most of the room.

He shrugged. "As I said, it was all they had. What are you concerned about? We'll be staying only a few hours, until dark. Don't you believe I can control my impulses that long?"

Her cheeks turned hot. "I don't think I'm that irresistible," she muttered. Facing away from him to deposit her bag on the luggage stand, she could still see him in the mirror. A smile flickered over his lips.

"More so than you think. However, all I want is sleep." She brushed a lock of hair away from her damp forehead.

"Well, maybe that's all you want, but I need food. We could order something from room service."

"Nothing for me." He sagged onto the bed, bending over to untie his shoes. "If you decide to order a meal, I'd prefer that you avoid any strongly spiced foods. The smells tend to upset my stomach."

"Sure."

"And don't open the curtains, please. The sun gives me a headache."

"Fine." Again she marveled at the incongruity of such a vigorous man having such a list of medical sensitivities.

The thought flew out of her head when he followed the removal of shoes and socks with pulling off his shirt. She hardly realized she was staring until he unsnapped his slacks and started to unzip them. Her gasp drew a quizzical glance from him. "Did you expect me to sleep fully dressed?"

Snatching her toiletries pouch and a handful of clothes from her bag, Linnet fled into the bathroom. She stood under the cool shower long enough to give him plenty of time to get settled—and hidden. Her bare skin still blushed deep pink when she got out to dry herself. Her nipples hardened not only from the friction of the towel but even more from the memory of her dream.

Why was she behaving like a kid with a crush? Max couldn't have any personal interest in her. He had to concentrate on finding his brother's killer. Just as she ought to keep her mind on Deanna, not on erotic fantasies.

In fresh shorts and blouse, with the ankh pendant again in place around her neck, she peeked through the half-open door. Max lay on his back with the sheet drawn up to mid-chest. His eyes were closed. Could he be asleep already? Linnet tiptoed into the bedroom and flipped through the guest services directory. She ordered a sandwich—chicken salad, surely bland enough for anyone—and a diet cola. The motel café might have offered a wider selection than room service, but she didn't put it past Max to leave without her if she let him out of her sight.

He did look genuinely dead to the world, though. He didn't stir while she talked on the phone, even though she had to switch on a light to read the number, nor did the rhythm of his breath change. In fact, she couldn't even hear him breathing.

After eating the sandwich, she tried vainly to concentrate on her paperback mystery. Fatigue made the words blur on the page. What harm would it do to lie down for a few minutes? Max didn't look about to wake up. Anyway, the width of the bed left her plenty of space to rest without getting near him. She folded down the bedspread just far enough to expose a pillow on the side opposite his. She lay faceup on top of the covers, taking her position with slow caution to keep from disturbing Max. He didn't move.

She forced her arms and legs to relax one by one. She was perfectly safe with Max. If he'd wanted to hurt her—or ravish her, for that matter—he'd had plenty of chances. The tension seeped out of her muscles. Her eyes and head felt heavy. Sleep crept over her....

Fingers caressed every curve and hollow of her body. Or maybe tongues. Tongues of flame. They scorched her flesh, but they didn't hurt. Far from it...

Linnet's eyes snapped open. Dreaming again. *What's with this crazy obsession?* She struggled to tame her rapid breathing. What if the noise woke Max? Carefully she turned on her side to look at him. The mattress dipped, but at least the springs didn't squeak. Despite the closed curtains, she could see his face clearly once her eyes adjusted to the dimness. He didn't react, not so much as a flutter of an eyelash. She told herself it was ridiculous to fear that he could sense her excitement. If he could, the vibrations emanating from her would have shocked him awake already.

On the other hand, he had talents she'd never seen in any other man. She'd read enough about hypnosis to realize that his effect on Nola's hanger-on hadn't been normal. If psychic powers existed, Max probably possessed them. Linnet had never believed in such things, though. As a science teacher, she ought to be ashamed of herself for entertaining the notion.

Yet how could the science she knew explain that boy's readiness to commit suicide at Max's command? Or the way he turned almost catatonic after Max got through with him? If a drug explained those reactions, why hadn't Max used the same drug on her?

A buried memory surfaced to form a cold spot in her chest. After Deanna had started spending so many evenings with Nola's group, she had often stumbled around the house in a daze the next day. She hadn't heard half the things Linnet said to her. Linnet had quickly realized her niece wasn't ignoring her on purpose. Rather, the lapses in attention were real. Worse, Deanna had suffered gaps in her memory. At first Linnet had assumed Dee just didn't want to confess the details of Nola's parties. Gradually, though, it had become obvious that the girl's vagueness arose from a genuine inability to remember much about those gatherings. Linnet had suspected drugs but never found solid evidence. Now she feared Nola had manipulated Deanna's mind the same way Max had controlled the young man's.

Could a normal human being do those things? But if Max and Nola weren't normally human, what were they? Though Linnet enjoyed reading the occasional science-fiction novel, she considered herself too levelheaded to confuse entertainment with real life.

She scanned Max, lying motionless beside her. Aside from his milk-pale skin in contrast to the dark hair, he looked normal enough. That coloring must have run in the family. His brother had had the same marble-like complexion. Her eyes fixed on Max, she waited for any sign of awareness. His chest didn't even expand visibly with his breathing. Struck by a ridiculous idea, she raked through her hair to snag a few loose strands. She dangled a couple of hairs in front of his face, inwardly laughing at her own silliness.

Of course he was breathing. A healthy man of no more than forty didn't lie down and die for no reason. Still, she stared at his nose and mouth, waiting for a breath to stir the hairs. Minutes went by. Surely at least two minutes, she thought, though she hadn't glanced at the clock. Her wrist cramped. *Give up. This is ridiculous!* she scolded herself.

Finally, after what felt like three minutes or more, the hairs wavered. She felt a light puff of air on her hand. *There, what did I tell you?* She dropped the hairs on the rug and massaged her wrist. Yet she remained less convinced than her rational side claimed. Could he have paused that long between breaths, or had she just failed to notice an exhalation? She plucked up the hem of the sheet and eased it down his chest. His right arm lay at his side, the left bent to cover his ribs. Linnet stretched her hand toward him, hovered an inch from his forearm.

Her heartbeat quickened. What was she doing? If she touched him, he would certainly wake up, and how would she explain her behavior? What if he got the wrong idea?

Well, it wouldn't be totally wrong, would it? She ordered the inner voice to shut up. Slowly she lowered her hand until her fingertips barely rested on his arm. No response. She curled her fingers around his wrist to find the pulse point. She couldn't feel any movement under the skin. She groped for the spot, fighting the impulse to squeeze, which would wake him for sure.

Her failure to find a pulse didn't mean a thing. She wasn't a doctor or nurse, just a biology teacher with a first-aid certificate seven years out-of-date. Her own heart raced, ignoring her sensible arguments. Again she noticed how cold his skin felt. Maybe he was sick, after all. Did he need medical attention? She visualized herself calling 911, then having Max wake up and laugh at her, while a paramedic team viewed her panic with pity or contempt.

She let go of his wrist and moved her hand over his chest, not quite touching. The triangular pattern of velvety hair tempted her with the memory of how it had felt when she'd touched it before. Instead of pausing to give temptation a chance to overwhelm her, she pressed her fingers to the side of his neck. Silently she counted, spacing the numbers with "thousand" between them. She passed two hundred before she felt a single pulsation. There, of course he had a heartbeat. And if she didn't stop groping him, he would catch her at it.

Yet she didn't back off. Instead, she caught herself laying her open palm on his chest. Could the coolness be caused by the air-conditioning? That seemed unlikely, since her own skin glowed with warmth.

Because of thinking hot thoughts, she chided herself. *Which you've got no business doing.* She skimmed down his chest, relishing the texture of the hair against her palm. *Stop that right this minute.* Her hand ignored her. She gazed at the landscape she couldn't resist exploring. His nipples pebbled up, even though she hadn't touched them. Her own suddenly ached.

His fingers clamped around her wrist. An involuntary gasp escaped her. Her eyes flicked up to his face and clashed with his, now wide-open. He was breathing audibly now, in shallow pants that her own breathing echoed.

"Sorry," she whispered. "I didn't mean to disturb you."

"Then what *did* you mean?" His voice, almost too low to understand, verged on a growl.

"I'm not sure. You looked so...still. I was afraid you might be sick." How ridiculous did that sound? But any excuse was better than admitting her actual thoughts.

"As you see, I'm perfectly well." He smoothed back the hair tumbling over her forehead. "Except for interrupted sleep. And acute hunger."

She tried to pull away. His hand kept hers imprisoned. "I could call room service again. What do you want?"

He bared his teeth in a not-quite smile. "Not that kind of hunger." His fingers crept under her hair to caress the nape of her neck. "And surely you can guess what I want."

Her throat constricted so that she could hardly talk. "I don't want—"

"Don't waste energy on lies." He sat up, still grasping her wrist in his left hand, while using his right to guide her head toward his. "You're as eager to be tasted as I am to taste you."

For a second she thought about how odd that remark sounded, but the fog in her brain kept her from focusing on the strangeness. His fingers traced spirals on the back of her neck. His tongue flicked at the corners of her mouth, never settling long enough for her to retaliate. Chills and flames chased each other up and down her body. Now the hand that chained hers began teasing tender spots on the inside of her wrist, places she'd never imagined as erogenous zones. He seemed to be feeling her pulse, the way she had tried to feel his. Except that his technique far surpassed hers.

He continued tantalizing her open mouth while evading every attempt she made to capture his lips. With rapid strokes of his tongue, he followed the curve of her jaw to her neck. She tilted her head, cupped by his open hand, to welcome his kisses on her throat. His lips burned, though his hands still felt deliciously cool on her overheated skin.

From deep in his chest that sound she'd heard before, almost a purr, rumbled through the mist that clouded her brain.

"Max," she whispered. No answer. She shifted her hand in his now-relaxed grip to press her nails into his skin. "Max, stop."

His mouth moved to her ear and painlessly nipped the lobe. "Why?"

"You know why. We're not supposed to do this." With her free hand she clasped the ankh. Its angles pressing into her flesh dispelled a little of the fog.

"You're absolutely right," he murmured into her hair. "We shouldn't make the mistake Anthony and Deanna made."

Linnet pulled back just far enough to keep his lips from touching her, though she still felt his breath. "Mistake? Being together, you mean?"

"Yes. Dangerous." His hand didn't stop rubbing the back of her neck.

"Because that's what made Nola send that guy to kill them." She had to force out the words between gulps of air.

"Not only that." He released her wrist and attacked the top buttons of her blouse.

"They were too young."

"That's one way to put it." He nibbled from her earlobe down her throat to the exposed V above her breasts. Her nipples tightened and tingled.

She squeezed the ankh. "Max, *stop!*" This time he obeyed. When he looked straight at her, she thought she glimpsed crimson flecks in his eyes. Imagination. An effect of the dim light. "You're saying the right words, but the tune doesn't match."

A hoarse laugh emanated from him. "True. Perhaps because I don't believe the words as completely as I should. Nor do you. I feel the glow you radiate." His hand skimmed over the front of her blouse, and she gasped with the electricity that sparked through her breasts. "And you respond in more obvious ways, as well."

She squirmed out of his loose grip. "That doesn't mean a thing. Just physiology. Automatic." She might have sounded more convincing if she could have calmed her breathing.

"Yet you were the one who touched me first."

"Well, like you said, big mistake." She glared at him, fuming at her own eagerness to throw her arms around him and beg for another "taste."

"I said it would be a mistake to get involved as Anthony and Deanna did. Unlike them, we aren't too young. Surely we have the self-control to enjoy each other without such entanglements." She couldn't tell whether he was making a serious proposition or teasing her. The wry smile suggested the latter, but at the same time he extended a fingertip to circle her parted lips.

Sighing, Linnet lapped his finger with her tongue. He paused long enough for her lips to close around the fingertip. She gave it a gentle bite.

A gasp escaped him. Blushing at her own bizarre impulse, she opened her mouth and drew back. "I didn't mean to do that. Really." She would have suspected him of laughing at her if it hadn't been for his ragged breathing. "That's the most blatant proposal of a one-night stand I've ever heard. You must have a great opinion of your own talents."

"You can judge my talents for yourself."

Shaking her head, she clutched the pendant as if it held the last scrap of her sanity. "No, thanks, I want entanglement or nothing."

He stood up. She was annoyed with herself for feeling disappointed when the removal of the sheet revealed a pair of shorts instead of nudity. "I could change your mind," he said. "Remember what I did to Nola's disciple."

"No, you can't, because I have this. You said so yourself."

"Just as well," he said, reaching for the clothes he'd left

on the nearest chair. "You're right, after all. It would be a mistake on every level."

Linnet nodded. "Absolutely. We have to concentrate on finding Nola. Nothing else."

"You shouldn't have touched me." He hurried into his slacks and yanked on a T-shirt.

"Me? Touch you? So now it's my fault you can't keep your hands to yourself?"

"My hands aren't the problem." With a wry smile, he sat down to put on his shoes. "You needn't worry, none of those *problems* will get near you from now on."

A flood of anger swept away her arousal. "Great! And you don't have to worry about me touching you again, either!"

"Excellent." He picked up a key card and stalked across the room, then whirled to face her. "Make sure you keep that promise. My self-control is not infinite." He walked out the door and slammed it behind him.

Chapter 7

Max's throat burned with thirst. He could hardly keep from snarling aloud as he flung the door shut and stormed down the hall to the stairway exit. He had no patience to wait for the elevator. Scarcely touching the steps, he half flew to the ground floor.

What was wrong with the woman? She behaved as if she *wanted* her blood drained. Touching him while he slept, with his defenses down... Of course he'd felt her fingers at the pulse point on his neck. It had been all he could manage to keep pretending to be oblivious. When she'd bitten him, the playful impulse had almost wrecked what little control he had left. Why would she be fool enough to act so seductively?

Emerging into the courtyard, Max glowered at the still-bright early-evening sun. It wouldn't set for at least another hour at this time of year. Fuming, he retreated to the shade of a flowering tree. The pool glinted in the center of the court. He had no intention of joining the sweaty human crowd and exposing himself to the blinding glare of the blue water. He needed to find a solitary female he could feed from in safety before returning to the room and facing Linnet's reckless allure.

He blinked in astonishment at his own thoughts. He was thinking like a human male—blaming the victim, as they called it nowadays. Linnet couldn't possibly guess what fate she'd tempted, nor had she intended her curious exploration as seduction. It was his own responsibility to keep a proper distance from her. Why did he crave her blood? After feeding on her the previous night, he shouldn't feel the need for at least another twenty-four hours. Proximity was artificially stimulating his appetite, he supposed. Also, the challenge of her immunity to his mesmeric power might have something to do with his interest.

For several reasons, he had to resist the desire. Emotional entanglement would impair their ability to work together, distract them from the mission. Repeated feedings at too close intervals would weaken her, and he needed his ally at full strength. Most important, if he tasted her too often, he risked becoming addicted, as Anthony had been with Deanna. Max never planned to fall into that trap. In one way Nola's strategy was sound. By taking her victims from a "harem" of a dozen or more, she never had to resort to the same one often enough to develop a dependency.

Furthermore, a passionate interlude with Linnet would hurt her—emotionally, even if not physically. He respected the woman's courage, no matter how foolhardy its expression. On some level, he liked her. Anthony had liked her niece. The attraction must run in the family. *Now you're thinking like a fool, Maxwell,* he berated himself. *She's a pet, at most, and you don't have time for a pet.*

Having argued himself into behaving rationally, Max surveyed the people strolling to and from the pool. Perhaps he could lure one of the young women away from the crowd. Blood from any live human prey would do, but a responsive female satisfied him best. Lacking the excitement of sexual polarity, a man's blood tasted little better than an animal's.

Lurking under his tree, eyes stinging from the sun, Max watched the people walking along the path a few yards away. A family, parents accompanied by a pair of little boys shoving each other as they ran ahead. A gaggle of teenage girls. Two women of about forty. No good, he needed one alone, who wouldn't be missed for a few minutes.

By the time a suitable target approached, his head was pounding from the sunlight. A girl of twenty or so in a two-piece bathing suit walked up the path, barefoot, blond hair dripping. No one else was nearby for the moment. Max stepped in front of her.

"Pardon me, miss, I believe you dropped your key." Capturing her eyes, he slipped the key card from her left hand, under a fold of the damp towel she carried, and offered it to her. Oblivious to his sleight of hand, she accepted the card and murmured confused thanks.

Having used the trick merely to entice her to look into his eyes, he held her gaze and whispered, "You aren't in a hurry to return to your room. You want to come with me into the shade, alone, where it's quiet." He clasped her hand and stroked from elbow down to fingertips, then back again, in a pattern of languid repetition. Her eyelids drooped. "Come with me. You will enjoy it, won't you?"

"Mmm-hmm." When he put an arm around her waist, she allowed him to guide her off the path and around the corner, where a taller tree provided deeper shade. At that moment a woman carrying a baby walked by. Max glowered at her, and she quickened her pace.

He focused on his prey again and curbed his impatience long enough to construct a bubble of illusion to hide them from anyone else who might stumble across them. Tucking the girl's wet hair behind her ears to expose her neck, Max caressed her shoulders in long swirls that wandered along her upper arms and back again. The scent of chlorine, mingled with her salty fragrance, enveloped him. She melted against him, her arms wrapped around his torso. Since she stood a foot shorter than he, Max had to bend over to lick and nibble her jawline and throat. He avoided her lips. Unlike Linnet, this girl inspired no desire for the intimacy of kisses. *Stop thinking about that woman!* he growled to himself.

Enough. The girl was lulled into a semiconscious erotic fog, and the enzymes in his saliva had numbed her skin. No need to risk further delay.

He pierced the tender flesh, avoiding the large veins and arteries where he would have done real damage. With a gasp, she pressed harder against his body. Tasting the salt-sweet trickle of blood, he stroked down her curves and insinuated his hand between her thighs. She convulsed against him, and her pulse raced. The heat of her life flooded through him.

He counted heartbeats to avoid losing track of time. The last thing he wanted was having to hypnotize some chance witness into forgetting this incident. Reluctantly, he lifted his head and applied gentle pressure to the tiny incision. "Go back to your room now. Drink a glass of water and rest. You will not remember meeting me."

She twisted away from his fingers at her throat and snuggled against him. "Don't want to go," she mumbled.

"Yes, you do," he said more firmly. He used her towel to wipe away the thread of blood and stop it from seeping afresh. "You need to forget about me and take a nap. You will have pleasant dreams and awaken satisfied, remembering nothing about this encounter." He allowed the psychic shield that surrounded them to melt.

He heard the voices of two boys coming up the path. "Go now," he ordered more sharply.

Finally she accepted the command and padded away. She might be perfectly satisfied, but he realized he wasn't. He'd enjoyed the few minutes of pleasure, sharing the girl's climax, but now that it was over, he still felt discontented. The best he could say for the experience was that the fires in his stomach and throat were quenched, and his head didn't hurt anymore. In this short time, he'd started to become obsessed with Linnet. All the more reason not to feed from her again. The quicker they found Nola, the sooner they could separate, and he could escape further temptation.

At any rate, now he could return to Linnet without the torment of hunger to undermine his resolution. Realizing how disheveled he looked—the girl's embrace had left blood on his shirt—he once again shrouded himself in a psychic veil to walk into the building and up the stairs. Doors that opened and closed by themselves, he decided, would arouse less curiosity than a man in a bloodstained T-shirt.

Still invisible, he paused at the door of the motel room, listening. He expected to hear only Linnet's breathing, or perhaps the television. Instead, he heard suppressed sobs. Damn it, what was wrong with the woman now? He doubted her crying arose simply from grief over her niece.

Slipping his card into the lock, he eased the door open a crack. Linnet lay on the bed, her face pillowed on her arms. He sensed the effort she made to keep from sobbing out loud. Anger as well as sadness radiated from her. Max felt an urge to take her in his arms and soothe away those negative emotions.

What an idiotic notion! If he touched her, the next thing he knew, he would end up kissing and caressing her, then getting thirsty all over again. Besides, where had he gotten the ridiculous idea that he ought to comfort a human female? She was just an ephemeral, whose emotions should mean nothing to him but a source of psychic nourishment.

Disgusted with his undisciplined thoughts, he pulled the door shut and, still veiled, stalked down the hall to a plate-glass window at the end of the corridor. Arms folded, he stared down at the freeway, where a stream of cars glinted in the sun. He punished himself with the glare, hoping the discomfort would drive away his irrational impulses.

When Max stomped out of the room, Linnet told herself she was glad he'd left. They both needed to cool off, didn't they? She didn't want to get sexually involved with a man she couldn't in a million years consider spending her life with, and she certainly didn't want a one-night stand. Even if she went in for that kind of fling, she would never choose Maxwell Tremayne. Their situation demanded an all-business approach. No distractions.

So why did she feel miserable? Just wounded ego from the fact that Max could so easily agree that they shouldn't get involved? Linnet hoped she wasn't *that* shallow.

Did she feel attracted to him, no matter how senselessly? She plopped down on the bed and picked at a loose thread on the hem of the cover. Sure, he turned her on. No doubt about that. But a grown woman's brain shouldn't get scrambled by a few incredible kisses. He seemed to feel that way, too. The moment she called time-out, giving him a few seconds to think, he jumped at the chance to escape from her. Well, let him. As far as she could tell, he regarded her as a nuisance he was stuck with against his will. Why had she demeaned herself for a single minute by kissing a man like that?

The thread she was twisting snapped off. She crumpled the bedspread in her hands and plucked loose another strand to fiddle with. A metallic scent wafted from the rumpled sheets. Max's aftershave? If so, she didn't believe the peculiar, though not unpleasant, aroma would ever become a best-seller.

Not that she wouldn't have enjoyed getting to know Max in normal circumstances. Suppose Anthony had lived, married Dee and introduced Linnet to Max? Not only was the man infuriatingly ravishing, he had a brain. He wrote books. He'd traveled all over the world. If the situation were different, he could show Linnet the Globe, Westminster Cathedral, the Paris Opera House, Notre Dame, all the places he knew as an art historian rather than an ordinary tourist.

Right, and he would get bored with her inside a week. She'd hardly set foot outside Maryland, aside from a few family vacations. She and Max fitted together about as well as a tiger and an alley cat. Why was she indulging in these wild fantasies?

Still, did he have to agree so emphatically when she declared that making love would be a mistake?

Don't know what you want, do you, girl? she mocked herself.

She wanted to go home, where life used to make sense. As if in a magical response to the wish, her cell phone beeped, announcing an attempted call.

She snatched up the phone. One message. When she pulled up the number, she sighed in dismay. Her mother.

She decided she had to return the call, or Mom would keep trying and interrogate her about it the next time they met. After all, she didn't have to volunteer her whereabouts. Mulling over possible alibis, she punched in her mother's number.

"Linnet, where have you been? I can't get anything at your house except the answering machine."

"Good grief, Mom, I left a message on yours."

"Some message! You've got business that'll keep you away from home for a few days? " said her mother in a sarcastic falsetto. "That doesn't tell me a thing. What business?"

"I ran into Anthony's brother. We had some financial arrangements and stuff to take care of." She braced herself for a scolding.

"Anthony's brother? You didn't think this was important enough to tell me about, not to mention Robin and Tim?"

Linnet swallowed a hysterical giggle at the thought of trying to explain Max to her sister and brother-in-law. "I didn't want to bother any of you. I'm sure Robin would rather have me deal with Anthony's one living relative than have to do it herself."

"That's still no excuse to up and disappear."

"I didn't disappear." She struggled to keep exasperation out of her voice. "I left you a message. I'll be home in a day or two."

"You never said where you are."

"Just in and out, nowhere special," she said with a vagueness she knew she could never get away with face-to-face.

"Do you even know about that crazy boy who went to the police and confessed to the murder?"

"Yes, I heard about that, but I'm not up to discussing it right now." She didn't have to fake the strain in her voice. "Look, Mom, I don't want to run up my cell-phone bill. I'll tell you all about what I've been doing next time I see you."

"And Robin. She'll want to hear about it, whatever it is, too."

"Not likely. She can't stand to hear Anthony's name mentioned. Besides, she won't talk to me in the first place."

A heavy sigh drifted over the phone. "She didn't mean anything by those things she said to you."

"Sure sounded like it to me."

"Hon, you have to understand, she's not herself. Her daughter was murdered."

Acid welled up in Linnet's throat. "What about my niece? And your granddaughter, for that matter? Robin's not the only one hurting, damn it!"

"Don't use that language to me!"

"Sorry, Mom." Her cheeks burned from the flare-up of anger. "But I loved Dee, too. Maybe not the same way Robin did, but that doesn't give her any right to take it out on the rest of us."

"You have to make allowances for her."

"Why do I always have to be the reasonable one and make allowances?" Catching the whine in her own voice, Linnet said, "I don't want to fight like this. We'll talk in a day or two." With a quick goodbye, she turned off the power before her mother could speak again.

Tears welled up. Sniffling, she grabbed a tissue and rubbed her eyes. She knew what she wanted. She wanted her parents and sister to forgive her for letting Deanna get murdered. Heck, while she was wishing, she might as well wish to have her niece back. Come to think of it, she could wish Deanna had never met Nola Grant or even Anthony, nice as he had seemed. She dabbed at the moisture streaking her face.

Nice? If she'd had time to get better acquainted with him, Anthony would probably have shown himself to be as arrogant and insufferable as his brother. For all she knew, Max might have decided he was fed up with her and driven to Monterey alone. Linnet flung herself down on the bed and hid her face in the pillow.

Several minutes later, a faint sound cracked the surface of her misery. The door? She rolled over and looked in that direction, just in time to see it close.

"Max?"

No answer. She stood up, wiped her eyes once more and scurried to the door. Opening it, she saw nobody in the hall. She knew Max could move fast, but disappearing that quickly seemed impossible. Yet who else would have peeked in at her? Not the motel staff, surely. Why had Max changed his mind and retreated?

Easy, because he was a coward. Afraid of emotional outbursts, like all men. A crying woman turned them into quivering blobs. He'd walked out in the middle of a fight, and now he was afraid to come back. Well, she wouldn't let him get away with it.

With just enough foresight to grab her own key off the dresser, she charged into the hall, barefoot. In the back of her mind a small voice chirped that at least he'd cared enough not to run off to Monterey without her. So far, anyway.

She glanced from one end of the corridor to the other. Had he had time to catch the elevator? In that case, she thought she would have heard the groan of the machinery. Not that long had passed before she'd opened the door. She headed toward the other end of the hall, with the stairway exit and a tall window.

When she got within a few yards of the window, the air shimmered. A heat mirage, she thought at first, until it darkened into a man-shaped blur in front of the glass. And then Max stood in front of her.

She jumped and clapped a hand to her chest. Her heart fluttered as if trying to fly out of her rib cage. "You—" She swallowed. "You did that in the woods, too. Appeared out of thin air."

He arched his eyebrows. "Surely you don't believe that. You're a scientist."

"So what do you expect me to believe? I know what I just saw. You weren't here, and now you are."

"I'm fast and quiet. Let it go at that."

"No way! I've been letting too much go on your word. I'm sick of being treated like a stray puppy who followed you home, instead of a partner." She put her hands on her hips and scowled at him.

He lowered his voice. "Then at least let's discuss this in private, not where anyone could overhear." He lightly grasped her elbow and steered her toward the room.

"Fine. Sure you won't run away again the minute things heat up?" Hearing that phrase slip out, she blushed. Though she'd intended *heat* in the sense of anger, the other meaning pounced on her at once, and she could only hope he hadn't thought of it, too.

As they entered the room, she got a closer look at Max. His shirt was not only rumpled but stained. Dark red stains.

"What's that?" She reached for him but stopped midway, remembering the last time she'd touched his chest. "Are you hurt?"

"No!" He turned from her to bolt and chain the door.

"Then what happened? Whose blood is that?"

"You don't need to know."

"Oh, yes, I do. For one thing, I have to know if I'm going to need a lawyer when the police barge in here any minute to arrest you for assault."

Max sat down with a decisive thud in the armchair by the curtained window, running a hand through his hair. "That won't happen. Damn it, woman, all this would be so much easier if I could hypnotize you into believing every word I say."

"The way you did poor Fred, and Nola did to Deanna and the other kids? Thank heaven you can't." She stood over him, her arms folded. "Give."

"Very well. Remember what I told you about Nola's blood fetish?"

"Yeah. She likes to drink blood." A lump of sickness congealed in the pit of Linnet's stomach. "And you said she's a cousin of yours. Blood on your shirt—you're like her?"

"It's more than a preference. It's a biological need."

"You're crazy." Linnet backed up until she hit the mattress, and then her knees buckled. Sitting on the bed, she stared at Max, who looked as cool as ever. "I'm alone with some kind of bloodsucking pervert."

"I concede the habit might constitute a perversion for a human being. Although there's some question about that. Certain African tribes who herd cattle use their livestock's blood, mixed with milk, for nourishment."

"Don't confuse the issue. The customs of exotic cultures are beside the point."

"So they are. Not that consuming blood is entirely exotic. Surely you've known people who eat blood sausage." He held up a hand to forestall another protest. "However, these facts have no direct relevance to Nola and me. We are not human."

She thought of his peculiar habits, his avoidance of sunlight and solid food, his aversion to garlic, his preference for sleeping in the daytime, his extraordinary talent for hypnosis. He really meant that incredible claim. Whether or not Nola was playacting, Max wasn't. He believed what he'd just said.

"You *are* nuts!"

He sighed. "The expected reaction. I suppose I should prefer it over an immediate rush for stake, cross and torch."

"Stake?" Now that he obviously wasn't preparing to leap on her and rip out her throat, fear gave way to outrage. "What are you saying? You're a vampire? How gullible do you think I am?" What she'd just seen in the corridor flashed into her mind. She smothered the thought. Now that she'd had a few minutes to recover, she knew she must have imagined that incident. She had to believe that or decide the universe, not just Max, had gone crazy.

"On the contrary, I think you're too intelligent to discount the evidence of your own eyes, even if it contradicts your ingrained beliefs about the nature of reality."

"You said it yourself, I'm trained in science. I don't believe in the supernatural. You're trying to scare me away with this wild story, aren't you? Well, it won't work."

"No, what will no longer work is trying to hide the truth from you. These few hours have shown that we can't share close quarters without the truth of my—anomalies—becoming obvious. Since I can't mesmerize you into ignoring an accumulating list of oddities, the simplest alternative is to reveal the truth. Then we can get on with the job at hand."

"Good grief, you really believe this stuff. You actually think you're a vampire."

Chapter 8

He shook his head. "We do not have time for this. After spending a night and a day trying to keep you from finding out what I am, must I now expend almost as much effort to convince you of the truth?"

"The way I see it, there are only two possibilities. You're feeding me this line to chase me away, so I won't slow you down going after Nola. Which I don't buy, because you're too serious about it. So you're mentally ill, a blood fetishist who thinks he's not human."

"Can you honestly say I look deranged?"

"How would I know? I'm not a psychologist." She had to admit, though, that Max looked more composed and rational than she imagined a raving psychotic would. After all these hours together, wouldn't she have noticed some hint of insanity? Or mental disability, or whatever the politically correct term was?

"Consider the things you've seen." He leaned forward,

hands on his knees. In the shadowed corner, his eyes gleamed with crimson-flecked silver.

"Your eyes," she said. "I didn't want to admit how they looked, but I'm seeing it right now."

He nodded. "Very good. You don't let preconceptions blind you. Normally that would be inconvenient for me, but in the present situation, I want you to make these observations."

"Doesn't mean you're a supernatural being. Could be tinted contact lenses."

"Why would I go to that trouble? And I do not claim to be supernatural."

"Whoa! Vampires are supernatural, right? Last I heard, anyway."

"Only in superstition. This is reality."

"Using the term loosely." Her heartbeat slowed to its normal rate. How could she fear a man who could argue so coolly on such a weird topic?

"The truth behind the superstition is that we're another species who prey on your kind. We look like you in order to pass unnoticed among you. Nothing that your science can't accept."

"I'm still not accepting."

"The blood."

Her stomach churned. She dug her nails into the bedspread. "You're admitting you attack people for their blood."

He frowned. "I did not attack the woman I just drank from. I lured her. She enjoyed the experience, and she won't remember it."

"Enjoyed? That's probably what every rapist thinks." Her protest lacked conviction, though, undermined by the memory of the way his lips had felt on her neck.

"Not rape, damn it, seduction. We give our donors pleasure, and they don't miss the small amount we take."

Trying not to squirm under his stare, she said, "So you're a blood fetishist, the way you claimed Nola was. That doesn't prove you're not human. Like you said, ordinary people can drink blood, too."

He leaned back, watching her. "You've seen other strange events in the last twenty-four hours."

She forced herself to consider the evidence impartially. His compliment on her powers of reasoning and observation had pleased her more than she wanted to admit, and she didn't want to destroy that impression. "The hypnotism thing. From all I've read about psychology, hypnosis doesn't normally work that way."

He encouraged her with a nod.

"And either I'm going nuts too, or I saw you appear out of thin air. Twice."

"Again, have you noted any other symptoms of incipient madness in yourself?"

"Sure." She dredged up a grin from somewhere. "To come here with you in the first place, I have to be crazy." The flash of humor faded. "At Fred's house, you moved so fast. I didn't see you, and you were suddenly—there."

"Not many people would allow themselves to notice that. We rely on human observers' inattentiveness, plus their eagerness to explain away anything that doesn't fit. Most ephemerals don't want their concept of reality overturned."

"Ephemerals? Oh, I get it. Us. People who don't live forever."

"Exactly."

Linnet shook her head. "You're losing me again. How can I seriously believe you aren't human?"

"You touched me." His low voice seemed to stroke her nerves.

Shivering, she wrenched her eyes away from his face. "You're always cold. That could be some obscure chronic condition. But I tried to feel your pulse…" With a jolt, she remembered the extended pause between breaths and heartbeats. On top of all the other anomalies, that one sent the final gust of wind blowing toward her mental house of cards. Could he be telling the truth? Inhumanly fast and strong, with psychic powers of which she'd probably glimpsed only a fraction, he could rip her to shreds on a whim. And if he were actually a member of another species, an intelligent predator, his motives might bear no relation to anything she could understand. How could she trust him not to turn on her?

She stood up, inching around the bed to put more distance between them.

He, too, slowly rose to his feet. "Come, Linnet, if you seriously think you have reason to be afraid, do you believe you have any chance to outrun me?"

"Good point." She drew a deep breath to stop her voice from trembling. "And you haven't tried to hurt me. Yet. But whether you're a vampire or just a lunatic, I know you could."

"We can't work together if you're terrified of me. You'd better save your fear for Nola." He took one step toward her. "Nor can we achieve our goal if you're confused. Frankly, I'd rather you consider me an alien monster than a lunatic. You'll be more likely to listen to my advice."

The remark startled her into a shaky laugh.

"Unfortunately, as we've already established, I can't calm you with hypnosis. And I've gone too far to back off and make you think the claim of vampirism was a joke. So my only choice is to show you something you can't explain away."

"Huh?" She lowered herself into the other chair, farthest from the bed, keeping her eyes fixed on him.

He didn't make any sudden moves, though, or even try to get closer to her. Instead, he peeled off his shirt.

"What now?" Surely he didn't plan to resume the interrupted seduction!

"Just watch, please. I can't do this in sunlight, but this late in the day, with the drapes closed, I can just manage it."

His outline blurred. Patches of darkness spread like spilled ink down his neck, over his shoulders and arms, across his chest. Linnet blinked, trying to dispel what must be an illusion. She found herself standing up, edging toward him to get a better look. His eyes glowed with brighter red at their centers. His ears grew pointed. Something in the collarbone region seemed to melt and reshape. She glanced in the mirror. There his image didn't blur and flicker. Instead, it changed from one stage to the next in fits and starts, like stop-motion photography. *So part of what I'm seeing is subjective perception.*

He turned his back to her. Wings sprouted from his shoulder blades and expanded until their mistlike outline coalesced into a fixed shape. Pale gray, they looked more like moth wings than bat wings. They unfurled to a six-foot span, flowing behind him like a cape.

"Oh, God." Openmouthed, she stared at him. Her legs crumpled.

Max glided across the floor and caught her. When he set her on the bed, she noticed a dusting of fine hairs on his face, not as heavy as the velvet fur that now covered the rest of his body. He flashed a sardonic smile that revealed a feline mouthful of fangs. "You won't faint, will you?"

"I'll try not to." She clutched his arms. "You have wings. And fangs. Is that how you bite…?"

"Certainly not. This shape is normally used only for hunting animals in the wild. Actually, it's seldom used at all in this civilized age, except for recreational purposes."

"Recreational," she parroted. It seemed strange to hear Max's resonant, faintly British-accented voice coming from that half-animal form. The now-familiar tone reassured her that he wasn't going to sink his teeth into her in the next few seconds. "You can't fly. You're too heavy. I don't believe you have hollow bones like a bird, or you couldn't be as strong as you are."

"We levitate. The wings are for gliding and steering."

Feeling dizzy, Linnet closed her eyes and bowed her head on one clenched fist. "Okay, I can accept that you have psychic powers like hypnotizing people. But levitation? That violates the laws of physics."

"Like the transformation itself? In both cases, I'm using my mental powers to alter my physical substance." He slipped out of her grasp, and she heard him move back. "I'm old enough to include clothing in the change, but it's more difficult. I wouldn't bother except in an emergency."

"That doesn't sound very scientific to me. Sounds more like magic." She opened her eyes to look at him. The wings were still there. Since she didn't believe she was losing her mind, she had to accept them.

He shrugged, making the silver-gray membranes shimmer. "Don't you have a saying about sufficiently advanced science being indistinguishable from magic? Anyway, many of your psychologists believe in extrasensory abilities."

"Yeah, and many more of them believe it's a lot of hooey." She rubbed her forehead. "Wow, what I could tell them."

His expression hardened. "I trust you're not one of those people who would jump at the chance to sell a story to the tabloids. I wouldn't have confided in you if you were."

"Of course not. I can just imagine all the lunatic-fringe elements coming after you with stakes, and the biologists locking you in a lab to experiment on. Not to mention the CIA trying to turn you into a secret weapon."

"Exactly. We have many reasons to hide our existence. Now that the various human ethnic groups are widely distributed and the average human height approaches ours, we don't stand out the way we used to. It is much easier to pass for your kind."

"How long have you existed?" Now more fascinated than afraid, she stood up and moved closer to him.

"At least ten thousand years. Perhaps longer. We have no culture except what we borrow from your kind, so perpetuating our own history is of little interest."

"I can understand your being evolved to live on blood." She reached out to run a fingertip along his arm. The hair, or fur, did feel like velvet. The temptation to stroke him like a cat struck her so forcefully that she had to pull back to keep from yielding to it. "But why would evolution give you wings?"

"We think this shape duplicates an ancestral form whose memory, so to speak, is stored in our genes. We can use hypnotic influence to make ourselves appear as other creatures, similar to the way I used that power to make myself invisible, but this is the only true shape change we can perform."

"So what good is it? Aside from recreational?" She folded her arms to resist the urge to touch him again.

"Most likely, in the hunter-gatherer and early agricultural stages, when human populations were small and scattered, we needed the ability to soar long distances in a single night, searching for prey. Then, as now, we probably didn't kill our human donors, nor did we want to frighten them by feeding too often in one settlement. We could glide over large areas using our night vision and infrared sense to find our targets." He must have sensed the chill those words gave her, because he quickly added, "Not that we feed on human prey every night. Much of our nourishment comes from animal blood and, as you've seen, milk."

She had to suppress a giggle. "Milk-drinking vampires?"

"A good many of your legends mention that."

"I wouldn't know. My vampire expertise pretty much begins and ends with the movies."

He bared his lips in a silent snarl. "The only good thing about that nonsense is the way it misdirects people so that they don't recognize the real thing when they meet it."

"You're an endangered species," she said. "Like most large predators in today's world. And I can't deny that predators are as much God's creatures as any other animals."

"Quite so, but few of your people would see us that way." His eyes raked her up and down. "You aren't afraid now."

"Not as long as you keep talking like, well, a normal person."

"You may touch me."

She felt a blush rising. "Do you read minds, too?"

"Only emotions. And yours are obvious enough." He flashed a teasing smile. "To read thoughts requires a two-way exchange of blood, the kind of bond young Fred had with Nola."

"Oh, yeah, he said something about that, but it didn't make sense to me at the time." Linnet took a step closer to Max, who moved toward her at the same moment. She skimmed her hand over his chest. The fur felt smoother than any cat's.

"I broke that bond with the posthypnotic command I gave him. She doesn't have access to his thoughts anymore." Max's breath caught in an audible gasp as she repeated the long, slow strokes. "I'm sure Anthony did the same thing with Deanna."

"Hold it." Her hand stopped moving. "You mean she drank his blood? They drank each other's?"

"Not for power and control, as Nola did with her followers." Taking her hand in his, he guided her fingers to the center of his palm. There she felt a patch of fine hair, sparser than anywhere else. He sighed when she explored it. "Enough," he said. "It's very sensitive, like a cat's whiskers. Pressure overwhelms the nerves so that I don't feel much, but light contact—"

She transferred her attention to the most fascinating feature, the wings. They felt like silk and quivered at her touch. "If Anthony didn't do that with Dee to control her, then why?"

"For intimacy." Max sounded faintly surprised that she had to ask. "To share their inmost thoughts along with the blood. It's said to be the most intense experience possible between lovers. I wouldn't know."

"You wouldn't, huh?" She couldn't stop running her hands over the upper curve of his wings. Their responsive vibration felt almost hypnotic in itself.

"I've never shared blood with an ephemeral. I've never known one I was willing to be that vulnerable to." He captured her arms. "You'd better stop. Didn't we decide not to repeat our earlier indulgence?" His voice was slightly hoarse, his breathing ragged. The wings must be as sensitive as those little hairs in his palms.

"You mean our mistake." She backed off and returned to the chair. "I know you think Anthony made a giant mistake falling in love with Dee." So much for her brief daydream about a relationship—which she didn't want anyway, she reminded herself.

Exhaling a long breath, Max allowed his body to melt back into human form, much quicker than the reverse transformation. She gasped at the sudden change. "I'm mature enough to hold that shape for several hours, but it does take energy, so I'd as soon not do it unnecessarily." He, too, sat down. "Yes, I've already acknowledged my feelings about their liaison. But it's nothing personal. I don't believe any of our kind should become intimate with ephemerals. Sometimes these affairs work. The male vampire near your home who notified me about the murders has a human lover. But more often than not, the attempt ends in disaster."

"Because we're inferior beings."

"I wouldn't be so discourteous as to put it that way."

"I'll bet you wouldn't mind putting it that way to your own people. Or to most of us lower animals, for that matter." She drew her feet up on the chair and wrapped her arms around her knees. "You're just being polite to me because you're stuck with me."

With a half smile, he said, "Your species isn't inferior in every way. You have creative gifts we lack. We don't make art and technology of our own, so we use yours. In many ways you're more flexible than we are. Direct sunlight doesn't make you ill. You don't sleep in a state of suspended animation. While that contributes to our long lifespan, it also leaves us open to attack. You can live on many different kinds of foods. Our diet is nearly as restricted as a koala's or a giant panda's."

She couldn't help smiling at the image of Max munching on eucalyptus leaves or bamboo stalks. "How can a human-size creature live on blood, anyway? Even with the occasional glass of milk?"

He shrugged. "Perhaps we synthesize some vitamins and amino acids. Our physiology has never been thoroughly studied. We've been too busy surviving. Our breeding rate has declined over the past hundred years. We aren't replacing ourselves. Our females go into estrus less often than in previous centuries, and they're more often infertile."

"Estrus?" The word came out as a squeak. "Your women go into heat?"

Openly amused now, he said, "Why does that strike you as bizarre? It's much more efficient than your way. No energy wasted on sexual activity except when reproduction is possible."

"Oh, yeah? What do you call that mistake we almost made?"

"Erotic dalliance with human donors is our primary sensual outlet. But it doesn't normally involve genital contact."

To her annoyance, she was blushing again. "Okay, it makes sense that long-lived animals wouldn't reproduce often. How long do you live anyway?"

"Thousands of years. Indefinitely. We don't become infirm with age, and I've never heard of a natural death."

It crossed her mind that he might be lying, playing with her to discover how many outlandish claims she would swallow. He looked serious enough, though. "Some reptiles and parrots live longer than human beings," she said, "but not that much longer. Some kinds of trees survive for millennia, but mammals, or whatever the heck you are, don't have the metabolism of plants. The whole idea boggles my mind."

He leaned back in his chair with a leisurely stretch. "You saw the transformation. Is our longevity that much harder to accept?"

"I'm still not sure I accept the transformation, even after I've seen it."

"Why not? Chameleons change color to match their backgrounds. Arctic foxes and hares become white in the winter and dark again in summer. The uteri of all female mammals enlarge to many times their normal size during pregnancy and shrink afterward. Some fish and amphibians change sex during their lifetimes. Caterpillars become pupae and then butterflies."

"But that's not the same thing. All those changes, except the chameleon, are gradual, not instantaneous. And the butterflies don't revert to caterpillars, and the sex changes aren't usually reversible."

"Nevertheless, the principle does exist in biology as you already know it."

"Okay, you can grow wings and reabsorb them, and you live forever. So how old are you, personally?"

"About five centuries." He spoke so matter-of-factly that she couldn't doubt him.

"Wow." Her head reeled at the thought. "Did you know Shakespeare?"

Max laughed. "As if anyone who happens to live at the same time as a celebrity must know him personally!"

She hugged her knees tighter, armoring herself against his laughter. "All right, silly question."

"At any rate, he wasn't Shakespeare then, the greatest name in English literature, just another hardworking actor. And actors didn't move in the same circles as rich country gentlemen like myself. I did see him in a private evening performance at a nobleman's home, and I was interested enough to brave London by daylight to watch that actor play the ghost in *Hamlet*. Later, I saw him as Prospero. But, no, we never met face-to-face."

"Still, all the things you could tell me… What your people could do for history, if you could let the world know you exist." She sighed. "Only you can't. No wonder you think of us as—what? An inferior race? Animals?"

"Most of my species regard yours as prey. Or pets."

Prey—the way Max had used some anonymous girl that very afternoon. "So much for our being at the top of the food chain and the lords of creation. I've never liked those cartoons where the creepy little mice infesting people's houses are the good guys and the beautiful cats who catch them are the villains. But the thing is, I've never been the mouse before. Probably best that most of us don't know about you. The human race would shrivel up and die from the humiliation."

"Not quite, I hope. We need you for nourishment, as well as the artifacts you make and the social infrastructure you maintain."

"Wow, some compliment."

Her sarcasm didn't seem to rattle him. "I meant it when I said you have talents we don't. And, to be honest, we're far too lazy to go to all that trouble. Your race is much more energetic."

"Useful animals." A tinge of bitterness crept into her voice. "So that explains why you didn't like your brother living with my niece. How old was Anthony, by the way?"

"He was born in 1893. Too young to know better."

"Better than to fall in love with a pet, you mean?"

"Enough of that!" The sharpness of his tone made her sit up straight. "More important, the relationship was dangerous. Not only for him, but for both of them. You saw the result. He could protect you, but not his lover."

"Anthony protected me? What do you mean?"

"That necklace you're wearing. He gave it to you and told you it would keep you safe, didn't he?"

She nodded, fingering the pendant.

"Thanks to his posthypnotic suggestion, you're immune to Nola's psychic influence—and mine, too, inconveniently. Anthony's mesmerism guarded you against falling under any vampire's control."

"No kidding. So that's why you can't hypnotize me. And why you're willing to take me along to face Nola."

"Yes. As I said earlier, if you can't be controlled, I'd better keep you in sight until this is over."

"Fine, I agree with that. Now that we're giving up all our secrets, tell me what you really have planned for that woman."

"What about her?"

"Come clean. I may not have ESP, but I can tell you've been holding out on me. What are you going to do with Nola when we find her?"

"Very well, you deserve a straight answer. Our law forbids me to kill one of our own species, aside from an outlaw condemned to death for that very crime. The one exception is self-defense. I intend to destroy Nola, but not by making myself a renegade in the process. I plan to set up a situation where she'll attack first and give me an excuse to kill her."

Chapter 9

"Sounds like a flimsy rationalization to me," Linnet said.

The frown of impatience reappeared, turning his thick eyebrows into a satanic V. "I already told you that your law-enforcement system can't deal with her. Now you surely understand why."

"Then what about *your* system? You have a rule against killing each other, and she murdered Anthony, even if she didn't do it in person. And what about killing humans?" In the increasingly dim light, she had to strain to get a clear view of his face. She walked to the window and opened the curtains. The view showed a purple sunset, with brightness fading from the sky.

"We have a rule against slaughtering human victims openly, in a way that might draw attention. Nola didn't commit any such indiscretion. That young fool did the work for her."

"Indiscretion!" A rush of anger set the pulse pounding in

Linnet's temples. "Is that all a human life means to your kind?"

"Not to me." He strode to her and clasped her hands. Her feeble attempt to break free brought no reaction. "Please, I sense emotions, remember. Your anger hurts me."

"Good! You deserve it, if that's the way you think of my niece's death."

"No. Many of our elders would see it that way, though."

"But there's still Anthony. Can't you bring Nola to trial for his murder?"

He gazed down into her eyes. "I wish I could. Do you visualize hauling her in front of some secret tribunal to answer for her crimes?"

"I guess that's what I imagined." His thumbs traced circles on her palms. Did he think he could derail her indignation that way? To her embarrassment, the waves of warmth creeping up her arms hinted that his distraction might work.

"We don't have a structure of law and government. You have those social entities because you're a gregarious species. We are solitary predators."

"You have rules, though. You said so."

"We formed a Council of Elders only a few centuries ago, in a rough imitation of the complex hierarchies that control human society. The elders do very little ruling. Aside from punishing those who turn renegade and kill our own kind, the Council's main function is to prevent your species from noticing the existence of ours."

"How would they punish Nola Grant?"

"If she had destroyed my brother by her own hand, she would be sentenced to death. Any of us who found her could execute her." He released Linnet and turned to the window. "Since her human disciple committed the murders, I'm not free to kill her unprovoked. Revenge isn't worth being outlawed and condemned myself."

"So you have to set it up to look like self-defense."

"That's what it will literally be. I'll make sure of it."

"You're not worried about getting arrested for murder? By the regular police, I mean."

"Nola didn't have any trouble getting your police to leave her alone, did she?" he said with a cold smile. "But I won't let the problem arise to begin with. She has nobody to notice she's missing, and I'll make sure the body won't be easily found."

"What do you mean you'll make sure it's self-defense, anyway?"

"Goading her into an attack shouldn't be hard. She's clearly unstable. And no wonder, since she was born in the eighteenth century, a dangerous time for us."

"What do you mean?"

He leaned against the window, arms folded, watching Linnet. Observing her reaction to his words, she imagined. "Many parts of Europe still had thriving vampire folklore then. Not only peasants, but representatives of church and state, destroyed our people whenever possible. Scholars soberly debated about whether vampires could exist. We'd made the tactical error of encouraging the superstition that we were human dead returned to life. The elders thought that belief might make people more sympathetic toward us." He shook his head. "They should have learned better from the witchcraft persecutions of the previous few hundred years."

"I'm not surprised people believed in the undead. When you're asleep, you do look dead."

"Yes. The industrial revolution and the rise of science worked to our advantage. By the time Anthony was born, most of Western civilization thought of us as a myth, a subject for horror tales. Unfortunately, many children of the generations born during the seventeenth and eighteenth centuries picked up human beliefs about our kind. Our young are highly adaptable, and such confusion is still a hazard even today. Nola may or may not have a psychosomatic fear of crosses and related symbols like the one you're wearing, but your psychologists would certainly call her neurotic."

"And your elders wouldn't want her locked up for being unstable? Or given some kind of treatment?"

He laughed. "Vampires do not subject themselves to psychoanalysis. The elders would intervene only if her instability threatened to expose her true nature. So far, she has been careful. The friend I telephoned to ask about her is one of the elders. He pledged to back me up if I can plausibly claim to kill her in self-defense."

"That's a plan?" Linnet sat on the bed, and Max returned to his chair. "Sounds pretty sketchy to me."

"The first step is to drive to Monterey and try to find her through normal channels, such as the telephone listings. After that, I shall go to her home and challenge her. Alone."

Linnet had half expected the "alone" part, and she didn't intend to let him get away with it. "Just like that? If you guys can sense emotions, won't she feel you coming and be prepared?"

"She might. What about it?"

"You need me for a decoy again. That's why you brought me along in the first place, remember? Nola would recognize you at first glance, even if she didn't sense you a hundred feet away. She wouldn't recognize me."

"Too dangerous. She isn't a harmless idiot like Fred Pulaski."

"What do you care about the danger? I'm just an ephemeral. I'm expendable."

"Confound it, don't twist my words! If nothing else, I care about you because my brother cared for your niece. In honor to his memory, I have to make an effort to keep you safe." His lips contorted in a self-mocking sneer. "It's obvious you've corrupted me, if I'm falling back on a sentimental argument like that."

"Gee, thanks." She squelched the flutter in her chest at the word *care*. An inhuman, immortal creature couldn't mean the same thing by that as she did.

"What is *your* plan, then? You go to her house and knock on the door while I lurk just outside her psychic range? Then what?"

"Maybe I wouldn't have to knock. If I went in the daytime, she'd probably be asleep, wouldn't she?"

"Very likely."

"I could break in, get well inside before she woke up. Then I could distract her while you bring in the reinforcements. I have a right to challenge her, too. I told you, I want a confession. I want her to admit what she did to Deanna, and why."

With his usual annoying half smile, Max said, "You're going to make these demands while she holds you immobilized with strength ten times your own and bares her teeth at your throat, I suppose."

"There must be some way to even the odds. Does garlic really work?"

He nodded. "Garlic powder thrown in her face would make her ill, but it wouldn't disable her for long. You'd have an enraged vampire instead of merely an annoyed one."

"Long enough for you to charge in and use your own superhuman strength to tie her up?"

"If we had anything sturdy enough to hold her."

"And then we could interrogate her as long as we need to."

"Have you forgotten that I plan to provoke her into single combat? Hard to do if she's tied up. Even your courts, much less our Council, wouldn't interpret that as self-defense."

"If you get her to attack you the minute you show up, how am I supposed to question her? Anyway, I still have my doubts about the whole killing thing."

A growl rumbled in his chest. "Haven't you got it through your head that she isn't human?"

"She's a sentient being, close enough to human. Not an animal you can put down like a rabid dog. I want that confession. Then we can talk about what to do with her next."

"You won't have any choice but to kill her, if you hope to live through another night after treating her that way."

Linnet rubbed her forehead to combat the ache building there. "I don't want her to go scot-free, but I can't see myself as an accessory to murder. Sure, she may deserve to die, but I don't know if I could live with that memory. Can't we confine her somehow, make her harmless?"

"My dear, you have no idea what you're suggesting. Imprisoning a vampire is a fate worse than execution. We can't starve to death or even suffocate. The pain would simply…continue."

"Then how would you kill her? A stake through the heart?"

"Not a very efficient method," he said. "A staked vampire takes a long time to die, and if the weapon is removed before the damage becomes irreversible, the body can regenerate. Decapitation or total destruction of the brain works best. Cremation would also be a viable method, except for the practical problem of sustaining a hot enough fire long enough."

"But not starvation."

"No. She would suffer unimaginable agony for days or weeks, until she finally lapsed into a coma. As long as no one released her, she would remain that way indefinitely."

"Fine, she deserves agony. I just don't want to kill anybody. Even a monster."

His eyebrows arched. "You have more of a taste for revenge than I suspected. If you insist on coming with me, we'd better make absolutely sure you can resist if Nola tries to control you."

"How do you mean?"

"Let me try once more to mesmerize you. I want to test the strength of your resistance."

"I'm not sure I like that idea." Did he hope to batter a hole in her shield and use the weakness for his own purposes? After all, he'd admitted how little his kind valued human life. What reason did she have to believe his claim that in some sense he "cared" for her?

"Afraid?" he said with a thin smile.

The taunt in his voice snapped her to attention. She curled her fingers around the ankh. "No way. Do your worst."

He rose from the chair and stood in front of her. She fought the urge to lean away from his looming height. He wrapped his hand around the back of her neck and insinuated his fingers under the hairline. She sighed, feeling her pulse accelerate.

Realizing what he was up to, she blinked to clear the gathering fog from her vision and squeezed the pendant until its sharp edges jabbed her palm.

He gazed into her eyes. "You don't actually want to fight me, do you?" He dropped his voice so that she had to strain to hear him. "Listen to me. Focus on my face. Nothing else exists."

She swayed toward him. The pressure on her mind, like waves beating on sand, threatened to wash away her grip on herself. Clinging to the pendant as an anchor, she whispered, "No. Stay out of my head."

His fingers traced spirals on the back of her neck. "Yield to me. Come into my arms. It's what you want."

"No, it's not." She could hardly speak. Waves of heat rippled over her body. *This was a very bad idea.* She had to lock her muscles to keep from flowing into his embrace.

She wrenched her eyes from his and stared at his chest. Not a great improvement, but at least she was no longer in danger of being paralyzed by his stare. "Back off, Max!"

With a bark of laughter, he took a step backward. "Brava! You did better than I expected."

She felt the pressure on her mind recede. Gasping as if a weight had been lifted from her lungs, she tried to dredge up a sharp retort. Before she could concoct one, a knock sounded on the door.

Max tilted his head as if listening. "One person, human, breathing rapidly, probably frightened. It should be safe to answer."

When she opened the door, a thin girl with a dragonfly tattoo and pale blue hair stood in the hall.

While Linnet stared with her mouth open, the girl said, "I'm looking for Max Tremayne. Do I have the wrong room?"

"He's here. Come on in." Linnet stepped aside to swing the door farther open before she stopped to think that the girl might have a weapon in the backpack she carried over one shoulder. "Jodie?"

"Hey, I saw you in the airport. You chased me." She sounded out of breath.

"I just wanted to talk."

"You look familiar. Hold it, aren't you Dee's cousin or whatever?"

"Aunt. I'm Linnet Carroll. You came to my house a couple of times."

Max cast a sharp glance at her. "You saw this person at the airport? And didn't mention it to me?"

She squirmed under his cool gray eyes. "I wasn't sure who she was. It didn't seem worth mentioning."

"We'll discuss it later." He stood up and moved toward them with long strides that reminded Linnet of a panther in the zoo. When Jodie cringed back and cast a glance at the open door, he…leaped? dashed? streaked? Linnet couldn't tell, except that he blurred into existence beside them and shut the door. Watching him fasten the bolt, Jodie crossed her arms over her chest and flattened herself against the wall.

"Relax, young woman. I don't intend to rip out your throat."

Though the curt tone didn't seem to calm the girl, at least she didn't lapse into hysterics.

"Come sit down." Linnet gently touched Jodie's arm, and she jerked as if zapped by electricity. "It'll be all right. Let me get you a drink."

All she had to offer was water. She guided Jodie to a chair, then went into the bathroom to fill a glass. After Jodie had taken a few sips, Linnet said, "What are you doing here? Did you bring us a message from Nola Grant?"

"Yes. Well, no—not exactly."

"Well, which is it?" said Max, leaning on the dresser.

She darted a nervous glance at Linnet. "I wasn't expecting you to be here, just Mr. Tremayne."

Linnet sat on the edge of the bed, trying to look unthreatening. "That's okay, you can say anything to both of us. I know the truth about Max and Nola." Not sure of Jodie's own awareness, she hesitated to speak more explicitly.

Jodie gave Max a quick look, then stared down at the carpet. "You know they're...not like us?"

"Not human." Linnet drew a deep breath to tame the shaking of her own voice. She hadn't begun to get used to the idea yet. "Vampires."

Since Jodie looked unsurprised, Linnet decided using the *V* word hadn't been a mistake. "Nola sent me after Mr. Tremayne. I mean Max. She didn't know you'd be with him."

Good, Linnet thought. Their plan of having her distract Nola could still work. "You said she didn't exactly send you with a message. What does that mean?"

Jodie gulped a swallow of the water. "She ordered me to lure Max into a trap. But I want to get away from her. I came here to ask him to protect me and help me escape."

Max spoke up. "You expect us to believe that you've run away from Nola? After months of groveling to her and feeding her with your blood?"

Jodie answered with a spasmodic nod.

"Why should I accept such a tale? Doubtless this appeal for help is part of the trap."

"No, I swear." Her eyes squeezed shut for a second. "I can't stand it anymore, the way she's draining my life. It was fun when there were lots of us, you know, so she drank from everybody. Now I'm the only one. It's awful." The girl shivered, a reaction visible even through the leather jacket she wore over her black T-shirt. "She keeps bags of pig blood in the freezer. But she still wants a taste of me almost every night. And I can't go anywhere. This is only the second time she's let me out. She sent me shopping for food once, but after that she kept me in the house."

"Why can't you sneak away while she's asleep?" Linnet asked.

"We're, you know, bonded. She made me drink her blood, like she did with Fred before she left him back in Maryland. She says she'd feel it if I tried to split, even in the daytime. I don't know if it's true, but I didn't want to take the chance."

"Why doesn't she know what you're doing right now?"

"Too far, at least I think so. After I got about two miles away, I couldn't feel her in my head anymore."

Turning his glittering eyes upon her, Max said, "True, you're out of range. She would sense your death or some other breaking of the bond, but she isn't old enough to have the power to spy on your thoughts or emotions from this distance. If the bond were longer established and deeper, the range would be greater. In this situation, however, you're safe for the moment."

"That's what I thought. So I figured, like, you're stronger than she is. You can protect me." Her voice sounded choked with tears. "Come on, guys, I'm being straight with you."

In the same fluid motion as before, Max blurred across the floor and loomed over her. One hand grasped her chin and tilted her head up. Chills prickled on Linnet's arms as she watched his eyes drill into the girl's. "Tell me again," he ordered. "Are you serving Nola, or do you want to break free of her?"

"I want to be free. Please!" The word trailed into a moan.

Max released her and darted back to his seat. "Very well, I see that you're sincere."

"Did you have to scare her?" said Linnet.

He shot her a cold stare. "I had to make sure." Turning back to Jodie, he said in a gentler tone, "How did you find us?"

"Something about Fred. The bond stopped working. Last night, all of a sudden, Nola's like, 'I can't feel him anymore.' And then she's like, 'It must be Max Tremayne,' because she said only a superpowerful vampire could break the bond, and you were the only old vampire who'd be interested in screwing around with her pets. You being Anthony's brother and all." A tremor crept into her voice. "She was so mad. I thought she might tear my head off."

"She left you unharmed," said Max, "because you're the only remaining pet she has. And she commanded you to intercept me in San Francisco."

"Yeah. Because of Fred, she knew you'd be coming after her."

The conversation was flowing too fast for Linnet. "Wait, how much do you know about Fred? Do you know what he did?"

"Uh-huh. He killed Dee and Anthony." Jodie rubbed her eyes. "I'm sorry. Really. I liked Dee. Liked them both. I didn't have a clue Anthony was a vampire until Nola told me about it last night."

"She told you? She admitted she sent Fred to murder

them?" It seemed bizarre to Linnet that Nola would discuss her crimes with a mere "pet." On the other hand, if Jodie was supposed to be completely under the vampire's control, maybe the conversation meant no more to Nola than a human woman's chattering to her cat.

"She was like, 'Did he have to make such a mess of it?' Then she said we had to get out of Maryland. That was a few nights ago. I kind of lost track of how many. She said she picked me to go with her because I was her favorite, after Fred. That's when she gave me a drink of her blood."

"You didn't mind that?" Linnet said.

"No way, it's the most incredible trip you can imagine." A dreamy expression stole over the girl's face. "But it's not worth all the other crap. Being a friggin' prisoner in that house, living with a monster who kills people." She threw a nervous glance at Max.

Living with a monster. A knot of cold congealed in Linnet's stomach.

"Nola brought you here," said Max, who seemed unfazed by the implied insult. "To her house in Pacific Grove?"

"Right. And then, like I said, she lost contact with Fred and freaked out. I think maybe she planned to let him hook up with us later, if he did what she wanted and kept his mouth shut."

"Yes, she would have wanted to rebuild her harem after she'd been back here long enough to get settled. As soon as she felt safe from attracting attention, she'd have started luring new disciples, so don't cling to the illusion that she thinks of you as something special," Max said. After a moment's thought, he asked, "How did she know when to send you to the airport, though? Surely you haven't been loitering around the terminal for almost twenty-four hours, making a circuit of the arrival gates?"

Jodie shook her head. "Nola went to the airport in Monterey and hypnotized one of the ticket guys. She made him search the computer for reservations in your name on all the airlines that fly here from Baltimore and D.C. He tracked down the flight you were taking."

"So you knew what plane to meet," Linnet said. "You watched him disembark and followed him to the rental-car counter. Then what?" This fresh evidence of Nola's power cast a shadow on her hope of defeating the vampire.

"I had a rented car, too, that I drove up from Monterey in. As soon as I saw what company Max was getting a car from, I waited outside their lot and followed you to the motel."

"And you haven't communicated with Nola in any way since you arrived at the airport?"

"No, I swear." Again she shook her head vigorously.

Linnet asked why she had waited several hours to contact them.

"I thought Max was by himself. I got a glimpse of you in the car, but I thought you were just somebody he picked up at the airport for, well, a quick snack. I figured if I knocked before sundown, he'd be asleep and wouldn't hear me."

"Then I take it Nola makes a regular habit of sleeping all day," said Max.

"Mostly. I didn't live with her full-time until a couple of weeks ago, but I don't remember seeing her up before sunset."

This confirmation that at least one facet of her plan made sense cheered Linnet a little.

"Now, young woman," said Max, "I acknowledge that you've given us useful information. However, do you expect us to go out of our way to help you?"

"Please, you're my only hope."

The desperation in her tone stirred Linnet's pity. "Max, we have to—" A glare from him silenced her.

"What, precisely, do you want of me?" he asked.

Jodie said, "After you've taken care of your business with Nola, get me out of town. Out of this state."

"Where do you plan to go?"

"I have a grandmother in Denver. I don't think there's any way Nola could know about her. Get me a ticket for Denver and, if she's still alive when you get done with her, protect me until I get on the plane."

Max leaned forward, staring into the girl's eyes. "Why are you so certain I can protect you?"

"Nola said you're a powerful vamp."

"Knowing what you do about her attitude toward the human race, why do you assume I would bother to help?"

"You can't be like her. You're Anthony's brother, and he was okay."

With a sigh, Max said to Linnet, "Dark Powers, another one!" To Jodie, he continued, "Regardless, you can't expect me to make that effort out of pure altruism. I want concrete proof that you've broken away from Nola."

"What kind of proof?"

"Do something quite simple for us in return."

Her eyes widened with eagerness. "You got it. Anything."

"Guide us to Nola's home. Not all the way, of course. We don't want her to sense your proximity. Just close enough."

"Sure, I can do that. I can do even better. I'll give you a key to the house."

"Excellent." He leaned back. Linnet felt him relax the pressure on Jodie's mind. "Jodie, Linnet and I need to confer in private. Go to the lobby and wait there. We'll be along in a few minutes. We are going to drive to Monterey tonight, and you will ride with us in the same vehicle."

"What about the rental car?"

"Whose name is on the agreement?"

Jodie shrugged. "I guess Nola's. She picked it up at the local airport and gave it to me."

"In that case, do you care whether she gets harassed for failing to return the car on time?"

A faint smile surfaced on the girl's face. "Hell, no."

Max walked over to her, at a normal pace this time. "Listen carefully. You will go to the lobby and wait for us. You won't go anywhere, and you won't get into conversation with anyone. When we come downstairs, you will be ready to travel. Is that clear?"

She nodded, her eyes wearing the dazed look that Linnet knew indicated a vampire-induced trance.

"Very well, go ahead."

Snapping back to ordinary alertness, Jodie snagged her backpack and headed for the door. On the way, she bent over Linnet and smirked. "You guys have to *confer* for a few minutes, huh?"

"What?" It took Linnet a second to absorb the implication. "It's not like that at all!"

"Yeah, right. I've been with a vampire long enough to know what it's like. I'm going to miss that part."

Her face hot, Linnet stalked to the door and slammed it behind Jodie. She whirled around to find Max watching her with a smug grin. "That girl is crazy!" She flung her hands in the air. "They've all got to be crazy, begging to have their blood drunk."

"Your niece, too?"

"She may not have been crazy, but I'll be the first to admit she was a little weird." The image of Jodie's dreamy expression, though, reminded her too keenly of Max's caresses. From what Jodie implied, those delicious sensations were only a mild hint of the potential rapture of a vampire's kiss. *Forget that! I didn't want to get involved when I thought he was a normal man. I sure don't now!* She plopped into a chair. "Okay, what do we have to confer about?"

"Our new friend, of course." His expression hardened. "You should have told me you'd seen her stalking us."

"Stalking *you*. Now that I think about it, she was watching you rent the car."

"And you said nothing." Did he actually sound more disappointed than angry? No, she couldn't believe she had the power to hurt him.

"I told you, I wasn't sure I recognized her. And even if I'd been sure it was Jodie, what could you have done about it? She gave me the slip."

"Damn it, those are just excuses." He grabbed her by the shoulders. When she flinched, he relaxed his grip. "You withheld the information because you didn't trust me."

She glared back at him. "Big surprise. Why should I? Like you haven't kept secrets from me? Big ones."

He shook his head and let go of her. "How would you have reacted if I'd told you right away that Nola, Anthony and I were vampires?"

"I didn't handle it all that badly, did I?" By then she'd had the evidence of her own eyes to convince her, though. "Okay, you have a point. But you could have tried to explain. In case you didn't know, we lower life-forms don't like being used."

"I didn't—" His protest died in midbreath.

"See what I mean? For all I know, I serve the same purpose for you that Jodie does for Nola. Just a convenient lackey." Though she wasn't sure whether she fully believed that statement, leaning in that direction was safer than falling into the illusion that he valued her as a friend—or something more.

"I won't even try to defend myself against that charge." He sighed. "At the moment, we have Jodie to deal with."

"You're going to help her, aren't you? You practically promised."

"If she upholds her side of the bargain."

"You aren't sure she will?" said Linnet. "You did your look-deep-into-my-eyes thing. You read her emotions, right?"

"Oh, she certainly believes her own story. She does want to escape from Nola, desperately so. However, I feel something…off…about her."

"Can't you be more specific? You're supposed to be the superhuman creature here."

"I'm afraid not. Her emotions feel murky, a whirlpool of confusion."

"She's been seduced and practically kidnapped by a vampire. Two of her friends have recently been murdered. Who wouldn't be confused?"

"I hope that accounts for it. Nevertheless, I have reservations about trusting her too far."

"As far as Nola's house in Monterey is the most we have to trust her. It's only a few hours, and you can keep an eye on her all the way."

"Granted. I would be more comfortable with a passenger who didn't share a blood bond with my brother's killer, though."

"You and me both." Although she didn't like the pleading tone she heard in her own voice, Linnet couldn't suppress it. "Max, we have to help her. We can't let Nola get her back and do God knows what to her."

"Why is this girl suddenly so important to you?"

"Because of Deanna. If anybody had gotten her out of Nola's clutches soon enough—"

"I should have known. More atonement." Max heaved an exaggerated sigh. "It seems I've acquired a destiny to avenge and rescue Nola Grant's victims. My softhearted brother has a lot to answer for."

Chapter 10

"One thing I don't get," said Linnet, as they gathered their baggage to leave the motel. "At Nola's place, when I chased you to your car, you could have turned invisible and lost me instantly."

"You might have noticed me vanish. I didn't think the risk of using the psychic veil was justified. For the same reason, I didn't resort to inhuman speed."

She wasn't sure she bought that explanation, since he'd shimmered into visibility right before her eyes in the motel corridor. Had their interlude in the room rattled him enough to make him drop his guard? The idea gave her a twinge of guilty satisfaction. "Why did you let me catch you invisible in the hall today?"

"You called my name, and I responded by reflex. I momentarily forgot I couldn't make you ignore what you'd seen. Or not seen."

"Forgot? You?" She tilted her head back to give him a skeptical look.

"Our kind have photographic memories for words and visual images, but we're as capable of repressing unpleasant truths as you are."

"All right, but how about when I caught up with you right after we left Nola's house? When I jumped into your car, you could have just shoved me out."

"Have you forgotten your threat to report my license number to the police? Having discovered I couldn't mesmerize you, I had no immediate way to ensure that you didn't carry out your threat. I could have handled police inquiries, but I didn't want the bother and delay." At the door, his hand closed around hers as she reached for the latch. "Also, I suspect I was already developing a weakness for you, an inexplicable desire to know you better."

"Inexplicable, huh?" His icy fingers suddenly seemed to scorch her wrist. She felt her pulse throbbing under his touch. She caught herself leaning back to gaze up at him.

"I'd never met a human female I couldn't fascinate at a glance. Are you surprised I responded to the challenge?" His head bent toward hers.

She watched him with wide eyes and parted lips. "Just a challenge?"

"A distraction," he murmured. "Definitely a weakness." Just before his mouth would have touched hers, he straightened up. "A weakness for both of us. Remember our resolution."

"Right." She opened the door, trying not to feel disappointed by his abrupt withdrawal. "Our guide's waiting."

In the lobby Jodie sat huddled in the chair next to the potted palm. She jumped when Max placed a hand on her shoulder. "Come along." Without a word, she picked up her backpack and followed Max and Linnet outside. Linnet sat in the front seat of the car, while Jodie, still wide-eyed like a trapped rabbit, crawled into the back.

Now that the sun had set, Max took the wheel. Linnet accepted his decision gladly, not eager to fight the downtown San Francisco traffic, especially at twilight. Even as a passenger, she caught herself clutching the armrest at every screech of brakes and abrupt lane change.

"Do you have a death wish?" she muttered after one dash through a yellow light. "Oh, yeah, you're immortal. Don't forget, we're not."

"Neither am I," he said, his eyes focused on the road. "We're long-lived and hard to kill. We are not indestructible. But you have nothing to worry about where the traffic's concerned. I have superhuman senses and reflexes."

"Easy for you to say," she muttered, prying her fingers off the armrest.

South of the city they picked up Highway 101, passing through San Jose, Salinas and mile after mile of farming and wine country. Scraps of popular songs and fragments of Steinbeck fiction tumbled through Linnet's brain. She wished they could have driven the route in daylight and seen the landscape clearly.

Jodie spoke up timidly from the back seat. "What are you going to do when you find Nola?"

"The same thing she did to my brother," said Max.

"Not necessarily." Linnet frowned at him. "We haven't completely decided."

"Man, I don't know if I want her dead." Jodie's voice quivered.

"You want to be free of her, don't you?" said Max.

"Sure, but—oh, God, I just wish I could be sure she's not inside my head right now. Like, hiding, you know."

"I don't believe she's powerful enough to reach more than a mile or two or invade your mind without attracting your attention. I could mesmerize you and break the bond, of course."

"Yeah, but then she'd—"

"She would notice the emptiness where that link had been. That is why I haven't suggested it."

"Yeah, she would." Linnet thought Jodie sounded relieved, as if she still felt an emotional tie to the vampire woman. Maybe Max's reluctance to trust the girl had some basis in fact.

"You're not planning to go in there tonight, are you?" Jodie said.

Linnet twisted around to look at her. "No way. I'm not about to act like the brain-damaged vampire-hunters in the movies. We'll go tomorrow. With your key, we won't have to break in. We'd like to catch her asleep."

"Besides directing us to the house," Max said, "you must give us a sketch of the interior, especially the location of her sleeping quarters."

"Okay, I can do that."

"Hold on," said Linnet. "Why don't you just draw us a map to her place?"

"I don't know the town well enough. Nola only let me out once, to buy some stuff we needed, and she planted the directions to the store in my head. She didn't trust me to run loose on my own." The girl's voice held a tinge of resentment. "So I don't know street names or anything. If you drive me around Pacific Grove, I'll recognize the area sooner or later."

"Very well, you'll have to guide us that way," Max said. "One thing we do want to accomplish tonight is to locate the house. You'll direct us there, so we can become familiar with the route."

"But Nola will feel my thoughts."

"I told you, I won't take that risk. Trust me to gauge how close we can get without any risk of making her aware you're nearby. Now what exactly do you recall about the area?"

Jodie gnawed on her lower lip for a minute before answering. "When we drove in the first time, I noticed a big tree with

a plaque in front of it. Nola told me it was called the butter-
fly tree, because every year the Monarchs land on it when
they migrate. It's on the road that runs right along the coast.
I think that's a couple of miles from her house, and I definitely know the way from there."

"Very well, that should do," Max said.

She cringed into the corner of the seat, obviously alarmed
by his impatient tone.

"And I'm not going to bite your head off, either. We have
rules against feeding on others' chosen prey."

"I know that." She sniffled, and Linnet handed her a tissue. "That's why Nola threw a fit when Dee ran off with Anthony. She said Anthony stole her pet."

"My niece was nobody's pet!"

Jodie shrugged. "That's how *they* think of us." She glanced
at Max. "You think he's any different?"

Linnet's chest tightened. All too probably, she had let herself be kissed and pawed by a creature who considered her
an entertaining animal with a few useful skills. "Anthony
was different. I know he loved her. He wouldn't have sacri-
ficed his life for a pet."

"Maybe. But all Nola saw was this young guy trespassing
on her turf."

"Enough of that." The rough edge in Max's voice reminded Linnet that even if he didn't care about human lives,
he must have loved his brother. "We have practical matters
to discuss."

"Right," Linnet said. "Like shopping. We have to make a
list of stuff we'll need. Garlic powder, for sure. What else?
Does Nola have a fear of religious objects? Would she run
from a crucifix?"

Jodie shook her head. "She laughed at all that lame hor-
ror-movie crap. Said it was a good thing people believed it,
because stuff like that made it easier for her kind to pass. You

know, like people thinking she had to be a normal human because she could go out in the daytime."

"Movies," Max snarled. "How long would we have survived if we burst into flames in a ray of sunlight?"

"What else?" Linnet said. "We'll need something super-strong to tie her with. For that we'll have to go to a hardware store. Chains and a padlock? Or just heavy cord?"

"Boat line," Jodie spoke up.

Linnet turned to look at her. "Huh?"

"The stuff you tie up boats with," Jodie said in a "duh" tone. "My folks have a sailboat. Those ropes are really strong."

"Not a bad idea," said Max. "Make sure the line is as heavy as possible while still flexible enough to wrap tightly around her. That will be my job, of course."

"Will we need weapons? I don't think we could buy a gun on the spur of the moment, but how about a stake in case she attacks?"

Max flashed her a smile. "I have trouble visualizing you driving a stake into a vampire's chest, even if she's doubled over with nausea from garlic fumes."

"Okay, so I'm not superwoman, and I've never used a spear. But I could swing a crowbar to bash her head in if things got desperate."

"Really? I thought you couldn't see yourself as a killer."

"That doesn't mean I'll stand there and let her rip me apart. Anyway, like I said before, I don't have a thing against causing her pain." Although the words popped out with little forethought, Linnet realized she meant them. Now that she'd heard from both Max and Jodie how Nola regarded people as nothing more than food sources, head bashing sounded like a fairly reasonable response.

"That shouldn't be necessary. Leave the hand-to-hand combat to me. I won't need weapons. I'm several centuries older than she, and therefore stronger."

"All right, this is the plan." Linnet paused to collect her thoughts. "Tonight Jodie gives us directions to the house and how to find Nola once we're inside. Tomorrow we use her key to get in, and I go to Nola's bedroom."

"We both do," Max interrupted. "If she remains dormant, I can stun her with a single blow to the head."

"What if she's active instead of asleep?" Linnet asked.

"Then I go in alone." His curt tone left no room for argument. "In that case, our only hope is that I can disable her in hand-to-hand combat."

"Okay, if that happens, I admit there isn't much I can do to help. Back to the dormant scenario."

"If she shows any signs of life, throw your jarful of garlic powder in her face. I'll follow a few paces behind, where I won't risk inhaling it," he said.

"Next you charge in, and then what?"

"Holding my breath to minimize the effect of the garlic, I'll knock her out. That will give me several minutes to bind her."

"With a break every few seconds so the smell won't make you too sick. Then we wait for her to wake up—or maybe dump a pot of water over her head—and I can get my confession. Hey, maybe I should take along extra garlic and threaten to give her a fresh dose if she doesn't talk."

"That might be counterproductive," said Max. "If she knows you aren't prepared to kill or even seriously harm her, petty torments will only make her more resistant."

Jodie said, "Then you aren't going to kill her?"

With a sidelong glance, Max said, "We haven't settled that. Linnet, have you considered how vengeful she's proven herself to be? If you let her survive and remain free, you'll have to live the rest of your life in constant fear that she'll find you. And since I doubt you're ready to give up your career and go into hiding, it may be a short life."

"Same thing applies to you, doesn't it?"

"Probably not. I don't think she'd want to suffer the penalty for murdering another vampire, nor would she risk her life attacking one who's older and stronger. She'll more likely take out her anger on you."

The image of Deanna's dead face on the steel shelf flashed into Linnet's mind. She closed her eyes, breathing slowly, until it faded. "We'll worry about that when we get to it. Maybe we should go with the idea of shutting her up someplace she can't escape from, somewhere she'll fall into a coma the way you described. Regardless, I'm determined to get her confession." For a few minutes she stared through the window at the dark fields, dotted with lights from widely spaced houses. "That reminds me of one more thing we need. A pocket tape recorder."

A few miles later, she heard Jodie sniffling. Linnet reached into her purse to get the girl a fresh tissue. Jodie dabbed her eyes. "Sorry. I know I have to get free of her, but I miss it already."

"You miss that monster?" Linnet's throat clogged with anger at the thought of anyone feeling sorry for Deanna's murderer.

"Not *her.* I miss, you know, the feeding." She threw a defiant glare at Linnet. "Don't look at me like I'm a freak. You don't know how great it feels, so don't judge me."

"She's addicted," said Max. "The fixation works both ways. I believe I mentioned that when a vampire feeds too often on one donor, a mutual dependency develops."

"That's why I have to get far away from Nola," Jodie said, "before I cave in and run back to her just for another fix." Crumpling the tissue in her fist, she leaned forward to speak over Max's shoulder. "You could…you know, to let me down gradually."

"No. Such contact would only make your condition worse. There's no point in prolonging the discomfort. You must withdraw 'cold turkey,' as drug addicts say."

"What good would it do anyway, if she's dependent on Nola?" Linnet asked.

"The donor has a bit more flexibility than the vampire in that respect," Max said. "She's addicted to vampire venom in general, as well as the emotional high of being fed on. Any vampire's bite would ease the pangs somewhat."

This conversation plunged Linnet into deeper gloom. Had Anthony and Deanna actually loved each other, after all? Or had they died for a passion no more noble than a crack habit?

They checked into a chain motel on the outskirts of Monterey. Jodie had a single room. Before leaving her there, Max gave her a hypnotic command to stay put until he came for her. He and Linnet shared a double room. Linnet suspected he still wanted to guard against her sneaking out to take action on her own. She didn't mind, since she harbored the same suspicion about him. For similar reasons, he wouldn't let her shop for supplies without him. They considered leaving Jodie behind, but rather than risk her vanishing if the "stay put" command wore off, Max decided to bring her along.

Linnet looked through the Yellow Pages until she found a supermarket and hardware store with addresses on the same block. She showed her notes to Jodie.

"Doesn't sound familiar. When Nola sent me for groceries the day after we got here, the store was pretty close to her house."

"Groceries?" Linnet said as they piled into the car. "For a vampire?"

"Well, I had to eat, didn't I? And she drinks milk."

Using the street index and a sketchy map in the phone book, they discovered the address was in Monterey rather than Pacific Grove. They found the location, a strip mall, in less than half an hour. Jodie, nervous about being spotted in spite of the presumably safe distance from Nola's place, waited in the car with Max there to watch her. Linnet found the garlic powder but noticed garlic spray, designed for flavoring Italian bread, and decided that would work better. As an afterthought she picked up a carton of juice, a bunch of bananas and a box of doughnuts. Even if Max didn't need solid food, she and their companion did. In the drugstore she found a cheap portable tape deck, small enough to carry comfortably in her purse, and a flashlight. At the checkout counter she added batteries and a local street map to the total. Last she zipped over to the hardware store. Despite Max's advice, she grabbed a hand ax. Wishing he had come along for this part of the expedition, she mulled over the different weights of boat line before choosing one and having the attendant cut a twenty-foot length. Hoping that would be long enough, she lugged the bags to the car.

Jodie, dozing in the back seat, blinked at her. "There you are. I thought maybe you chickened out."

Linnet shoved her purchases into the seat beside the girl, who wore her leather jacket like armor despite the season, then got into the front. "Don't be silly. I just had a little trouble at the hardware store. And I still think maybe I should have bought a crowbar."

"It wouldn't do any good," said Max. "Nola would rip it out of your hands in the first five seconds."

"Big encouragement you are." She jerked her seat belt tighter and folded her arms. "I guess you thought I'd decided to take off, too?"

"Certainly not. You don't have the directions to Nola's lair yet."

"It's great to know you trust me." Jumpy with the anticipation of confronting the other vampire, crabby from lack of sleep, and irritated by Jodie's weepy-rabbit expression, Linnet felt as if imaginary ants were scuttling up and down her arms.

Back at the motel, they off-loaded the supplies, then gathered in the double room. Jodie sketched the floor plan of Nola's house on a sheet of motel stationery, which Linnet tucked into her purse for safekeeping.

"Now, here is what we're doing," said Max. "I'll drive. Young woman, as soon as we reach a landmark you recognize, such as the tree you mentioned, I'll stop the car, and you'll explain the rest of the route in detail."

Linnet said, "And then we come back here for the night."

"Yes. Tomorrow morning, Jodie, we'll take your key and go to the house, leaving you here at the motel."

"There's an alarm system. I'll have to give you the security code," she said.

"Very well," Max continued. "You will stay here until we return, no matter how long it takes. After we've settled our score with Nola, and only then, I'll make arrangements for your flight to Denver. Understand?"

Jodie nodded.

Out front, Max drew Linnet aside for a second after Jodie got into the car. "I didn't expect our earlier conversation back in the motel room to be cut short so abruptly. I would like to spend more time with you, alone, after we've finished with our young…friend."

"Time for what?" she murmured, conscious of Jodie watching them from the back seat. "I thought you didn't want to get addicted."

"I said nothing about physical intimacy." His eyes flashed crimson. He exhaled, as if forcing himself to calm down. "Oddly enough, I've discovered I value your good opinion. I'd like to give you a further chance to understand our species, to ask whatever questions you have in mind. As for addiction, I don't want to leave you with the idea that Anthony didn't care for your niece as genuinely as any human lover could."

Linnet blinked away tears. "This is no time to talk about that stuff. Let's get going."

They reentered the car and cruised in search of landmarks Jodie could recognize. Linnet wished she'd come to the area for an innocent purpose. The pine-scented air felt cool compared to the muggy heat of Maryland in summer, cool enough that she almost envied the girl's leather jacket. She'd glimpsed interesting shops during their drive through downtown in search of the strip mall. Steinbeck's Cannery Row beckoned only a few miles away, as did Carmel, a short ride down the coast. She could tour the aquarium or watch sea otters from the wharf. She would have enjoyed visiting as a tourist instead of an amateur vampire-hunter. In the moonlight that sparkled on the bay as they drove along the shoreline to Pacific Grove, the whole adventure struck her as bizarre. Maybe she'd lost her mind, listening to Max's claims and Jodie's story.

Was it too late to abort the whole mission and go home? Or first she could spend a couple of nights in one of those bed-and-breakfasts in Carmel Valley advertised in illustrated color brochures in the motel lobby. One glance at Max's face, jaws clenched in concentration, shattered the fantasy. Jodie's low voice, murmuring an occasional "left" or "right," reinforced the truth that Linnet had fallen too deep into this nightmare to pull out.

They passed rows of Victorian houses on the inland side of the road, gnarled cypress trees shaped by ocean winds on the bay side. "There's the butterfly tree," Jodie piped up at one curve, pointing to a large specimen that grew on a promontory jutting into the water. "Now I know where we are."

A couple of minutes later, she told Max to pull over. "I'm afraid to get any closer."

He turned the car into a park across the street from the gabled, 1890s-style houses. Benches and picnic tables were scattered among the pines and cypresses. Paths wound over the grass to a gravel-surfaced playground consisting of a swing set and two slides. Other paths led down to the beach. Max found a parking space as far as possible from the single light that illuminated the small lot.

"Do you feel Nola's presence at all?" he asked, opening his door.

"Not yet," Jodie said. "I guess it's okay."

He opened her door and ushered her out of the car. "We should be safe. Nevertheless, I'd rather we get away from the light." Holding on to Jodie's elbow, he guided her toward the water. Linnet followed, wondering why Max still didn't trust the girl out of arm's reach. Sure, she acted nervous, but who wouldn't? If she'd meant to betray them into a trap, she could have taken them the whole way to Nola's place.

"Now, Jodie, tell us the address," he said in the shadow of a spreading pine tree near the verge of the rocky strip of beach.

"I don't remember the street name, just the house number." She recited it.

He released her arm. Linnet noticed the red gleam in his eyes. "Describe the rest of the route."

"It's easy." Jodie rubbed her elbow where Max's hand had squeezed. "Keep going on this road and turn left two corners down. Follow that street until it makes a T, then turn right. Make the first right after that. It's a dead-end street, and her house is by itself at the end. You can't miss it."

"Excellent. That's all we need from you. The sooner we get you well out of Nola's range, the better. Both of you need a decent night's sleep, anyway."

Jodie scooted away from him and headed for the car at a brisk walk. Linnet couldn't blame her for not wanting to stay anywhere near the vampire woman's home, even if it meant hurrying back to a stuffy motel room. With the girl pulling ahead, Linnet found herself walking side by side with Max. "Have you considered my earlier proposal?" he said, too softly for Jodie to hear.

"Don't you mean proposition?" Linnet whispered. "After this is over, I want to go home and forget the entire trip." Not that she truly wanted to forget Max, a fact that must be obvious to a man who could read emotions, but she knew she ought to. She quickened her pace to get away from his side.

A few yards ahead of them, Jodie stopped, turned, and fumbled inside her jacket. From her waistband, under the hem of her oversize T-shirt, she pulled out a pistol.

Linnet froze, her heart hammering.

"Move over!" Jodie said in a shrill tone. "I don't want to shoot you, just him."

"Why?" Linnet felt Max behind her, his breath on her hair. Her vision went gray. *Don't faint, for God's sake!* she ordered herself.

"I have to!" Jodie's whole body trembled, making the gun shake in her hand. "I don't want to, but I can't help it!"

Max's low voice rumbled in Linnet's ear. "Jodie, put that down. If you don't want to shoot us, you do not have to."

"Yes, I do, she told me to!" Sobs blurred the words. "Linnet, move, please!"

Her wail was blotted out by a crack of thunder. Linnet's ears rang. At the same instant, she saw Max appear in front of her, then collapse to the ground. She darted around his fallen body and charged at Jodie.

The girl swung the gun at Linnet, but the blow didn't connect. Linnet dived for her knees. The gun fired again. Her head spinning, Linnet knocked Jodie to the ground with a thud. Her own breath jarred out of her, she lay on top of the girl for a second, unable to move. Only when Jodie started to struggle did she manage to strike again. She pushed herself up and punched the girl in the jaw.

Linnet scrambled to her feet, ears still buzzing from the two shots. Jodie lay flat on her back on the grass. Stomping on her wrist and wrenching the pistol away from her, Linnet brandished it at the girl. A few feet away, Max knelt, one hand pressed to a dark stain on the front of his shirt.

Chapter 11

Max's eyes blazed. Over the ringing in her ears, Linnet heard a growl rumble in his chest. "Bring her here."

"Max, you won't…?"

"Here, I said!" His voice rasped so hoarsely she had trouble understanding the words.

Still squeezing the gun in her right fist, though she wasn't sure she would know how to use it, Linnet hauled Jodie to her feet. "You heard him. Move!"

The girl staggered forward. Max's hand lashed out to grab her wrist and jerk her to the ground in front of him.

A cry burst from Jodie.

"Quiet!"

"Please don't—"

"Quiet, I said." The girl's whimpering trailed off. Max's eyes drilled into hers.

Hovering over them, with Jodie's panting and Max's harsh breathing loud in her ears, Linnet decided she didn't need the gun anymore. She tucked it into her purse. "Max, you claimed you were sure she really wanted to help us."

"I was." He forced out the words between painful gasps. "I still believe it." He grabbed Jodie with both hands, shifting his grip to hold her upper arms. She stared into his glowing eyes. After a few seconds, she swayed, her eyelids drooping. "Enough. You have questions to answer, girl."

Jodie nodded. Still kneeling on the grass, she hung rag-doll limp in his grasp, all resistance melted away.

Surprised at the sudden firmness of Max's voice, Linnet said, "What did you do to her?"

"Borrowed some of her energy to suppress the pain and bleeding." She shivered at the thought that he could drain someone's life force through his hypnotic stare alone. "Now, Jodie," he continued. "Why did you try to shoot us?"

"Not Linnet, just you. I didn't want to hurt her."

Max glanced at Linnet. "Which explains why you disarmed her so easily. She felt conflicted. Her heart wasn't in it."

Easy, huh? Linnet grumbled to herself, with her knees and elbows bruised from the scuffle.

To Jodie, he said, "Why me, then? Nola ordered you to kill me?"

"Not kill. She knew—" the girl's breath hitched "—knew I wouldn't be able to, anyway. Just knock you out for a while."

"Yes, and then?" he prompted, giving her a brisk shake.

"Then I was supposed to go get her. Don't know exactly what she planned to do with you after that."

"But when I questioned you earlier, I sensed you meant us no harm."

"That's right," came the reply in a thready whisper. "I didn't remember until just now. Then it came back to me, and I had to shoot you. But I didn't want to."

"Wait a second," Linnet said. "This is the weirdest part yet. Is she saying Nola planted some kind of posthypnotic suggestion for Jodie to shoot you and then made her forget about it?"

"Is that what happened?" Max said.

Jodie nodded. "I meant it when I asked you to help me. For real, I swear."

Linnet wrapped her arms around herself to keep from trembling. "Nola can do that?"

"With the blood bond between them, she could make the girl do or think almost anything," said Max. "Jodie, listen to me. Are you in mental contact with Nola at this moment?"

Jodie shook her head, her pale blue hair tangled around her face.

"Have you communicated with her in any way since you first met us?"

"Noooo." The moan trailed off into a sigh.

Max hauled her to her feet. "We'd better get away from here before someone comes along to investigate the disturbance."

Until that moment, it hadn't crossed Linnet's mind that somebody might have heard the shots. If they had, they must have mistaken the noise for a car backfiring or a neighbor's TV. "Max, you need to get to a doctor."

"No!" When she flinched, he continued more quietly. "Have you forgotten what I am? What your doctors would find if they examined me? I could mesmerize one at a time into ignoring my differences. Handling a whole emergency-room staff would take more energy than I can spare."

"But the bullet—isn't it still in your chest?"

"It didn't penetrate any vital organs. It will work itself out within the next few weeks. Uncomfortable, but not a real problem. And I've temporarily suppressed the pain, as I said." He silenced her attempted protest with, "We have more important things to worry about at the moment."

At the car, Max shoved Jodie into the back seat and joined her there, leaving Linnet to drive. When they got to the motel, he instructed her to park at the edge of the lot away from any direct light. Instead of getting out, he turned Jodie to face him. "Nola gave you the gun?"

"Yeah, when she sent me to meet you. She told me to forget about it until I needed it."

Linnet still had trouble with that concept. Wincing at the soreness in her side from landing on the ground, she twisted around in the driver's seat to watch them. "How could you forget you were carrying a gun?"

"I don't know. It was in my backpack all the time, but it's like I didn't even see it."

"And when we left the motel this evening," said Max, "did you recall your mission then?"

"No way. I wanted to lead you to Nola so you'd help me get away, that's all. I remember now that I hid the gun under my jacket back in my room, but at the time it was like I didn't even know I was doing it."

Linnet studied her wide-eyed expression. "Max, is that possible? Are you sure she's not making this up so you won't punish her?"

"Considering the power Nola has over her through the bond, it's quite plausible. It explains why I felt no hostility in her until the moment she pulled out the weapon. The situation triggered the command Nola had lodged in her unconscious mind."

"So what now?"

Max said to Jodie, "Does Nola expect you to report to her tonight?"

"Not really. She told me to wait for the best chance, that I'd know it when I saw it. And I did. That was my chance, and I blew it. Linnet being there screwed everything up. I thought maybe I could fix it by bringing you, too." She glanced at Linnet. "Kind of an offering, like. Then maybe

Nola would get interested in you, so I could still escape. My head was totally messed up." Linnet hardly knew whether to believe the pleading tone or not. "So anyway, Nola shouldn't get too suspicious if I don't contact her right away." Her eyes turned away from Max's, then drifted back as if magnetically compelled. "Are you going to kill me now?"

"Perhaps I should." He bared his teeth, and the girl cringed. "But I am not like your mistress."

"So what are you going to do?" Linnet asked. "Not wipe her mind like Fred's?"

"No. Aside from your probable objections, that would alert Nola that I've exposed her plot." He heaved a long sigh, making Linnet wonder whether his pain-suppression technique was wearing thin. "Jodie, do you still want to flee to Denver?"

A quick nod.

"Then you shall." He leaned closer, looming over her. "Your transportation will be arranged. I'll supply you with funds. You will not contact Nola in any way. You will never come near her, myself or Linnet's family again. Understand?"

"Yes," she breathed.

He pulled out his wallet and passed a credit card to Linnet. "Take Jodie up to the room to collect her belongings. Call the airport and use my card to book a flight. If there's no direct flight to Denver, get her somewhere, then book her on the first connection, which may not be until morning." He gave Jodie a handful of cash. "This should cover cab fare and incidentals. Linnet, you call the taxi and wait with her until she's been picked up. No, on second thought, you'd better ride with her to the airport. I believe it isn't far."

"Okay, I'm on it." She felt almost as dazed by the flurry of commands as Jodie looked.

"Young woman, go with Linnet and don't give her any trouble. Do whatever she says. This is your only chance to escape without your deserved punishment. Is that clear?"

"Right," Jodie whispered.

He squeezed her wrist and bored into her eyes with his own. "You will wait quietly for your flight. Then you will go to your grandmother's home in Denver and stay there. You will begin that new life you spoke of. Understand?"

"Yes." Jodie nodded, her eyes wide.

"Good. Now get moving." He let go of her arm.

"Aren't you going in?" Linnet asked him.

"Looking like this?" He touched the bloodstain on his chest. "Deflecting observers would take too much effort in my present condition. Bring me a clean shirt, please." He leaned back and closed his eyes.

Just in time she remembered to turn off the car's dome light before getting out. She nudged the girl across the quiet parking lot to the main entrance. At this late hour the lobby was deserted except for the desk clerk. Half-afraid Jodie would bolt as soon as they got out of Max's sight, despite his hypnotic coercion, Linnet held on to her elbow while they walked to the elevator. Jodie trudged along with her eyes downcast, though with no sign of rebellion. In the room she stuffed her personal items into her backpack, working sluggishly, fumbling and dropping things. Linnet almost screamed when a metal deodorant can bounced onto the bathroom tile. Soon enough, though, Jodie finished packing, and they moved over to Max and Linnet's room.

Linnet waved Jodie to the bed. "Wait there."

Jodie sank onto the bed, her head drooping. How much energy had Max drained from her with a mere touch, anyway?

"Where's the key to Nola's house?"

Jodie listlessly fished the key out of her backpack, then returned to her inert position on the bed. Linnet shoved a pen and notepad into her hands. "Here, write down the security code." After Jodie scribbled the numbers, Linnet tucked the slip of paper in her purse and opened the phone book to the Yellow Pages.

She phoned several airlines, tapping the desk with impatience while minutes dragged by on hold, until she found a seat on a direct flight to Denver. Luckily, it was the last one departing that night. She wouldn't be stuck with Jodie for hours longer. After that she called a cab, and finally they were ready to leave. On the way out, she snagged a towel and damp washcloth from the bathroom, and a sport shirt from Max's bag.

Out front, she watched Jodie standing at the curb, weighed down by the backpack dangling from one shoulder. The light from the front of the motel revealed a gleam of tears on the girl's face.

"Jodie, what's wrong?" Linnet gave her an awkward pat on the back. "It's okay now, nobody will hurt you."

Jodie swiped her hand across her eyes. "I know. But I'm still scared."

"Of Max?"

She shook her head, sniffling.

Linnet dug a tissue out of her purse and gave it to Jodie. "You're afraid Nola will catch up with you?"

"Not that. I know this sounds way dumb to you, but I'm freaked about leaving her. Scared I'll go back to her, that I won't be able to stop myself."

"Why would you want to?"

The artificial light made Jodie's eyes look gray shadowed. "You don't understand! It's not just that addiction Max talked about. Nola's…I know she did awful things, like what happened to Dee. But before that, I thought she was way cool. We all did."

"You really liked being her pets?" Linnet's stomach cramped. "Even Deanna?"

"We didn't think we were pets. It was like we were all her favorites. Or pretended we were. Even Dee, until Anthony took her away."

The warmth in Jodie's voice made Linnet queasy. "So if I'd tried harder to get Dee away from Nola, maybe barged in on one of those parties and dragged her away—"

"That wouldn't have worked. She'd just have sneaked back there the next night."

"I couldn't have stopped her," Linnet murmured, to herself rather than the girl. "It wasn't my fault." Recognizing Jodie's fascination with the vampire woman, Linnet realized that once Deanna had fallen under Nola's influence, nobody could have rescued her against her will.

I don't have to be ashamed to face Robin and the rest of the family, she thought. *It wasn't my fault.*

When the cab pulled up, Jodie squeezed her hands. "Thanks, really, I'm sorry about everything, I just—well, thanks." She crawled into the back seat. Linnet joined her there and gave the driver their destination.

He drove them through town, inland a few miles, to the small regional airport. As Max had predicted, even at the low speed limit allowed in downtown Monterey, the trip didn't take long. They didn't talk during the ride. At the terminal, Linnet sat in the cab at the curb until Jodie vanished into the building. She hoped Max's hypnotic command would stick long enough to override the girl's craving to return to Nola. Brooding over that point, Linnet rode the cab back to the motel, paid the driver and headed for the parking lot.

Hurrying to the rental car, she found Max slumped in the back, his eyes closed. Her heart hammered. What would she do if he'd fallen unconscious and she couldn't wake him? The moment she opened the door, though, he stirred. She caught the glint of crimson in his half-open eyes.

"Max, look at me!" She crowded into the back seat with him, almost kneeling on his legs. He groaned faintly when she bunched up his shirt to check the bullet wound. "You won't die on me, will you?"

"Hardly." He pushed himself from a reclining position into a half-sitting one, wincing in obvious pain. "Then I wouldn't be able to show you the Globe."

Her breath caught in her throat. "What are you now, delirious?" With the still-damp cloth, she dabbed around the wound until she'd wiped off most of the dried blood. After a quick look out the window to make sure nobody was passing nearby, she switched on the overhead bulb to examine the injury. She saw a ragged hole with no sign of fresh bleeding. Patting the area dry, she said, "I don't have any bandages, but it looks like you'll be okay without them." She turned off the light.

"Yes," he whispered. "We heal quickly." His fingers curled around her wrist, pressing her hand against his chest. His fingertips caressed the pulse point.

She had to brace herself with the other hand to keep from falling onto him. The red gleam in his eyes made her heartbeat stutter with mingled fear and excitement. "Max, what are you doing?"

His tongue flicked out to lick his lips. His fixed stare showed no sign that he'd heard her at all. She caught herself swaying toward him. She focused on the weight of the ankh dangling from the chain around her neck. "Stop," she whispered.

He blinked. "I need you. Please." He sounded almost hurt by her rejection.

Did he mean to drink her blood? He'd already taken it without her consent, invaded her dreams. Why did he bother to ask now?

Because now, alert, she had the ability to resist. Because his wound made her the stronger of the two.

If he'd wanted to drain her life, he could have done it many times already. Asking permission showed his good faith. She let out a pent-up breath, easing the ache in her chest. "All right." She braced herself for the onslaught of his hunger.

Leaning forward, he nuzzled her throat. Though his skin

felt as cold as a mountain stream, the shiver that convulsed her was pleasant, not chilling. The piercing sting she expected didn't come. Max pulled away, his eyes drifting shut, and he drew a deep breath. A wave of warmth surged through her. Sparks flashed before her eyes, and for a second her head seemed to float.

When the faintness subsided, she said, "What was that?"

"Forgive me," he breathed. "I…borrowed…from you."

"The way you did from Jodie."

A cautious nod.

"It didn't hurt." On the contrary, it had left her with an echo of tingling pleasure.

"No, you're healthy enough to spare some of your life force. But it's only a temporary stopgap. I need blood to complete the healing."

She stiffened and drew her hand out of his loose grip. "Okay, if you have to."

"Not yours. More than you can give. Animal blood."

She reminded herself that many creatures in the natural ecological balance fed on blood, and that such a diet was no grosser than eating a chunk of animal flesh. "Where do you plan on getting it?"

"I think I know a source. You'll have to drive."

She moved into the front seat and started the car. "Okay, where?"

"Remember the route we followed into town? Go back that way. I'll give you more detailed directions later."

Over the past few minutes, fog had begun gathering. She cautiously pulled out of the lot and crept along under the speed limit. Away from the motel, driving along two-lane streets with scant traffic, she said, "Thanks for saving my life."

"Pardon?"

"When Jodie shot at us. You jumped in front of me on purpose."

"Oh, that? Purely a reflex response in the heat of the moment."

She smiled at his gruff tone. He actually sounded embarrassed. "You'd do that for any mortal, right?"

"Not mortal," he said. "We are mortal, too. We can be killed. We call you ephemerals."

"Oh, yeah. Makes it easy to dismiss us as unimportant, I guess." She felt a little ashamed of needling him. He was hurt, and, after all, he really had saved her life.

"Hardly. If it comes to that, you may have saved me, too, tackling her that way. Reckless as it was."

"If we saved each other, we're even. About Jodie. Are you sure it's safe to let her run loose?"

"I believe so. Her true will is invested in getting free from Nola. I only commanded her to do what she herself wanted."

Recalling Jodie's conflicted tears, Linnet wasn't so sure escaping represented the girl's deepest will. But this was no time to harass Max with her doubts.

After they'd passed through downtown, they picked up Route 68 around the perimeter of the Fort Ord Army Base. About half an hour away from the city, following secondary highways toward Salinas, they moved into farming country. The fog thinned as they left the coast and finally dissipated altogether. After an extended drive along poorly lit roads, they passed the shadowy silhouette of a house and barn. "Here's a likely prospect," said Max. He directed her to pull onto the shoulder under a tree. "With the lights off, the car won't attract much attention from anyone driving past."

"So what's here?"

"Horses. Three of them, in this field."

She peered through the window, but in the dark she could distinguish only vague shapes that could be animals, trees or tractors, for all she could tell. "Right, you have super night vision."

"And I see into the infrared range. Their body heat is obvious to me." He opened the door to get out. Linnet did the same. "You should stay here," he said.

"Wait in the car by myself? No way. Anyhow, I can stand as your lookout in case somebody wanders by." She hugged herself, surprised by the nip in the air. The temperature had dropped noticeably since the earlier part of the night.

Since Max didn't persist with his objections, she followed him to the split-rail fence. When he bent over to crawl between the rails into the pasture, she had second thoughts about wanting to stick with him. But she made it through with no worse damage than snagging her hair on a splinter.

She stumbled trying to keep up with his long stride. He paused to wait for her. "I forgot you can't see the ground properly." He took her hand in his cool, firm grip and led her along.

A couple of minutes' walk brought them to a pond sheltered by a cluster of trees. "Now we're not likely to be spotted from the road." He let go of her hand and stretched out his arms, crooning a wordless hum. Linnet felt the hair on her arms lift as if stirred by static electricity. The strands at the back of her neck rustled, and a faint buzz vibrated her teeth.

Three dark forms trotted toward them from the middle of the field. "Good girl. Come here," he murmured. "Yes, you."

Two of the horses stopped, while the third walked up to Max. Linnet swallowed with nervousness at the animal's bulk. Her last close-up experience with the species, a pony ride at the county fair when she was ten, hadn't prepared her for the size of this creature.

The mare didn't pay any attention to Linnet, though. Max stroked the animal's back, and she whickered softly as if she'd known him all her life. When he resumed his hypnotic hum, more quietly now, she hung her head, pressing close to him. He ran his hands over her neck, apparently feeling for a vein. Linnet couldn't see much of his face other than the red glow at the centers of his eyes.

"You're going to bite into it just like that?" she whispered. "Doesn't look very clean."

He flashed her a smile. Now that her eyes were adjusting to the dark, she could see the whiteness of his teeth, as even and humanlike as ever. "Do you imagine my ancestors roaming the Alps and the Himalayas with bottles of disinfectant to sterilize the skin of their prey? Our saliva contains a mild antiseptic. There's no danger of infection for either the animal or me."

He wrapped his arms around the mare's neck. With his face hidden from her, Linnet couldn't see him pierce the hide, but she did hear faint lapping sounds. She turned her back, performing her nominal duty as lookout, and reminded herself not to indulge in humancentric prejudice. As a biology major, she'd dissected enough frogs in college that she shouldn't be fazed by Max's comparatively neat, nongross feeding habits.

Nevertheless, when he touched her arm and she turned to face him, she was glad she couldn't see any bloodstains on his mouth. In fact, he didn't look any different from the way he normally did. "No fangs?"

"Only in the transformed shape I showed you earlier. That's not necessary for drawing blood. My teeth are razor sharp and leave a thin incision that will disappear in a day or two." True, the mare didn't look injured. She whinnied a farewell as if nothing had happened. As for Max, his voice sounded stronger. He took Linnet's hand and led her back to the car. Now his flesh felt simply cool, not icy.

"You may as well keep driving," he said. "I need to rest."

"You said you heal quickly." She belted herself in and started the engine, with Max reclining in the front passenger scat. "How quick, exactly? How long do we have to put off our visit to Nola? When Jodie doesn't report soon, she might get suspicious."

"Don't worry, one full day of sleep should restore me to full strength. We'll talk about it later." He closed his eyes. Linnet doubted he would fall asleep in the car, but she decided not to pester him. She focused on retracing their route and coping with the fog when they neared the coast again.

In the motel parking lot he changed into the clean shirt. Linnet wished she had thought of spare clothes for herself, after rolling on the ground with Jodie and crawling through fence rails. The clerk didn't give them a second look on their way to the elevator, though. Back in the room, she grabbed her nightclothes and ducked into the shower.

When she came out, with her nightgown discreetly covered by a terry-cloth beach robe, Max was lying on his bed, still dressed except for his shoes. He'd left the bedside lamps off. "I'll rest as much as possible," he said, "but I can't actually sleep until dawn. You should try to, though."

She looked at the clock. "I can't believe it's that long after midnight. I'm too wired to sleep yet. We should be safe here, right?"

"Yes. If Nola had another minion or two waiting as backup, Jodie would have mentioned it. And I sensed it was true that she hadn't made contact with Nola."

"Well, yeah, but—no offense—you were sure about what you sensed earlier, and you were wrong."

"I don't think Jodie would have dared to communicate with Nola while I was within range. Jodie would have expected me to be aware of any such communication. Remember, I'm older than Nola, and for our kind, age means power."

"Five hundred years." Linnet sat on the other bed, running her fingers through her hair. "I can't imagine it. You were alive when Elizabeth's navy defeated the Spanish Armada. You saw Shakespeare and Ben Jonson."

"Yes, and I meant it when I offered to show you the Globe."

As tempting as the offer sounded, Linnet didn't seriously believe he would give her a second thought once they had completed their quest. "We can talk about it after we defeat Nola Grant. So the plan's changed. We have to wait until tomorrow evening, when you're rested and healed up. It'll be more dangerous than invading her space in daylight, won't it?"

"Yes. That is one reason I'm making another change in the plan. *We* are not going to her house. I'm going alone."

"Now, wait a minute! We have a deal!" She felt heat flood her skin.

"I'm changing the terms. I'll take along that ridiculous tape recorder, if you insist, and get the confession you have your heart set upon. But I can't allow you to confront her when she's at full strength. Especially now that we know how far she's willing to go."

"What are you talking about?" She felt like hitting him. Even if it weren't for his bullet wound, though, the prospect of humiliating herself with a futile attack would have stopped her.

"Nola sent her pet after me with a deadly weapon. It's highly unlikely that the girl could have killed me, but not impossible. A lucky shot—or unlucky, depending on your viewpoint—could have damaged my brain beyond repair. If Nola would take that risk, after one of her disciples had already killed Anthony, what would she do to an ephemeral who got in her way? If she's a threat to her own kin, imagine how dangerous she'd be to you."

"So I'm just a liability, a human weakling you have to protect." She stomped over to the bed, clenching her fists against the temptation to smack him after all. "I know you think ephemerals are worthless, but damn it, we had an agreement!"

Max sat up. "Linnet, please—"

"Don't go 'please' at me, as if my opinion made one bit of difference to you." Her eyes burned. She rubbed away tears of anger. "I wouldn't be surprised if you planned to dump me all along. Don't you people have a concept of honor? Or are ephemerals just animals, so honor doesn't apply?"

"Linnet, stop this!" He grabbed her arm and forced her onto the mattress. She yielded, mainly because she knew fighting him would be hopeless. "I don't consider you an animal, much less worthless. I do value the arts your people produce. And I value courage and devotion such as yours."

"Oh, I get it, some of your best friends are ephemerals."

"Not until now." He sighed. "If you'll calm down enough to listen, I'll try to explain my feelings about the human race."

"Sounds like a tall order in twenty-five words or less." Her heartbeat slowed, and the pounding in her head faded. She momentarily wondered whether he was sneaking in some kind of hypnotic influence despite the necklace she'd dutifully put on again right after her shower. "Okay, I'm listening."

He clasped her hands between his. "Anthony was much younger than I. He was born in the 1890s, in the eastern part of Germany near what is now Poland. Although the sibling bond is vitally important to us, ordinarily I wouldn't have had much contact with him until he entered adolescence."

"Why not?"

"With our extended lives, we don't have the kind of family structure common among you. We don't marry. Females go into estrus and mate at rare intervals and are fertile even less often. A woman cares for her infant alone until weaning, at three or four years. Then a mentor takes over the child's upbringing, an uncle or aunt if one is available and old enough for the responsibility. Otherwise, one of the elders assumes the role."

"What about the father?"

"We don't know our fathers. The male's role is purely genetic."

"So this mentor sort of fills the role." Again Linnet reminded herself that she shouldn't be shocked. Vampire family dynamics sounded conventional compared to the way some animals bred and reared their young.

"The chosen mentor serves as a guardian until maturity, about age thirty, and as an adviser for the next century or so. We have little contact with our mothers after early childhood. A brother or sister helps to fill what you'd doubtless consider a painful gap in the kinship network."

"That's hard to imagine. Sure, Mom and I have had our differences, but to leave her at age four—that's something else."

"As I mentioned, your kind of family wouldn't suit our long lifespans. Can you visualize the intensity of that mother-child relationship if it continued for millennia?"

Linnet shook her head. "I'm having trouble visualizing any of it. So what's all this leading up to? There was something different about you and Anthony?"

"Yes. When he was not quite a year old, I received word from one of my mother's servants, the old steward who had managed her estate." Max's eyes turned cold, staring past Linnet. "Belief in vampires as monstrous undead wasn't quite extinct in that time and place. A mob had slaughtered her and burned the house."

"Oh, God!" When she tried to pull her hands free, Max tightened his grasp. From the distant look in his eyes, she thought he wasn't aware of the act.

"The steward and his wife escaped with Anthony. They didn't know the truth about us, of course. They thought the baby's pair of needle-shaped teeth were merely a natural anomaly. Still, they knew they couldn't take proper care of him. I journeyed there to claim my brother."

Linnet tried to imagine Max taking care of a toddler. "Normally, you wouldn't have had that responsibility."

"Exactly. In the nearest large city I found a young, unmarried woman whose infant had recently died. Without a position such as I offered, she would probably have turned to streetwalking. I hired her as Anthony's wet nurse and took them back to England."

"I can see why you wouldn't think much of the human race. But we aren't all like the superstitious people who murdered your mother."

"I'm well aware of that. I don't dismiss all your kind as rabid beasts."

"Only the majority, is that it?"

"Would you blame me if I did think that way?" Now his eyes met hers straight on. "Look at the way you treat each other."

"But we're improving. At least, we're trying…" Her voice trailed off under his level gaze. One look at the headlines would effectively undermine her argument. "Did the nurse know what you and Anthony were?"

"No. I kept her mesmerized so that she didn't notice he sampled her blood along with her milk. When he lost his baby fangs and began to look and behave more like a human child, I gradually loosened my mental control over her. She saw him as a delicate invalid who had to avoid the sun and live on a restricted diet. She became genuinely fond of him."

"Well, I should think so. He was the only baby she had."

"Of course, as a human female, you understand better than I could." He released her hands. "Anthony cared for her, too. He knew she wasn't his birth mother, but he couldn't help becoming attached to her."

"That's why he didn't have any trouble falling in love with a human girl."

Max nodded. "The woman stayed in our household until

Anthony reached his teens, when animal blood stopped satisfying him. Once he started needing human donors, keeping the truth from her would have become unnecessarily difficult. I settled her in a house of her own with a lavish pension."

Linnet let out a pent-up breath. She didn't quite believe Max would have killed his brother's nurse, but that fear had nagged at the back of her mind anyway. "I'll bet Anthony kept in touch with her."

"Until she died, at a comfortable old age. So you see why he found ephemerals attractive and wanted to protect them from predators like Nola."

"And why you prefer to avoid us."

"Not all of you." He ran his hand over her hair. "Certainly not you."

"Well, I'm glad you want to protect me instead of putting me in the dangerous-beast category. But I still want my chance at Nola."

"Stubborn." He drew her close, his breath ruffling her hair. "I want to do more with you than protect you."

She wondered whether he could hear the tripping of her heart as well as her ragged breathing. "If you want me for a pet, that's out."

"Not that, damn it!" His breath sounded as labored as hers felt. "Anthony didn't treat Deanna as a pet. I'm beginning to think he was right."

"Are you saying you see me as a friend?" She didn't dare suggest more than friendship. With his cool fingers wandering through her hair and teasing the nape of her neck, she could hardly gather her thoughts at all.

"I suppose I do." He sounded mildly surprised. "Blast it, I always warned Anthony that caring about an ephemeral meant leaving oneself vulnerable. Now I'm doing the same thing."

"Then treat me like an equal. Don't shut me out of the quest." She tried to pull away from him. When his arms tightened, though, her will to resist evaporated.

"As your friend, I should keep you from risking your life for no purpose."

Linnet shook her head, trying to ignore his lips brushing her forehead and trailing down the side of her face. "You told me it's forbidden for you—vampires—to kill your own kind. The only way you can get around that is to force Nola to attack you, right?"

"Yes," he whispered.

"You're going to provoke a fight with a murderer while you're weak from a bullet wound. *I* should stop *you* from risking your life."

"By tomorrow night I'll be sufficiently recovered."

"I think you're bluffing. No matter how much older and stronger you are, you still shouldn't face her alone in this condition."

"The subject is closed." His tongue flicked the corner of her mouth. "This isn't what I want to spend the night talking about. I told you I want to do more than protect you—" His lips alighted on hers, then instantly withdrew. She reacted with an involuntary whimper. "Or be your friend—" Another mothlike kiss. "Linnet, I'm thirsty for you."

With her eyes closed, she clung to him, her head spinning. "You said you didn't want my blood."

"I said I wouldn't take it then. It would have been dangerous for you, when I was wounded and ravenous. But I've wanted it all along, from the first night."

"The first night...I dreamed..." She opened her eyes to gaze into his silver-gray, crimson-flecked ones and felt herself blushing. "Did you drink from me then?"

"Twice," he said, still tantalizing her with spiral caresses on her neck and shoulders. "In your living room, and later while you slept."

"How dare you...?"

He wrapped his arms around her to keep her from squirming free. "You enjoyed the experience. You can't deny that."

No, she couldn't deny that. Treacherous heat pooled between her thighs. "But I didn't know. You ignored my free will." She clutched her necklace, struck by a sudden realization. "Hey, you said you couldn't hypnotize me."

"I didn't. The first time, you responded to my touch, and it was easy to keep you from noticing a painless nip. The second time, you were already asleep."

"That's no excuse."

His hand swirled over her back, making her melt like ice cream in the sun. "I admit it was a mistake. I haven't done it since. Now that I know you as an individual, I want your consent. Even though it's against my better judgment."

"What's that supposed to mean?"

"We shouldn't risk becoming dependent on each other."

The sensations rippling through her congealed into a cold lump in her chest. "Like Jodie. I could turn into a puppet the way she did with Nola."

Chapter 12

"No, *not* like Nola and her disciples!" His arms caged her.

"I saw the way Jodie acted. And Fred—"

"Listen to me. Whenever a vampire drinks too frequently from the same donor, and especially when they're bonded by mutual sharing of blood, a dependency develops. Call it addiction, if you like, but it doesn't have to be a negative experience."

She pushed against his unyielding chest. "Then why are you so anxious to avoid it?"

"Because if I cared too much about an ephemeral, I would give a hostage to fortune, as Bacon says—someone who could be used to hurt me. Nevertheless, I don't deny that such a relationship can produce intimacy of the most ecstatic kind."

"Yeah?" The memory of her "dream" burned through her veins. If anything more ecstatic existed, she didn't think she would survive it. "Have you ever personally seen that kind of relationship that didn't turn out badly?"

"Yes, a few, including the couple in Maryland I mentioned earlier. And so have you. Anthony and Deanna. Given the length of time they cohabited, they were certainly addicted to each other in a physiological and emotional sense. But he also cared for her. His letters to me made that clear."

"Cared, huh? You're afraid to say 'love'?"

"That's a human word," he murmured into her hair. "And your people give it so many incompatible meanings."

"I've heard it defined as making somebody else's happiness as important to you as your own. Hostage to fortune is close enough. Some people—human people—feel the same way about animals. They won't have a pet because it might die."

"An attitude I can well understand. But I've already said that I don't regard you as a pet."

"You're not saying you love me, either." His caressing hands stilled on her back. She said, "Don't worry, I'm not asking you to. I'm not looking for anything permanent, either. I'm here to deal with Nola, not start an affair with a man I've just met and who isn't even human." She spoke the words almost firmly enough to convince herself.

"So we understand each other." He resumed the languid, swirling strokes up and down her back.

She arched her spine, rising on her knees to meet the kisses he sprinkled on her lips, neck and shoulders. An involuntary "mmm" escaped her.

"Regardless of how little time we have, I still want you. Admit you feel the same desire."

"Well…" Her head fell back, exposing her throat to the flicker of his tongue. One of his hands circled around to the front of her body and cupped a breast through the robe and nightgown. The satin slid over the nipple, teasing it to a peak. "You're cheating."

"I can't mesmerize you. Whatever you feel springs from

within you. But I can read your emotions and sensations, touch and taste wherever it gives you greatest delight."

"Taste?" A warm fog muffled her thoughts. "My blood."

"Only a taste, to bring us both to fulfillment. My satisfaction depends on yours. I do not…experience love as human males do. My focus, so to speak, is elsewhere." He gently eased her onto the pillow. She didn't resist.

His hands rested on her shoulders, swept down over her breasts and the curve of her hips. While his tongue parted her lips, he opened the robe, then pulled up the nightgown, inch by inch, his fingers brushing her skin. Beyond thought, she arched her back to let him undress her. She let him lift the necklace over her head. It was a bit late now to worry about succumbing to his influence. She eased his shirt off, running her hands over his chest, carefully avoiding the wound. The silken hair made her palms tingle.

Catching his breath, he nibbled from her mouth down to her throat. His tongue flickered like a painless flame. He stroked between her legs, probing for the bud that throbbed with need. She melted.

She felt a sting at her throat just as his fingertips found the center of her desire. He lapped at the hollow of her neck, while his fingers traced circles faster and faster around the aching tip, until she convulsed with an arc of electricity between that spot and the place where he was kissing her.

Before she spiraled down from the height, he began again. "What about you?" she murmured. "You didn't—" She reached for his zipper.

He stopped her. "That isn't necessary now. My pleasure will come from sharing yours. Your fulfillment flows into me with your blood."

"I've never felt anything like that."

"Nor I. It's been a very long time since I drank from a conscious, willing donor. I'd forgotten—no, I don't think it has ever been quite like that." He silenced her with a kiss, then returned to her throat and increased the tempo.

Her fingers curled. She dug her nails into his flesh, involuntarily raked them down his chest. She felt a spasmodic tightening of his muscles. Slitting her eyelids, she realized she had opened the gunshot wound.

With an "oh!" of dismay, she twisted in his arms to press her lips to the trickle of blood. He let out a hiss when she licked the spot clean.

"Sorry," she murmured. "Hurts?"

"No. Not pain." She could hardly understand the hoarse words. "Don't stop."

With one of her hands rubbing the back of his neck, he turned his head to capture the skin of her wrist between his teeth. He nibbled at the fresh incision, while her tongue mimicked the movements of his. His blood effervesced like champagne on her tongue.

The world shattered into a explosion of prismatic colors. Abruptly, she found herself looking down on her own bowed head and tasting the tart sweetness of her own blood. The next moment, back in her own brain, she "heard" Max's voice reverberating in her skull and resonating through her internal organs.

No, we can't do this, we must stop!

Despite that, he continued to hold her tightly with one arm while his fingertips goaded her to new heights of rapture, and his lips feasted from her wrist. Her release triggered his, which she felt echoed in every cell of her body.

Linnet, please stop. This is a mistake. Yet he skimmed over her breasts and hips with his open hand. Purring, she savored the sensations that swirled through her, while at the same time she felt the tiny hairs in his palm tingle with electricity.

At last he pushed her away, holding her at arm's length.

Max, what's happening? She formed the words without speaking aloud.

You drank my blood. I told you what would happen.

I didn't mean to.

I know. And I could have stopped you. Should have. His pain pierced her the way his ecstasy had a moment earlier.

She swallowed hard and forced out an audible question. "Why do you think this is so wrong?"

"You felt the same thrill I did. You sensed the power of the bond." His voice rasped. "Now I understand, a little, why Anthony risked everything for his bond-mate. Even why Nola was so determined to cling to her thralls. The experience is...incredible." He cupped her chin, gazing into her eyes, and a fresh wave of delight swamped the pain. "But you and I don't want to be trapped in this bond."

"No, we don't." The heat in her veins screamed *Liar.* "We can fight it."

"After tonight, we can part, if that is our choice." She felt his mood veer back from pleasure to distress. "After I tend to Nola's execution."

Shadows blotted out the rainbow shimmer. Linnet sensed that this new anguish didn't relate to the "trap" they had fallen into. The prospect of killing Nola caused him pain. Or possibly fear? She sent inquiring tendrils into his mind.

A kaleidoscope of memories whirled in her head. A little boy, who she somehow recognized as Anthony, with his arms wrapped around Max's neck. Anthony bending over a bed where an old woman's body lay, his face contorted with sorrow. Max in the hushed anteroom of a funeral parlor. Agony like a shard of ice in the heart. *I never should have tried to be his guardian. My incompetence killed him.* A wave of grief washed over her. The face of a glowing-eyed, dark-haired woman brought on a surge of rage, followed by a second plunge into the abyss. Fear? Self-doubt? Another fragment of a thought brushed her mind: *If I claim my vengeance, am I a kin slayer, too?* Linnet realized she was witnessing Max's memories, sharing his emotions about his brother's death.

Nonhuman predator or not, he feels as devastated about Anthony as I do about Deanna.

Max repulsed her with a mental snap. An invisible door slammed shut. "Enough! We have to resist this temptation. The more we communicate mentally, the deeper the bond will grow, the harder to break."

"Yes, of course you're right." But from the brief glimpse of his thoughts, she knew that argument was only an excuse. He didn't want her to read his doubts, his nauseated revulsion at the thought of killing Nola.

"Sleep." He guided her down onto the bed. "Rest. You have nothing to worry about. The problem is mine now." As he soothed her with slow strokes from shoulders to hips, over and over, she spun down toward oblivion.

He lay on his side and drew her into a firm embrace. "That's right, rest now."

Woozily trying to focus on how she felt about the past hour, she dozed off.

When Linnet woke, her first thought was to wonder whether Max had used some psychic power to make her sleep. Probably not, she decided, since she'd been tired enough from…everything. A blush rose to her cheeks.

Rising on one elbow, she looked at Max, who lay asleep beside her on his back. Gray half light seeped through the curtains At least he hadn't sneaked out to face Nola alone.

But he planned to do that very thing at sunset. Linnet couldn't allow him to carry out that plan. Not without her.

She lightly touched his wrist. He felt cold, with no discernible pulse. He would probably remain dormant all day. He'd claimed he needed that rest to finish healing. She would have plenty of time to visit Nola by herself.

The intention had sprung into her mind full grown between sleep and waking. If Max killed a member of his own species, he might become an outcast. His plan to set up the "execution" as self-defense sounded awfully tenuous. In the few seconds when his mind had lain fully open to her, Linnet had sensed his horror at the deed he planned. She couldn't let him do that to himself.

Not only that, no matter what he said, she was convinced that the wound would undermine his chance of vanquishing Nola. As would waiting until dusk, when they couldn't hope to catch her off guard. By surprising her in her diurnal coma, Linnet hoped to dispatch her without involving Max and letting him become a murderer in the eyes of his own people.

She'd decided Nola couldn't be allowed to live.

I guess that makes me a murderer, doesn't it? Linnet thought. Well, if Nola could handle the police in Maryland, surely Max could do the same thing here. She grabbed fresh clothes and shuffled into the bathroom, where she tried to wake herself with cold water on her face. She drank several glasses, realizing the thirst must be a side effect of Max's feeding. In the mirror, she examined the tiny incision on her throat. It looked no more conspicuous than the mark left by donating at a blood bank. The bite on her wrist wasn't much bigger. The bruises from tumbling on the ground at the park looked worse and ached more. No wonder she hadn't noticed any traces the morning after Max's first "taste." Her skin tingled at the thought of what they'd shared.

She impatiently shook off the memory. She had to concentrate on dealing with Nola. Max had been right all along, Linnet thought, while she dressed as quietly as possible and restored the ankh pendant to its place around her neck. The vampire woman was too dangerous to leave at large, and there was no way the conventional legal system could handle her. Jodie's programmed attack proved those points. Linnet collected her supplies—gloves, garlic spray, rope, ax, flashlight, tape recorder, spare batteries. She tied each length of rope into a slipknot, grateful for the summer when she'd worked as a camp counselor during one of her "catching up with Robin" phases. She had the security code and the key to the house. Max would be furious, of course, but by the time he woke, the act would be accomplished.

She dumped the personal items from her carry-on bag and stuffed the vampire-hunting equipment into it, except for the miniature tape recorder and the slip of paper bearing Nola's alarm code, which she carried in her purse. At the last minute she remembered her cell phone, abandoned on the dresser. She scooped it into the carry-on bag. With Jodie's gun still in her purse, she stepped into the hall, easing the door shut with a click. A minute later she was driving out of the parking lot. Fog shrouded the streets. Shivering in the cool air, she wished she'd brought a sweater. She sipped from a juice box and munched on a granola bar, hoping a little food in her stomach would tame the queasiness. Could she actually kill a woman, even an inhuman murderer? Her lack of firearms training wouldn't matter when all she needed to do was hold the barrel to the vampire's head and pull the trigger, but could she force herself to fire? And suppose the police tracked her down afterward and Max couldn't lull them into leaving her alone? Would wiping out Nola be worth life in prison?

Though Linnet's mind shuffled the risks over and over, her body kept driving toward Pacific Grove. A part of her brain below the level of consciousness must have decided that, in the unlikely event the authorities connected her with Nola's death, the penalty would be worth it.

Not used to driving in fog, she found her hands cramping from her tight grip on the steering wheel. Ghostly shapes of trees and other cars loomed up at every curve. The "butter-fly tree," a faint silhouette in the mist, reassured her that she hadn't made any wrong turns. She passed the waterfront park and crept up the side street Jodie had pointed out. When she pulled over to park near the corner of the dead-end lane where Nola's house was supposed to be located, Linnet paused for a second to reflect that she ought to give thanks for the fog. Though rapidly turning pearl-white rather than gray, it was still thick enough to hide her from any casual observers.

She suppressed a shiver, wiped her damp hands on her jeans and stepped out of the car, her purse slung over one shoulder and the tote bag over the other. The gabled fronts of Victorian houses loomed across the street. She hoped their inhabitants were still asleep.

As described by Jodie, a single house stood alone at the end of the lane, its lot backing onto an inlet of the bay. The crash of waves drifted to Linnet's ears, along with the call-ing of sea otters. A wrought-iron fence surrounded the yard, shadowed by several cypress trees. She drew on the garden-ing gloves and pushed open the gate, wincing at its creak. Tip-toeing up the brick-paved front walk, she scanned the faintly visible facade of the house. Unkempt shrubbery crowded next to a wide porch. When she got closer, she could make out bay windows on either side of the porch and gables on the top floor.

Nobody challenged her when she walked up the porch steps. She might actually make it inside safely. If Max's hyp-notic power over Jodie, not to mention the girl's own desire to escape, could be trusted. If she hadn't lied to them about Nola's sleeping habits or somehow warned the vampire woman about their plan of attack.

Linnet checked the folded paper with the security code one more time. She got out the key and unlocked the door, then scurried across the foyer to the control panel and punched in the numbers. She leaned against the wall, panting, afraid the alarm would scream out her intrusion anyway. Nothing happened. She closed the door, hitched her bag into a more comfortable position and turned on the flashlight.

Can I actually do this? Now that she'd made it this far, she paused to review her plan. According to Max, Nola had at least ten times the strength of a human woman. Linnet's idea of disabling her with a squirt of garlic juice suddenly seemed ludicrous. She would probably have to shoot the vampire to immobilize her, the way Fred had done to Anthony. And not being any kind of marksman, she would have to do it while her target lay inert in bed. Sickness welled up in her throat. *Who am I kidding? No way will I be able to pull the trigger.* Max had a point about goading the woman into attacking first. Wounding or killing someone in the heat of combat had to be easier than doing it when the enemy looked helpless.

Once more she conjured up the image of Deanna's face, masklike in death. *If I have to shoot her while she's asleep, I will.* As for the next step, chopping off Nola's head, Linnet couldn't force herself to think of it yet. First, she would get the woman's confession. Nobody else would ever hear it, not even Robin, Linnet reminded herself, but she needed it for her own satisfaction. Put a bullet in Nola's chest, tie her up for extra insurance, and keep the garlic handy just in case.

According to Jodie, Nola slept in a finished space in the attic, with the window boarded over. Linnet walked from the foyer into the front hall, careful not to slip on the Persian rug at the foot of the curved staircase. Though her eyes had begun to adjust to the dimness, she still welcomed the flashlight. She crept upstairs, forcing herself to breathe normally. If Max hadn't awakened when she'd touched him, or when she'd run water in the bathroom and opened and closed the room door, Nola shouldn't wake just from the sound of footsteps.

The upstairs hall felt a mile long. Plagued by memories

of low-budget horror films, Linnet visualized zombies shambling toward her from the shadows of the empty bedrooms. But she reached the end of the hall without incident and found the closed door Jodie had described. Opening it, she saw a steep, narrow flight of steps leading up. The tremor in her hand made the flashlight beam skitter ahead of her. She tiptoed up the stairs, ducking her head to avoid the slanted ceiling. The air smelled stale and dusty but not outright unpleasant.

At the top, she emerged into an open space cluttered with boxes and trunks. An unpainted wooden floor covered the beams underfoot, she noticed. She wouldn't have to worry about accidentally stepping through the ceiling of the second story. An unidentifiable machinelike noise hummed in the background. She turned in a slow circle, casting light over every part of the chamber. On each end, a plasterboard wall sealed off a section of the attic. The door to each closed-in area was shut. Jodie hadn't mentioned which end held Nola's lair.

Linnet took the pistol out of her purse. Earlier she'd examined it and found the safety, which she now clicked off. With the gun in her right hand and the garlic spray lying on top of the items in the unzipped tote bag, she edged toward the door on the right. "Lady or tiger?" popped into her mind from an old story she'd read in college. In this case, the lady and the tiger were one and the same, and neither door hid a prize.

She tugged at the latch. Locked? She pulled harder, with her heart beating so rapidly she felt light-headed. The door sprang open. She stumbled backward into a footlocker and barely escaped a fall. For a few seconds she sat on the trunk, gasping, sure the vampire would come charging out of that dark cavity. Nothing happened, though. She got a fresh grip on her supplies and slipped into the walled-off space.

Her flashlight shone on bookshelves, floor to ceiling. Near

the round window sat the source of the noise that had puzzled her. The compact device on the floor looked like a dehumidifier. Besides books, many of them leather bound, the shelves held record albums and eight-track tapes. Some of the records looked like the old 78s Linnet had seen in her grandmother's house many years before. The musty volumes tempted her, but she knew better than to let herself get sidetracked. She had no guarantee of how long Nola would sleep.

Backing out, she closed that door and threaded her way between boxes to the opposite one. Unlike the first, this latch opened easily. The flimsy barrier was clearly designed for privacy, not protection.

A queen-size bed almost filled the space under the steeply slanted ceiling. A box-style fan circulated air. The only other furniture was a nightstand with a reading lamp. A thick burgundy carpet covered the floor. Plywood was nailed on the end wall, apparently to block sunlight from another circular window.

On top of rose-colored satin sheets, Nola lay on her back, naked. Creeping into the chamber, Linnet stared at the woman, almost luminously pale against the bedclothes, as thin as a fashion model, with a high forehead and sharp chin. Her black hair, waist length, flared under her like a cape. She brought to mind Sleeping Beauty in the enchanted tower, awaiting Prince Charming's kiss. Only one detail marred the image, a triangle of silken, dark hair that began under her small breasts and dwindled to a point at her navel.

Linnet propped the flashlight on the nightstand to shine on the bed. Then she quietly set down her bags, tightened her grip on the gun, checked that the coiled ropes weren't tangled and readied the spray bottle in her left hand. For a second she considered trying to bind Nola's arms before resorting to violence. She dismissed the idea as wildly reckless. Her...intimacy with Max made it possible to touch him without waking him. She'd better not try that with this creature.

When she pointed the gun at Nola's chest, Linnet's hand shook. She drew a deep breath and exhaled it, forced her muscles to relax, and curled a finger around the trigger. She stepped closer to the bed, afraid of shooting off center.

Just as she prepared to squeeze the trigger, Nola's eyes flew open.

Linnet screamed. Her hand jerked, and the gun fired. The sound reverberated in her head, making her ears buzz.

Nola spasmed, blood spurting from her left shoulder. Her eyes blazed. Roaring like a panther, she grabbed Linnet's right arm.

With her left hand, Linnet shoved the spray bottle in Nola's face and squirted. Nola emitted a shriek and curled up on her side, hands over her eyes. Linnet sprayed her again. The vampire convulsed, retching.

Dropping the gun and bottle, Linnet stooped to pick up the ropes. She grasped one of Nola's arms and slid it into the noose. When she tightened the knot, the woman rolled onto her back.

Nola's free hand shot up and fastened around Linnet's throat.

Trying to scream, Linnet felt the pressure squeezing her windpipe. Her vision grayed. She saw the woman's mouth moving but couldn't hear the words over the ringing in her ears.

Nola flung her onto the bed, stopped choking her and pinned both her arms. She struck like a snake. Her teeth sank into the inner curve of Linnet's elbow.

Linnet cried out at the searing burn, nothing like the gentle sting of Max's bite. Nola clamped on with painful suction.

Within less than a minute, though, the heat faded to a warmth that spread from Linnet's arm up to her throat and breasts, then through the rest of her body.

No! Mustn't give in to this! It seemed like a worse violation than the pain, to feel pleasure at having her lifeblood stolen like a deer's or rabbit's. Tears prickled her eyes. *Max!*

She thought she heard the echo of his voice in her head, calling her name. She felt his anguish at her suffering. Before she could cling to the impression, it faded.

After some immeasurable time, Nola rose to a crouching position. She reached to the nightstand for a handful of tissues and cleaned the blood off her own shoulder. The bullet wound visibly shrank as Linnet watched. "Who the hell are you, and how did you get in here?" Nola snarled.

The ringing in Linnet's ears had subsided by now. "I'm Deanna's aunt. Jodie told me how to find you."

"Jodie!" Nola spat the name like a curse. "Where is that treacherous little bitch?"

"Gone where you can't find her."

Nola's eyes captured Linnet's. "Tell me."

"No."

Nola stared at her in evident surprise. "You can't hide the truth from me."

"Yes, I can." Linnet fingered her necklace.

"What's that?"

"A gift from Anthony."

"That weakling." Nola stood up, snatched a burgundy satin robe from the bedpost and shrugged into it, her eyes never leaving Linnet's face. "Tell me. Tell me everything."

Her will battered at Linnet's mind. Anchored by the necklace and, more important, the memory of her time with Max, Linnet fended off the attack.

With an outraged growl, Nola yanked her to her feet. "You couldn't have planned all this by yourself. Maxwell Tremayne sent you, didn't he?"

"No, he doesn't know I'm here."

"He never struck me as the kind to be soft on ephemerals. But he's obviously fed on you. Your aura might as well be flashing a neon sign." She shoved Linnet toward the door. "Go on. Downstairs."

On the way out Linnet snagged her purse. Nola just gave it an amused glance. "You don't have another weapon in there, do you? Or a cell phone?"

"No." Unfortunately, Linnet had left her phone in the larger bag, where it might as well be back in Maryland, for all the good it would do.

"Hang on to it, then. I know human females use handbags like security blankets, and you'll probably need one."

"What are you going to do with me?" Stumbling down the attic steps ahead of Nola, Linnet dismissed the fantasy of escape that crossed her mind. She'd had glimpses of how fast a vampire could move.

"Keep you, of course. Max robbed me of my pet. Now I've got his."

"I'm not—" She cut off the end of the sentence. No point in arguing with this creature.

"What happens to you will depend on how long Max takes to come after you and how he reacts when he does. I ordered that halfwitted girl to shoot him. Obviously she screwed up." On the second floor, she steered Linnet into one of the bedrooms.

"Why did you do that?"

"To even the odds. Max is older and more powerful than I am. It would be stupid of me to face him when he's at full strength."

Half-open curtains let in the gradually brightening daylight. Linnet staggered to the bed. Though woozy, she felt no pain from the incision on her arm. She suspected that, like leeches, vampires secreted an anesthetic as well as antiseptics and anticoagulants. A vampire's venom, though, apparently bestowed pleasure instead of just blocking pain. An elegant adaptation, making the victim enjoy the attack instead of fighting it.

I guess I'm not in such bad shape, she thought, *if I can think like a biologist at a time like this.*

"Are you planning to fight Max? Try to kill him?"

Nola laughed. "Max must've told you it's taboo for us to kill each other." She backed through the door. When it was almost shut, she added, "But there's no rule against killing you, pet."

Chapter 13

After the door closed, Linnet heard the click of a lock. Nola must have a bolt on the outside of the door. Why would she equip a bedroom that way? To keep her "pets" caged?

A frantic search confirmed that guess. One door led to a half bath with a cramped shower stall retrofitted into a corner. The other door opened onto a closet full of clothes whose dominant black-and-silver motif suggested that Jodie had occupied this room.

Linnet's heart pounded from her hurried shuffle through the closet and the drawers. She'd found no tools suitable for vampire slaying or jailbreaking. She wasn't in the mood to enjoy snickering at Jodie's taste in skull-shaped silver jewelry, bikini panties or black lace camisoles. Crowding up against the single window to peer outside, she prayed for a porch roof to climb onto or at least a network of vines with sturdy stems. She saw nothing like that, only a view of the back lawn and a rocky beach.

She peeled off the gloves and collapsed on the unmade bed

in a trembling heap. She felt light-headed and thirsty. Bruises showed where Nola had grabbed her. On the inside of her arm, she found a ragged mark like the bite of a cat or small dog. Linnet buried her face in her arms. How could she have hoped to overcome Nola single-handed? She'd had no real concept of a vampire's strength. *Please, God, help me get out of this!*

Raking her hair back from her forehead, she reflected that she didn't deserve to have her prayers answered. Not only had she acted like an idiot, barging into a predator's lair, she had been prepared to commit murder. Her earlier arguments against killing Nola outright still made sense, and she must have gone temporarily insane to think otherwise.

Max is right, even if he has a twisted way of getting to the conclusion. If she makes us kill her in self-defense, that's one thing. But chopping off her head while she's asleep, the way she had Anthony killed...

A shudder racked Linnet, and her stomach lurched. She rushed to the bathroom and gulped a glass of water. Washing the bitten place on her arm, she remembered the moment of Nola's attack. For a few seconds she had felt Max inside her head, sharing her fear and pain. Or had she?

Linnet closed her eyes and reached for him. She encountered sheer blankness and silence, with no hint of the immersion in his thoughts she'd experienced when they made love. She decided she must have imagined his presence in her mind up in the attic. Wishful thinking. Hadn't Max estimated that Nola's bond with Jodie wouldn't work over a distance of more than a mile or two?

A few minutes later, standing at the window and watching sunlight on the waves, Linnet heard footsteps in the hall. She dashed to the bed, groped in her purse and switched on the miniature tape recorder. Just in time, hoping that she looked innocent enough and that Nola would attribute her nervousness to simple fear, she crouched on the bed with the purse open beside her. The bolt clicked, and Nola opened the door.

Her hair hung to her waist in a single braid. It looked damp at the edges, as if she'd taken a shower. Over white slacks, she wore a loose blouse embroidered with a fern pattern. She closed the door, leaned against it and surveyed Linnet with a thin smile.

Linnet didn't have to fake the quaver in her voice. "Are you going to kill me?"

"I didn't say that. I only said I could."

"Max told me you have a rule against killing people."

"If he said that, he fudged the truth to keep you quiet. We have a rule against killing conspicuously, leaving evidence that might make ephemerals suspect us."

"Yeah? Then what about Deanna and Anthony?" She clenched her fists around folds of the bedspread, half expecting Nola to fly into a rage.

Instead, the woman just arched her eyebrows in apparent curiosity. "Deanna? What's she to you?"

"My niece. You murdered her. Max's brother, too—one of your own people."

Nola folded her arms. "You're mistaken. One of my young friends killed them."

"I know. Fred. But he was following your orders."

"Not quite. He exceeded them."

"Are you trying to claim you didn't order him to commit murder?"

"I didn't, if it matters now. I just told that idiot boy to teach them a lesson. If I had him here, I'd—" She bared her teeth. "Thanks to him, I had to abandon a perfectly good setup in Maryland."

Linnet felt a rush of heat to her face. "That's all their lives mean to you? A little inconvenience?"

Nola shrugged. "All ephemerals die sooner or later. As for Anthony, he had to be punished, but I regret his death."

"Punished, why?"

"For trespassing. He stole one of my donors. That violates our custom."

"Deanna wasn't a thing to steal. She had free will. She wanted to get away from you, and she loved Anthony."

"Love." She emitted a laugh like the ripple of icy water. "He seduced her the same way I did, except that he was more successful. They had a mutual addiction."

"I don't believe that. He wouldn't have risked his life if he hadn't loved her." Linnet felt a cold lump in her chest, though, recalling Max's mention of that same dependency. Could vampires love at all? "I met Anthony a few times. He wasn't like you. He didn't collect human victims like—like bottles in a wine cellar."

Nola shook her head in mock pity. "You romantic dreamer! Anthony hovered around the edge of my little group to pick up my leavings. I didn't mind sharing. The young ephemerals didn't mind, either. They came to my home to immerse themselves in the glamour of the vampire lifestyle. I couldn't drink from all of them every time. Anthony was welcome to feed on the ones I wasn't using at the moment."

Linnet still couldn't imagine kids like Dee wanting to be used that way. "They didn't know you were a real vampire, did they?"

"Of course not. How stupid do you think I am? Most of them would have run screaming into the night if they hadn't thought it was a game. A few would have begged me to convert them, which is impossible, and they would've caused even more trouble. Fred figured it out. That's why he knew how to destroy Anthony. I don't think Jodie guessed until we left Maryland."

"I'll bet they still don't understand the whole truth. More

likely they think you're some undead demon like in the movies." Linnet felt a little better knowing that Jodie hadn't acted as even a passive accomplice to the murders. Discovering what Nola was capable of had probably incited the girl's desire to escape.

"So Max has told you the truth about us?" Nola frowned. "Incredibly careless of him."

Linnet's heartbeat stuttered. She shouldn't have dropped that remark. Now Nola would consider her more dangerous than if she'd appeared ignorant. "If you're not planning to kill me, what are you going to do?"

"Hold you here until Max shows up, naturally. You're my bargaining chip."

"Then you're wasting your time. Max doesn't care what happens to me."

"Nonsense. I tasted him in your blood. When he wakes up and realizes I've got his pet, he'll come running."

"I'm not—" Linnet cut off her protest in the bleak awareness that "pet" was the most she could expect to be for Max. He might treat his "donors" better than Nola treated hers, but Linnet knew she herself was only one in a long succession over the centuries. "He won't give you what you want just because you have me."

"I told you, we have a rule against poaching. He'll want his possession back, whether he cares about you or not. It's a matter of pride. He stole Jodie, so I've taken you in return." She stepped closer to the bed and stared into Linnet's eyes. "Tell me where that girl is."

She shook her head.

"Speak!" Nola bared her teeth in a snarl, and the pressure of her mind bore down harder.

Closing her eyes, Linnet reached for Max. She found only a void, but the attempt distracted her from Nola's attack. The pressure faded.

"Damn you, look at me!" When Linnet ignored the command, Nola's voice continued. "So he's somehow made you immune to mesmerism. Well, no matter, I can still use you." The door opened and closed, and the bolt snicked into place.

After she heard Nola's footsteps disappear down the hall, Linnet opened her eyes. She turned off the tape recorder and collapsed onto the pillow, fighting tears. If her safety depended on Max's caring enough to bargain for her, she might spend whatever was left of her life as Nola's pet.

To her surprise, only a couple of minutes later she heard steps in the hallway again. Two sets this time. *Max?* She sprang up, turning on the tape, and sat on the edge of the bed. Voices, male and female, argued in the corridor. Though she couldn't make out the words, she felt sure she recognized Max's voice.

The bolt snicked again, and Nola flung the door wide-open. "There, you see, I haven't hurt your pet. Satisfied?"

Max stood beside her on the threshold. He glowered at Linnet from under his dark eyebrows.

She gazed into his eyes, probing for his thoughts. She felt nothing, as if she'd imagined their union of the night before.

He glanced away from Linnet toward Nola. "Given your track record with donors," he said, "I had to make sure you hadn't damaged this one. But that isn't why I'm here."

"I know. It's about your brother."

"You ordered his destruction. Can you give me one reason not to haul you before the elders?"

"Hmm…" Nola pretended to think over the question. "Because I've got your pet? If you're threatening me, think what I could do to her."

"She isn't my pet, only a temporary traveling companion." His casual tone chilled Linnet. "I could demand your death for murdering Anthony."

"Planning to tear me limb from limb for what Fred Pulaski did? How would the elders feel about that?"

"Pulaski belonged to you. You're responsible."

"What do you want from me? I can't bring your brother back to life."

Linnet held her breath, waiting for his response.

Folding his arms, Max turned sideways to face her. "Since I can't have your death, I'll settle for banishment."

"What do you mean?"

"I want you to disappear, somewhere I won't have any chance of meeting you. Leave the country. Whatever remnants of a harem you may have in this area, you'll have to abandon them. Start over anywhere you like, as long as I don't see you again."

Nola grasped the doorjamb for support, as if fighting the pressure of Max's will. "How long?"

"Let's say a complete human generation. Twenty years."

With a quiver of anxiety in her voice, she said, "You have no authority to pass that sentence. The elders would never back you up."

"Oh, really? Would you like to check with Valpa on that? He'll stand by me. He gave me permission to execute you if it could pass for self-defense. Consider yourself getting off easily."

"You're lying." Her voice turned shrill. "Drop your shield and let me read whether you're lying."

Their eyes met for a second. Nola flinched as if lashed by a whip. "There," said Max, "that's all you're going to get. Believe me or don't."

"I believe you. I'll go."

"Leave immediately. Don't wait for nightfall."

"But—" She shifted her eyes away from his cold stare. "All right. But I'm taking the woman along. If you have a change of heart and decide to attack me, she'll suffer."

"Do whatever you want with her. She isn't my property. She's been convenient, but I don't need her anymore." His cold stare scanned the room, passing over Linnet without meeting her eyes.

Her breath congealed in her lungs. She mentally reached out, groping in a fog for any trace of Max's thoughts. She hit a blank wall. *Max, please, look at me! Tell me you don't mean that!* Nothing. Her eyes burned. She blinked to hold back the tears. Even if the two vampires could read her emotions, at least she didn't have to make a spectacle of her humiliation.

He flashed from the door to the bedside. "I need the keys to the rental car, though. I took a taxicab here." With his hands moving so fast they blurred, he rifled through Linnet's purse and shoved the keys into his pocket. In an eyeblink he returned to the doorway. "If you violate my terms," he said to Nola, "I'll know it. You'd better start packing." He disappeared, his steps fading toward the stairs.

Nola slammed the door. Hardly noticing the sound of the bolt being locked, Linnet swallowed an upsurge of sobs and dashed to the window. She couldn't see the street from this point, but the window wasn't locked. Pushing it up, she listened to the car starting in front of the house. When she heard the engine noise die away around the corner, she had to let go of the hope that Max would lurk nearby to rescue her.

He didn't care. She'd been only a "convenience" to him, as any other mere mortal would be.

A couple of minutes later, Nola reappeared. "Well, you heard what Maxwell the Great said. We're leaving. You have ten minutes to get ready." She tossed Linnet's tote bag, obviously empty, into the middle of the floor. "So you did have a telephone in here after all. But not in your handbag. What a sly thing you are." She stalked to the window and stared down at Linnet from her willowy height. "Why can't I mesmerize you? Is it something Max did?" Linnet didn't answer. "Or is it this thing?" Her hand hovered over the ankh pendant but didn't touch it. "Suppose I take it away from you?"

Linnet stared back at her without moving. Nola's fingers crept closer to the necklace, then retreated. "Never mind. I may not be able to hypnotize you, but I can still hurt you. Remember that and behave yourself." She hurried to the door, repeating, "Ten minutes," before she withdrew from the room.

Picking up her bag, Linnet wondered whether Nola had a neurotic fear of religious symbols. Not according to Jodie, but Jodie couldn't have known everything that went on in Nola's head, and maybe the she-vampire had lied to her disciple on that point. Max had mentioned that some of his people suffered from such phobias. Immersed too deeply in human culture, some of them had become infected with superstitions about their own kind. Obviously Max had made sure Anthony escaped that problem.

Linnet dropped the bag on the bed and glanced inside her purse before closing it. The key ring wasn't the only item Max had taken. The tape recorder was gone.

She suspected he meant to destroy it and the evidence of vampires' existence that it contained. No time to worry about that now, though. The information on the tape meant little compared to her life. She rummaged in the bathroom cabinet and dresser drawers for any useful items she might be able to collect in the allotted ten minutes. Since she didn't know how long Nola intended to keep her—she pushed the phrase "keep me alive" to the back of her mind—she might as well be prepared.

She pitched deodorant, toothpaste and an unopened toothbrush into the bag, then gathered a few items of clothing. Bras and camisoles meant for Jodie's slender torso were useless, but Linnet found some underpants that might fit. Keeping in mind the cool nights, she took three oversize sweatshirts, along with several pairs of white socks. As for a distraction to stave off panic through hours of helplessness, the paperback books on the dresser fell into the horror category, the last thing she wanted to read while in Nola's clutches. She did take a few music magazines from a stack under the bed. After topping off the heap with a box of tissues from the nightstand, she couldn't think of anything else worth packing. She certainly didn't need makeup or hair spray.

At second glance, the aerosol can reminded her of the garlic spray. Regardless of their inhuman nature, vampires needed to breathe, and their eyes must be as sensitive to caustic substances as anybody else's. She dropped in the hair spray, too. As a weapon, if the chance arose, it would work better than nothing.

Why am I bothering with all this? My hours are probably numbered.

Just as she zipped the bag, Nola, wearing sunglasses and a broad-brimmed straw hat, opened the door and said, "Ready? Get moving."

Trailing behind her, Linnet said, "Where are we going?" She noticed a strong aroma of coconut. It took her a minute to realize Nola had rubbed sunscreen on her exposed skin.

To Linnet's mild surprise, Nola answered her. "To Canada. I'm going to lose myself in the wilderness with Bigfoot for twenty years or until Max gets over his vendetta, whichever comes first. Damn him."

She led the way downstairs and out the front door, shutting it behind her with an emphatic slam. Gripping Linnet's arm, she hauled her around the side of the house to a carport that sheltered a sky-blue sedan, adorned with large fins and sparkling with chrome in the midday sun. "Damn if I'll drive eight hours in daylight. We'll find somewhere to hide out until nightfall, then head for the border." She shoved Linnet into the back seat, otherwise empty. Nola must have loaded her own luggage into the trunk already.

"What do you need me for? You heard what Max said. I'm

no good as a hostage." Linnet made no attempt to soften the bitterness in her tone. Yet even though Max's caring had turned out to be an illusion, she was in no hurry to die. If she had the slightest chance of talking Nola out of using her as a shield or a mobile blood bank, she had to make the attempt.

"He wouldn't let me read his emotions, so I'm erring on the safe side. Anyway, do you think I'd set you free to run to the nearest phone and call the police? I could handle them the way I did in Maryland, but I don't want any more trouble." With her lips curled in a snarl, she backed out of the carport, turned the car toward the street and used a remote control to open a vehicle gate in the wrought-iron fence. The well-tuned engine of the vintage sedan made surprisingly little noise. "Bad enough that I have to abandon both my homes and go live in the middle of nowhere." She pulled onto the street with a screech of tires, pausing only to signal the gate to shut before she headed for the road. Linnet huddled against the luxurious leather upholstery and gazed out the side window.

The car followed a coast-hugging toll road called Seventeen Mile Drive past expensive-looking gated communities and several golf courses. At Carmel-by-the-Sea Nola turned inland, navigating through narrow streets lined with quaint art galleries, shops and restaurants. When the first intersection forced a stop, Linnet watched the steady stream of tourists walking by. She considered leaping out of the car. With a hand on the door latch, she glanced at Nola, who seemed unconcerned about possible escape attempts.

Linnet let go of the handle and sat back in the seat. She had some idea of how fast a vampire could move. If Nola jumped out and grabbed her on the sidewalk, would a scream for help do any good? Or would Nola just hypnotize any would-be rescuer into forgetting the whole incident? The most likely result of making a run for freedom would be that

Nola would watch her more closely, spoiling any future chance to escape.

Outside the downtown tourist district, Nola pulled into the parking lot of a convenience store, where she ordered Linnet to pump gas, standing over her while she did so. Nola then escorted her inside to the ladies' room, standing guard at the door. Naturally the tiny, disinfectant-drenched cubicle had no handy window to escape through. Linnet used the facilities, on the premise that one should never pass up a chance, and soaked a paper towel to wipe nervous sweat from her forehead. When she emerged, Nola's cold fingers grabbed her arm and kept hold of it while buying a sandwich, a giant-size soft drink and two bottles of spring water.

Back in the car, she thrust everything except one container of water into Linnet's hands. Taking a long drink from the water bottle, Nola said, "Don't look so surprised. I have to keep my food source well nourished." She pulled onto the highway.

Linnet struggled to hold her voice steady. If she could resist expressing her fear, maybe she wouldn't feel it so intensely. "How long do you plan to hang on to me?"

"Until I get well away from civilization. I don't trust Max not to change his mind and come after me. Cheer up, we'll travel through the night and the end might come as early as dawn tomorrow."

"Then what?" Linnet's throat felt dry despite the iced cola.

"I'm not planning to rip your throat out." The woman sounded amused. "We're not supposed to leave evidence, remember? I'm going to drop you in the woods. If you find your way to a town, well and good. You'll be too late to do me any harm. If not, the authorities will never connect me with your death from exposure."

Twining her fingers together in her lap, Linnet fought to suppress the scream that tried to erupt from her. Minute by

minute, the panic faded, until she became calm enough to reflect that it was too bad Jodie hadn't kept a compass in her
bedroom. Summer camp had taught Linnet survival tech-
niques for the tame woods of central Maryland, but except
for the unlikelihood of meeting Bigfoot, she knew almost
nothing about the Pacific Northwest.

The car headed east on a winding road through Carmel
Valley. In other circumstances, Linnet would have enjoyed
the glimpses of antique shops and ethnic restaurants, the deceptively rustic houses that probably cost far more than anything comparable in her own neighborhood, the occasional
field dotted with grazing horses, and the view of the hills in
the distance. Now she could only wonder what Nola's constant scanning of the road on either side was in search of.

About half an hour from the coast, Nola turned into a private lane marked by a real estate agent's faded For Sale sign.
Another few minutes of driving brought them to a rambling
two-story house with redwood siding, camouflaged by a cluster of pine trees. A detached garage, apparently a converted
barn, stood near the house.

"This looks promising. Get out."

Linnet obeyed, snatching up her things, remembering to
tuck the water into the carry-on bag. Immediately seizing her
hand, Nola dragged her across the overgrown front yard to
the porch. The steps were littered with petals that had blown
off the flowering shrubs on either side. Dust coated the windows.

"Good, this should do," Nola muttered. She led Linnet to
the garage. "We're spending the day here."

Rather than struggle with the main entrance, she circled
around to the side and forced open the small door. Linnet
began to feel like a puppy on a leash. Her fear had shriveled
from sheer fatigue, now that the vampire obviously didn't
plan to slaughter her on the spot.

Inside, she blinked in the dim light and sneezed at the dust. Taking off her sunglasses, Nola steered Linnet to a ladder that led to a loft covering half the upper part of the interior. "Perfect. Climb up."

"What?"

Nola gave her a brisk shake. "You heard me. We're resting up there."

"You've got to be kidding."

"Move." The sharp edge in Nola's voice rekindled Linnet's fear.

She clambered up the ladder with the purse and tote bag thumping against her sides. Nola followed. "Yes, this will do nicely." The loft had a sturdy-looking floor of unfinished planks. A window at one end let in daylight, but the other end lay in deep shadow. Aside from a stale, dusty scent, the place seemed clean.

To Linnet's surprise, Nola leaped down to the main floor. As Linnet peered over the edge, Nola removed the ladder and laid it on the concrete. She then unlatched and opened the large front door. While Linnet watched, she drove the car inside and closed the door. With her eyes adjusting to the dimness, Linnet could see Nola taking an armful of cloth from the car trunk. Nola sprang up toward the loft.

No, Linnet thought, almost forgetting to breathe. *She levitated.*

Backpedaling from the edge, Linnet watched Nola unfold the bundle, which turned out to be a pair of blankets. "Here." She tossed one across the floor. "Close your mouth before flies get in. You seem to think I'm out to torture you. Unlike some of my kind, I don't think pain makes blood taste better." She jumped down again. Linnet heard her banging around below. A minute later, she reappeared, carrying a bucket.

"What's that for?"

Nola set the bucket down in a corner. "I don't see a bathroom up here, do you?"

Linnet's cheeks burned at the thought of such a makeshift chamber pot.

After spreading one of the blankets in the shadows farthest from the window, Nola lay down on it. "I have to get some sleep. Rest over there and don't bother me." Apparently confident that Linnet didn't have any weapon capable of hurting her, she closed her eyes at once.

Since she had no intention of sleeping, and the thin blanket wouldn't make much of a mattress anyway, Linnet folded hers into a pad to sit on. Hunkered down next to the grimy window, she thumbed through one of Jodie's magazines. One gushing celebrity interview later, she tiptoed across the boards to check on Nola. The vampire slept literally like the dead, with no visible rise and fall of breathing.

Linnet reflected that this would be an ideal time for escape, if any escape route were available. The floor of the garage was a good ten feet below, maybe more. She imagined jumping and breaking an arm or leg, lying on the concrete slab in agony until Nola woke at twilight. Crawling back to her spot, Linnet leafed through the magazine again.

A few hours later she could have passed an exam on platinum-selling heavy-metal bands. Her head ached from the stuffy atmosphere. A fly buzzing in the rafters had found her and kept landing on her sweaty arms. Though she sipped sparingly from the water bottle, eventually she had to resort to the bucket. Not that she worried about modesty, with her captor in suspended animation.

Hunched against the rough wall, she caught herself dozing off. The first couple of times her head sagged, she resisted. Finally she decided staying alert was pointless, given the vampire's strength and speed. She let herself drift into oblivion.

The sound of a car engine snapped her out of the stupor. At the same instant, she thought she heard someone call her name.

"Who…?" she whispered. *I must have dreamed that. Linnet!*

She scrambled to her feet, stifling a yelp of surprise. *Stay calm, Linnet. Be very quiet. I'll need your help. Max?*

Chapter 14

Aching all over, Linnet eased onto her feet. She stretched, wincing at the stiffness in her neck. *Max, where are you?* Her heart raced.

Outside. Show me your surroundings and Nola's position.
How?
Let me see through your eyes.

Bracing herself as if opening her mouth for a dentist's drill, she opened her mind to him. Rather than a rough intrusion, his entry felt as smooth as a hand slipping into a glove. For a second she was tempted to relax into his mental embrace. Resisting the impulse, she scanned the loft. The sun must have just set, for the sky visible through the window had faded to gray. Nola's inert body looked like a vague lump in the far corner.

Very well, came Max's silent voice. *Get as far away as you can from her and from the window. And cover your head. Quickly, before she wakes.* He withdrew, leaving Linnet alone in her skull again.

She retreated to the edge of the loft, crouched on her knees and wrapped the blanket around her head. The crash of shattering glass assaulted her ears. She stared at the window, now a jagged hole with shards of glass scattered below it. A streak of darkness shot across the loft.

With a lupine howl, Nola sprang up. Max, his wings furled, collided with her and knocked her down. Her nails ripped his bare shoulders. The wings melted into his back, but the fangs and fur remained. Dark fur spread over Nola's face and hands. The air around her blurred, and her nails elongated to talons like his. Her teeth grew sharp.

Her head pounding, Linnet watched them grapple on the bare wood. They clawed at each other like a pair of tigers. Almost at the edge, Nola flung Max off her and rolled away from him. He dived at her and knocked her down again. In the heat of combat, the fur vanished from both of them. They still had the fangs and claws of beasts, and each one growled when a talon drew blood.

Red streaks scored their arms and Max's chest. Over and over he pinned the other vampire to the floor, but she slithered free every time.

Wedged in a corner, Linnet watched with her hands pressed to her mouth. *Nola's as strong as he is!* She had a recent bullet wound, but so did he, and his was more serious. Though both their chests were heaving with labored breathing, Max's breath sounded harsher. Now he fought more like a bear than a cat. He lumbered rather than pounced, and half his blows swung wild. Nola tripped him, and this time she landed on top. Her hands encircled his neck, the nails gouging his skin.

While Linnet wasn't sure one vampire could kill another with bare hands, she didn't want to bet his life on her guess. With neither of them paying attention to her, she sidled toward her bag. The hair spray rested on top of the clothes. Linnet grabbed the can, pulled off its lid and edged toward the combatants with a finger on the nozzle.

She crouched beside the snarling pair. Her own pulse thundered in her ears. She raised the can to eye level. "Nola!"

The she-vampire whirled toward her with a growl. Linnet sprayed her full in the face. Leaping up, Nola pawed at her eyes. Linnet rolled out of the way.

Max felled Nola with a blow to the temple and knelt on her chest. He squeezed her head between his hands and wrenched her neck halfway around. Hearing the crack of bone, Linnet screamed.

Max lifted Nola's body and threw it to the floor below. He turned on Linnet, who dropped the spray can and backed toward the window. A growl rumbled in his chest, gradually subsiding to drawn-out, rasping breaths. The fangs and claws receded into humanlike teeth and nails. Blood stopped oozing from the scratches on his chest and arms. He took a step toward her.

She backed farther, her hands splayed on the wall behind her.

"Linnet?" His voice sounded human, though hoarse.

"You killed her," she whispered.

"No, she's comatose, not dead."

"You broke her neck."

"Yes." He glided closer. When she flinched, a shadow crossed his face. Sensing the tentative brush of his mind against the edge of hers, she thrust it away. "Listen to me, Linnet. She isn't dead. I haven't broken the law against kin slaying. She'll need weeks, possibly months, but she will heal and revive, unless I take precautions. Do you want her to revive?"

Linnet shook her head. In a mouselike voice that hardly sounded like her own, she said, "What precautions?"

"Confine her in a small, enclosed space."

"Like a coffin."

"Not having a coffin in reserve, I have another idea." He reached her side, and she didn't cringe from him. "First, let me take you down from here."

"Okay." Without stopping to think, she put her arms around his neck when he picked her up. The strength of his embrace gave her a treacherous feeling of comfort.

Holding her, he floated to the ground floor of the garage. He set her on her feet and glowered at her. "What possessed you to attack her on your own? We had an agreement. Why didn't you wait for me?"

"Wait for dark, when she'd have her full strength? While you were still recovering?" Linnet didn't think telling Max she'd sensed his buried scruples about killing another vampire would improve his mood.

"You could have consulted me, explained your reasons."

"Yeah, and I'm sure you would have listened and been perfectly reasonable about the whole thing."

"You objected to my keeping secrets from you. Then you did the same and put your own life in danger."

Since she was keeping her thoughts firmly sealed against his, she couldn't tell what emotion lurked behind those words. "Why do you care whether I'm in danger? You got what you wanted. You defeated Nola."

He ran his fingers through his already mussed hair in a nearly human gesture. "If that's what you want to believe. Now, I have things to take care of. Will you be all right for a minute?"

"Sure, why not? I see vampires fight to the death all the time."

Ignoring the remark, he guided her to the side of the room, then leaped back up into the loft. When he reappeared, he held Nola's purse, with a handkerchief shielding the leather from direct touch. Linnet was baffled until he extracted car keys from the purse. Unlocking the huge trunk of Nola's sedan, he moved two suitcases and an overnight bag into the back seat. He heaved the woman's body into the trunk and closed the lid. "There. I suspected this vintage monstrosity she drove would have ample room."

Linnet noticed how carefully he kept the handkerchief between his skin and Nola's belongings. "You're worried about fingerprints?"

"As far as I know, mine aren't on file, but why take chances?" He rifled through Nola's wallet to remove the driver's license and other cards, tucking them in his back pocket. He hid the purse under one of the seats. "Wait here." He opened the garage door, settled behind the wheel of the car and backed out.

Her strength flowing away like water down a drain, Linnet slid to the concrete floor. Braced against the wall, she sat on the concrete with her eyes shut and knees drawn up to her chest. She tried to shape a prayer of thanks but doubted whether the attack of a berserk vampire counted as divine intervention. Her head ached along with assorted bruises.

She wasn't sure how much time had passed when Max's footsteps jolted her out of a mental fog. When she opened her eyes, he was leaping down from the loft once more, carrying her purse and airline bag. She pulled herself upright, ignoring the hand he offered. "What did you do with the car?"

"Hid it in the woods and obliterated the tire tracks."

"But somebody's still bound to find it soon. And her."

"Not if I buy the property." He went outside, and she followed, waiting while he lowered the garage door. "The rental car is farther down the driveway. Can you walk that far?"

"Sure." She didn't want him to carry her again. She didn't trust her own reaction to that closeness.

His eyes traveled over her. "Nola fed on you. Damn, I wish I'd done worse than break her neck."

"I'll be all right." Her legs wobbled, and her throat felt raw with thirst, but those effects would wear off. "She had you figured. She suspected you'd have a change of heart about following her."

"What change?" He headed down the lane, with Linnet hurrying to keep up. "I never intended to let that woman escape unpunished, much less leave you in her power."

"You could've fooled me. Oh, wait, you did." Anger welled up afresh, making her head throb and her hands curl into fists. "I was a convenience you didn't need anymore."

"That was for Nola's benefit. Did you expect some kind of signal? I couldn't give her any clue to my real intention."

"You could have sent me a telepathic message, right? You wouldn't let me read your mind. You shut me out."

He halted and turned to her, clasping her hand before she could evade him. "Don't you understand that I had to? Nola could read your emotions. If you hadn't believed in my rejection, she wouldn't have, either."

"I see your point." His fingers encircling hers sent shivers up her arm. She pulled free, and he didn't try to stop her. "But understanding that doesn't change how I feel. You could've at least contacted me right after you left, when Nola wasn't around to sense the link."

His expression went blank for a second. "The truth is, I didn't think of it."

"Which you would have, if I'd been important enough to you."

"Damn it, Linnet, I was too busy thinking about saving your life!"

"Yeah, right."

"I had to make *her* believe you weren't important to me. I wanted her to let you go, leaving me free to attack her without putting you in danger. I never expected her to keep you as a hostage anyway."

"She decided to abandon me in the Canadian woods like

an unwanted puppy. That way it wouldn't be her fault if I happened to die."

Max growled a curse. "Fine, if she stays undead until her car crumbles into a heap of rust, that won't be your fault or mine." They reached the rental car and got in.

"You said she could recover eventually."

"Not without oxygen or blood."

"So she's as good as dead, but you didn't kill her." Linnet belted herself into the front passenger seat.

"Exactly. It's in the hands of fate. Nor did I let you kill her. If you'd managed to pull that off, the deed would have given you lifelong nightmares."

"How do you know?"

"I know how your people in this time and place feel about violent death. I know how *you* feel. I touched your mind, remember."

"Invaded it!"

He let go of the steering wheel and put one hand on her shoulder. "You shared in that merging. You enjoyed it as much as I did."

"How can I be sure of that?" She shrugged off his touch. "Maybe I was just feeling your emotions all along."

"Open your thoughts to me and I'll prove that isn't so." She felt him leaning on the door of her mind, whispering through the keyhole.

"No." She clutched the ankh, not because she believed it could shield her against him if he made a determined assault, but to strengthen her resolution to lock him out. "There's no way you can prove you aren't trying to control me."

With his jaws clenched as if fighting the temptation to batter her with arguments, he started the car and turned it toward the road.

When they passed the For Sale sign, now barely visible in

the gathering dark, Linnet remembered his earlier remark. "You're actually going to buy the house?"

"And the land around it, which covers five acres, according to that notice. Judging from the condition of the sign and the building, the listing agency will be more than glad to get the place off its hands."

"But won't they still do inspections and all that?"

"Most of those procedures are required only for a mortgage loan. I'll pay in full by cashier's check. A walk-through tomorrow for appearances' sake, and closing as soon as I can get the funds from my bank."

Linnet could only gape at him in astonishment. "Big spender," she murmured.

"I'll tell the agent I want it as a summer home. Eccentricity and wealth aren't uncommon in this area. I won't attract any particular notice. As soon as the property is mine, I'll lock Nola's car in the garage and forget about it."

The revelation that he could drop six figures on a house just to keep Nola's "undead" body hidden struck Linnet with the depth of the difference between Max and herself. That level of wealth seemed almost as alien to her as vampirism. Though the terror of watching him fight like a wild beast had faded, the gulf between them felt wider than ever.

Halfway to the motel, another question occurred to her. "How did you know I needed rescuing from Nola this morning? Lucky guess? I thought you'd sleep till sunset."

"You woke me."

"Huh?"

He glanced at her, his eyebrows arched as if her question puzzled him. "I shared your pain when she drank from you, of course."

"I thought I imagined that, feeling you in my head for a second. How could you? Wasn't it too far?"

"What makes you think that?"

"What you and Jodie said last night." Linnet frowned, try-ing to recall the conversation. "You implied Nola wouldn't be able to sense her from more than a mile or two away."

"That was different. The bond she had with the girl was superficial, imposed for control. Nola wouldn't tolerate the kind of depth that would allow an ephemeral to plunge below the surface of her mind. She would have noticed the break-ing of the link over any distance, but otherwise, the range was necessarily limited."

"You're claiming we have some deep, intimate, whole dif-ferent kind of bond?" She wished she had the power to sharpen those words to barbs that would make him bleed.

"Do you deny it?"

"Damn right I do. If we did, you couldn't shut me out at will. If we have this mystic union, then I don't believe you could stand to hurt me the way you did back at Nola's."

He shook his head, glowering through the windshield. "If you don't believe I care, how do you explain the fact that I saved you from her?"

"For all I know, that was just a byproduct of taking revenge on her, which you said you planned to do all along. Nola gave me a good idea of what you people think about us. To her, we're no more than useful animals. From what you said about Anthony and his weakness for ephemerals, you've always felt pretty much the same way. Right?" She heard her own voice turning shrill and fought to clamp down on the rising hyster-ics.

"That was before—"

"Before you met me? I'm the big exception? Why should I buy that?"

He sighed. "If you refuse to open your mind to me, I can't convince you otherwise."

A few minutes later they arrived at the motel. Snatching up an armful of clothes, Linnet slammed into the bathroom.

A hot shower eased the bruises but couldn't wash away her inner turmoil. When she emerged, Max was reclining on one of the beds, his hands laced behind his head. By the lamp shining over the other bed, she saw that the scratches on his chest and arms had almost vanished. The smears of dust and dried blood were gone. He must have cleaned up at the sink in the alcove outside the bathroom door. His eyes, roaming over her, glowed with what looked like hunger.

She caught herself blushing. "I almost forgot. You must need blood, after all that."

With a quiet laugh, he said, "Not from you, when you can hardly stand the sight of me. Besides, you need to recover from Nola's theft." He swung his legs to the side of the bed and gestured toward a chair. "Don't worry, I fed on a squirrel after I hid the car. Please, sit down. We have to talk."

"Classic scary words." She sat, keeping her back rigidly straight. "What's to talk about? Mission accomplished. I'm going home."

"Before we discuss that, I have some things for you." He crossed the room to the dresser and came back with a couple of items. One was Linnet's cell phone. "I broke into Nola's house after she left and retrieved it."

"Thanks. What about all the vampire-hunting supplies?"

"I wiped them down for fingerprints and left them in the attic. Nothing to identify you there, even in the unlikely event they're ever found. And when I took the car keys out of your handbag, I also took this." He gave her the tape recorder.

"Yeah, I figured that." She popped it open. "Hey, the tape's still here."

He said with a humorless smile, "Did you think I'd destroyed it?"

"Well, that was my first thought, yes."

"I know how important this record is to you, even though

you can't share it with anyone. At least, I hope you don't plan to share it."

"Who with?" she said with a shrug. "You've already rubbed my nose in the fact that the police couldn't arrest Nola, even if they didn't think it was a weird hoax. And forcing my sister and mother to listen to this stuff is the last thing I'd do."

"Then what will you do with the tape?"

"Keep it, I guess, for my own satisfaction. To prove to myself, when these couple of days fade into a blur, that I didn't imagine it all. Even if I can't tell anybody else what really happened to Dee, at least I'll know."

"Good, I felt sure you'd be sensible." He leaned back, arms folded. "But what is this about the memory becoming a blur? You talk as if you never expect to see me again."

"Why should I? All I want is to get back to normal." She barred the door of her mind against any possible invasion. She didn't want him to feel the anguish behind that lie.

"What is normal? Surely you don't expect your life to return to its former equilibrium?"

"I can sure give it a try."

"I don't want to return to what my life was before you. I want to revisit that union we shared—and deepen it."

She sensed no attempted mind-touch this time. So why did she feel an urge to throw that door open on her own? She suppressed the feeling and said as coolly as she could manage, "Don't waste energy trying to convince me you care."

"Don't you understand how much trust I showed by giving you this tape?"

"The way I see it, I'm entitled. After all, I'm the one who risked my life to make the recording in the first place."

"You bloody exasperating female!" He flung his arms wide and sprang to his feet. "Very well, what do you want to do?"

"Go to San Francisco right now and catch a plane back East. I don't care how many connections I have to make. I want out!"

"If you insist." He took out a credit card and picked up the phone.

She dumped Jodie's things in a dresser drawer. By the time he hung up from booking a flight, Linnet had finished packing her own belongings.

"Incidentally, how will you explain this expedition to your family?" he asked. "Someone must have noticed you weren't home for the past few days."

"I talked to my mother once, while you were out of the room. I claimed you and I were going over Anthony and Deanna's joint financial arrangements and so on. She won't question that story, because talking about Anthony is way down on her list of fun things to do."

"Wise of you, since that aspect does need to be dealt with." He opened his checkbook. "What is your sister's full name?"

She was so taken aback that she answered him automatically. When he handed her a four-figure check made out to Robin, Linnet said, "Wait a minute, she won't take this."

"Yes, she will, when you explain that it comprises her daughter's share of their bank balance."

"Come on, Dee never had this much money at once in her life."

"Nevertheless, it is half of her joint account with Anthony, so you won't be lying. It isn't as if I need it, and you do require something concrete to show for our supposed consultation, don't you?"

She grudgingly nodded. "Okay, I'll take care of it."

"As for the apartment, I've already removed the few things of Anthony's I wanted. Dispose of the rest of the contents any way you see fit. The rent is paid through the fifteenth of next month."

Stuffing the check into her purse, she said, "You think of everything, don't you?"

He arched one eyebrow. "Is that a reason to resent me?"

She flushed. "Sorry, I guess that was uncalled for."

"In my existence, any small lapse might expose me to danger. I've learned to think of everything." He unzipped his carry-on bag and took out an envelope. He unfolded the papers inside, extracted one sheet and handed it to her. "Here's another item you should have. A note your niece enclosed in Anthony's last letter to me."

She read silently.

Dear Max, It feels funny to call you by your first name when I've never met you. But we're going to be in-laws, so I guess it's okay. Anthony says you don't approve of us being together. My parents wouldn't, either. I hope we can change your mind—and theirs, too—because we really love each other. I'm looking forward to meeting you in person and proving it. Someday I'll be able to go home and introduce Anthony to my folks. Mom probably thinks I hate her, but I don't. I miss her and Dad, even if I haven't talked to them in a long time. I just want Anthony and me to be together, and for his family and mine to accept us.

It was signed, *Your new sister, Deanna.*

Tears burned Linnet's eyes. She dabbed them with a tissue, angry at herself for showing weakness just when she was trying to break away from Max. Tucking the note into her purse, too, she muttered a reluctant word of thanks.

Max caught her hand. She felt her pulse quicken under his fingertips. "Please, Linnet, don't shut me out."

"Must be hard for you to plead with an inferior being."

His eyebrows drew together in a scowl. A surge of impatience crashed like a wave against her mind and instantly receded. "If that's how you see it, you must realize it proves my desire for you. Just as you desire me."

"Desire isn't a good enough reason to turn my life upside down." Her racing heart and unsteady breath mocked the words.

Curling one hand around the nape of her neck, Max drew her close. "Are you sure?" His fingers wove through her hair to massage her scalp in languid circles. "I know you share my hunger."

"I can't ever be sure with you," she breathed. "What does it matter how you make me feel? How do I know you didn't plant those feelings in the first place?" She flattened her hand against his chest to push him away. A mistake, for now her palm touched the silken hair. Before her brain realized what her body was doing, she stroked down to his waist, back upward, then down again. He arched his back with a sigh. Capturing her hand, he moved it from his chest to his shoulder and pulled her tightly to him. "You see?" he murmured, his breath on her hair sending warmth through her veins. "We belong together."

Heat crept over her arms and breasts, down her body to the sensitive places that remembered his touch and kiss. Light-headed, she hugged him and rubbed against him like a cat.

"Stay with me," he whispered. "I want you."

The verb cut through the warm mist in her head. Not "love," or even "care." Even if he was sincere now, eventually their unequal power would distort their union. After what she'd seen of Nola's relationship with her "pets," Linnet knew that in the long run she would become the same thing to Max.

She removed her arms from his waist and lashed out with a mental slap. Letting go of her, he stepped back. *Linnet, don't do this to me.* His pain jabbed her like a needle.

With a shove she ejected him from her mind and threw up a mental barrier. She visualized a stone wall without a door, as high and blank as the wall he'd raised against her earlier. "Stay out!" Hearing the snakelike hiss in her own voice, she breathed hard until she managed to settle her outrage and speak normally. "Try seducing me again, mentally or any other way, and I'll take a taxi to the airport. I don't care how much it costs."

Sighing, he turned away, his shoulders slumped. "Don't do that. I'll drive you, and I won't interfere with you again." After picking up the keys, he faced her again. "You know I could force my way into your mind. That shield wouldn't hold against my full strength, especially when part of you wants to surrender."

With a defiant lift of her chin, she grasped the necklace. "Yeah, you're probably right."

"I won't do it, though. Using force would only reinforce your belief that I see you as inferior. Let's go."

On the drive to San Francisco over dark highways, she tried vainly to sleep. All she managed was a half doze that made her head feel clogged. The flash of lights appearing and vanishing as they sped past made her eyes ache. She had to make a pretense of resting, though, to resist the impulse to get into another circular conversation with Max.

When the car pulled up to the curb at the terminal, he stopped her as she reached for the door latch. Taking her hand, he kissed her palm, the flicker of his tongue sending sparks along her nerves. "You insisted so strongly that my brother loved your niece. If you believe that, why can't you accept that I care for you?"

She snatched her hand away. Even if he couldn't control her mind with hypnosis, his every touch threatened to ensnare her. "Don't you see the difference? When Anthony helped Dee escape from Nola, he risked his life for her. Not just on a second's impulse, the way you did when Jodie shot at us, but deliberately. When I saw them together, it was obvious they meant everything to each other. But you...you've stayed in control all along. You can read my emotions, even with that shield keeping you out of the deeper levels, but you can shut me out of yours at will."

"I offered to open my mind to you. I begged for that, remember?"

"Too late. How can I ever be sure if you're really baring your soul or just showing me the parts you want to display? We made love, or so I thought, and I've never even seen you naked."

His eyes gleamed in the shifting light and shadows. "We shared passion, didn't we? Is nakedness required?"

"You know what I mean."

"Yes, I know." He folded his arms. "Travel safely, Linnet."

She scrambled out of the car, slammed the door and stalked into the airport without looking around. All the way, though, she felt his eyes on her back.

Chapter 15

As soon as she got home, Linnet buried the ankh and the mini cassette recorder under a pile of old letters in a shoe box on her closet shelf. She'd played only enough of the tape to reassure herself that Max hadn't tricked her by erasing it. Otherwise, she had no desire to relive those conversations, and hiding the tape from herself would remove the temptation. Just the few phrases she'd heard had made her chest ache as if a giant boulder were crushing it. On the other hand, she couldn't discard or destroy the recording after all the risk it had cost.

Any hope that hiding the evidence would bestow instant forgetfulness of her time with Max proved futile. She crawled into bed long after midnight, East Coast time, and slept past noon, ravaged by dreams. Ghastly visions of Max's tigerish fangs ripping into the she-vampire, searing dreams of his lips on her own throat.

Waking in the afternoon racked with headache and thirst, Linnet muzzily realized that her nightmare of the death struggle hadn't been accurate. Max and Nola hadn't used their teeth, only their claws. Because drinking blood signified intimacy, she decided.

Why am I thinking about this at all? After chasing the sleep fog with a shower and coffee, she found that the dreams had already splintered into fragmented images. Within a few days, she hoped, the actual experience would feel like a dream. She could return to a normal life.

First, though, she had to smooth things over with her family. If nothing else, the past few days had hammered the uncertainty of life into her head. She phoned to ask if her mother would be home for the rest of the afternoon. "I've got something for Robin. Maybe you could give it to her."

"Why don't you give—"

"We'll talk about it when I get there, Mom. Bye." Linnet hung up before her mother could interject another word.

An hour later she parked in front of her mother's row house in a gentrified section of Baltimore. Finding an open space in the same block instead of having to walk from the next street over struck her as a good omen.

Her mother opened the door before Linnet got halfway up the walk. On this hot, humid day, her mother wore Bermuda shorts with a T-shirt and had her shoulder-length, graying blond hair pulled back in a ponytail. They hugged, her bony shoulders feeling brittle under Linnet's hands, and she drew Linnet into the crisp coolness of the air-conditioned living room. "Sit down, hon, and I'll get you a glass of tea."

Wearily, Linnet sank onto the comfortably dented couch cushions and waited. When her mother brought in two glasses of iced tea, Linnet automatically placed hers on one of the cork coasters stacked on the coffee table. In the context of this routine action, the past few days began to feel like her imagination. Now if only she could avoid talking about them.

No such luck. "Linnet, where on earth have you been? I tried to call you again yesterday."

After a sip of the tea, artificially sweetened and garnished with lemon and mint the way she'd always liked it, she said, "I told you, Anthony's brother and I had some things to work out. I didn't think you or Robin would want to be bothered with the details."

With a "hmph" sound, her mother said, "That brother who didn't even show up at Deanna's funeral?"

"He couldn't help that. He didn't find out until too late."

"And he didn't want to meet her parents?"

Linnet tried to visualize bringing Max to Robin's house for a cozy visit. Her mind boggled. "Come on, Mom, Robin and Tim wouldn't want that, either, considering what happened."

"You're right, but he could have asked. So does he know about that crazy boy who confessed to the murders?"

Linnet nodded.

"I just don't understand that—why anybody would—" Her voice broke. After wiping her eyes with a napkin, she went on in a steadier tone. "Does the brother have any idea why that lunatic killed them?"

Shaking her head, Linnet said, "When we heard, Max was as shocked as I was." She had no intention of trying to explain Fred's motive to her family.

"Now the boy claims he's sorry, of course. And some jury will let him off with an insanity plea."

"Please, let's not talk about that." Next thing, her mother would probably veer into a harangue about the law being soft on criminals, which Linnet didn't want to hear, either. "How's Robin doing?"

"How do you think? She can barely drag herself out of bed in the morning. But having the crime solved seems to help a little. At least the newspapers aren't pestering us for comments anymore." She put her glass down and leaned forward to pat Linnet's knee. "Listen, hon, I know what happened wasn't your fault. Deanna was a grown woman, even if Robin had trouble seeing her that way. And now that the cops have the murderer locked up, Robin's starting to realize it wasn't your fault. But you have to give her time."

"How much time?" Linnet could barely suppress a sigh. The memory of many a "don't you take that tone with me, young lady" rebuke from childhood was all that kept her face blank. "I don't want to fight with her. That reminds me, I brought you something to give her." She took Max's check out of her purse. "It's from Anthony's brother, half of Dee and Anthony's joint bank account."

"What? Your sister doesn't want that man's money!"

"It's not Max's money, it's Deanna's. Robin has a right to it."

"Max, huh? You must have gotten to know him pretty well, with nicknames and all."

"It was just business, Mom. I'll never see him again." She tried to ignore the pang in her chest at the thought.

"Good. He may be a fine man, but after what happened to Deanna when she ran off with his brother…"

"Mom, that's not fair. Anthony was trying to protect her."

"I guess this Max person told you all about it. What did you two do together besides divide up bank accounts?" The edge in her voice reminded Linnet of being quizzed after dates in high school.

"Nothing much. We discussed what to do about the stuff in the apartment. He already moved out Anthony's things."

"And that took two or three days? What don't you want to tell me?"

Linnet fought the urge to squirm under her mother's narrow-eyed stare. *Stop that. I'm thirty-four, not sixteen. I don't owe her a blow-by-blow script.* "Nothing. Too dull to bother with."

The front door opened, saving her from further interrogation. She glanced up and almost choked on an ice cube when Robin walked in. Though her short platinum hair was as tidily waved as ever, she wore jeans and a loose blouse. Apparently she hadn't started back to work yet.

"Mom!" Linnet yelped. She set down her glass with a thump and stood up.

Robin stopped short in the foyer and stared at her. "Mom didn't tell me…" Her voice trailed off.

Linnet glared at their mother. "You set us up."

Her mother shrugged. "You expected me to wait till next Christmas for you two to get together on your own?"

Linnet fumbled for her purse. "I'll go." Her stomach churned at Robin's cold frown.

"You sit right down." Her mother pointed at Robin. "And you come over here and say hello to your sister. She's got something to give you."

Both sisters sat down, their mother shifting to a chair to make room on the couch. Robin murmured a barely audible "hi."

"It's no big deal," said Linnet. "Just a check for Dee's half of her and Anthony's bank account."

Automatically accepting it, Robin said, "Who the heck is Maxwell Tremayne?"

"Anthony's brother."

"I know my daughter never had this much money." She tossed the check on the table. "What's he trying to do, buy us off?"

An unexpected spasm of anger choked Linnet. Swallowing it, she said, "Where do you get that from? You've never even met him. I promise, he's as devastated over this whole thing as we are."

"Then why didn't he stay around long enough to face me? Where is he?"

"Back home in Colorado, I guess." At least, he would be after disposing of the problem with Nola's house. "And the reason he didn't want to meet the rest of the family is probably because he thought it would just upset you more." Why was she bothering to explain Max's behavior? She was supposed to be forgetting him.

"Good guess. If Dee had come home instead of moving in with a guy from that crowd of perverts—"

"You don't know what you're talking about!" Feeling the heat on her face and hearing the shrillness in her voice, Linnet forced a lid onto her anger. "Anthony wasn't like the others. He was trying to save her life. Don't forget, he died trying."

"I don't care about him!" Robin slammed a fist into the couch. "All I care about is my daughter, and he let her get killed."

"Like I did? Come on, that's what you've been hinting at ever since it happened."

Their mother held up a hand like a traffic cop. "Girls, don't—"

Linnet shook her head. "Let her say it, Mom. That's what she's been thinking. Like I didn't love Dee enough or something."

Staring down at her fists clenched in her lap, Robin nibbled on her lower lip. "I never thought that."

"Did it occur to you that maybe the reason I've spent the past couple of days with Max is because he's the only person I could talk to who didn't blame me? He felt the same way you did, only the other way around. He thought Anthony threw his life away because of Deanna. When we talked about it, we both realized they really loved each other."

The harsh lines on Robin's face softened. "Listen to you defending that Max guy. You must have really spent some intense time together."

"That's what I said," their mother put in.

Linnet felt herself blush. "And I told you, I never expect to see the man again."

"Then why are you blushing?" Robin said.

"Am not," Linnet mumbled, sipping her tea to avoid their eyes. "I'm just trying to be fair to him. He feels guilty about what happened. He's worried that he neglected his brother, just the way I feel about—" She gulped, afraid she would start crying. "He gave me something for you." She rummaged in her purse and pulled out Deanna's letter to Max.

Robin stared at it blankly for a few seconds, then began to read. Gradually her cool mask melted, and silent tears trickled down her cheeks. When she tried to speak, her voice shook, and she swallowed visibly a couple of times before she could get the words out. "Dee wrote this to Anthony's brother instead of me because she thought I wouldn't listen?"

Struggling against sadness and anger, Linnet heard a harsh edge in her own voice. "Okay, if I'd taken better care of her, paid more attention, tried harder to get her to talk to you, she might've still moved in with Anthony, but maybe we wouldn't have lost her. I'm sorry. I know it doesn't help, but how many times do I have to say it?"

"Oh, Linn, you didn't neglect her!" Trembling, Robin clasped Linnet's hand. "I know you loved her as much as I did. I didn't mean all those things I said."

"You don't have to apologize, not when I thought the very same about myself."

"Well, you're wrong, and so was I." She sniffed and rubbed her eyes. "After the murderer turned himself in, I talked things over with Reverend Hale. He recommended a counselor, and I'm going to see her, but meanwhile, he helped me understand some stuff. I accused you because I felt guilty myself."

"You? What for?"

"For giving up on my daughter, practically throwing her out of the house because I couldn't handle her. Like I should have expected you to keep her out of trouble when I couldn't. And then she got mixed up with a gang of crazy people and got herself killed." She buried her face in her hands.

Linnet put her hands on Robin's shoulders, stunned into silence for an instant. "That wasn't your fault," she whispered. "She could've met those people no matter where she was living."

"Cut it out, both of you." Their mother rapped on the table like a judge calling them to order. "It wasn't anybody's fault except that insane young man's. Stop beating yourselves up."

Robin gave Linnet a quick, stiff hug. "I thought you dropped off the face of the earth because you were mad about the way I treated you at the funeral."

"I'm not mad," Linnet sighed. She hugged Robin back, feeling her sister's tears dampening her shirt. "We're a mess, aren't we?" she said with a shaky giggle.

"So what about Anthony's brother?"

"Oh, go on!" Linnet waved at her like shooing a fly.

"No, seriously. Maybe if I'd made an effort to meet Anthony and get to know him, instead of thinking he was as bad as the rest of that screwed-up bunch, things might've turned out different. Did his brother tell you much about him?"

Linnet took a long drink of tea and gathered her thoughts to concoct an edited version of her conversations with Max.

Submerged in a warm tide, she luxuriated in the lapping of the waves on her breasts and thighs. A sting at her throat convulsed her like an electric shock, and ripples radiated over every inch of her skin. Max's face floated into her view. She reached for him. His lips brushed hers. She melted....

Her eyes opened in the darkness of her bedroom. She threw off the sheet and sat up, shivering as the air-conditioning blew on her sweat-dampened arms. Why couldn't she forget Max in sleep as easily as she did while awake? By day, the experiences she'd had with him seemed as far-fetched as some weird movie she'd watched in the dim past. Except for the transformations she'd seen with her own eyes, she could almost believe she had simply run afoul of deranged cultists who played at being vampires. At night, though…

She turned on the overhead light, blinking until her eyes adjusted. After dragging a chair to the closet, she lifted down the shoe box full of high-school love notes and old birthday cards. She ignored the recorded minicassette but dug out the ankh necklace. After putting the box away, she sat on the bed with the chain looped around her fingers.

Thanks to Anthony's posthypnotic suggestion, the necklace was supposed to provide a mental anchor and protect her from vampiric influence. Maybe it would drive away the dreams and give her back her normal life. She squeezed the ankh in her fist until it gouged her palm.

Who am I kidding? If anything, the talisman would only keep the memory alive. She shoved it into a drawer under a pile of scarves and crawled into bed, tears scorching her cheeks.

Almost three weeks after leaving Monterey, Max couldn't clear his mind of his last conversation with Valpa. He had phoned the elder to report what had happened to Nola. Valpa accepted her "undead" condition as a valid compromise between slaughtering her and letting her escape unpunished. Max wouldn't be hauled before the council for judgment and ostracism.

Not that such a concern had significantly preyed on his mind. What haunted his days' sleep was his final glimpse of Linnet marching away from him into the airport. Her strength added to her appeal for him, but why did that strength have to include the power to reject him? He oscillated between outrage that an ephemeral would dare frustrate his will, and thirst for the taste of her and the touch of her mind. He soared through the night for hours, howling like a lost wolf, whenever he felt safe from human eyes and ears.

Valpa's indulgent chuckle echoed in his brain. The elder

vampire enjoyed the irony of Max's fascination with an ordinary, short-lived woman, after the way he'd scorned his brother for a similar infatuation. Max had itched to reach through the phone and strangle the old man. To Valpa's question about his feelings, he'd indignantly retorted, "Of course I'm not in love with her. That's a human delusion."

"A weakness, I believe you've always said."

"Exactly. A weakness that got my brother killed. I'm not likely to fall victim to it."

"Of course not." That blasted amusement had tinged Valpa's answer. "If you did happen to fall, though, I'm not the one you should ask for help."

"I don't need help!"

"Certainly not," Valpa had agreed in a tone suitable for humoring a lunatic. "If you do, however, I suggest you speak to Roger Darvell. Not only has he made a success of such a relationship himself, he is trained to give counsel to others."

"Voodoo! I might as well hire a phrenologist to read the shape of my skull."

"Quite so. Nevertheless, if your problem arises from a human relationship, you might want to seek advice from someone accustomed to dealing with human problems."

At that point Max had hung up. Yet Valpa's words lodged in his brain with inconvenient persistence. Well into July, he still dreamed of Linnet every day, though a healthy vampire should hardly dream at all. He couldn't delude himself that her thoughts were invading his over thousands of miles. The obsession came from within. The anonymous women he fed on slaked his thirst for a few hours, but the hunger always seared his throat anew the following night.

Finally he called Roger Darvell in Maryland and left a message on the psychiatrist's voice mail, then paced a circuit of his house in a froth of impatience until the other man called back.

He bit off the first words that sprang to his lips, a rant about the time he'd had to wait for the return call. Instead, he thanked Darvell for informing him of Anthony's death.

"It was the least I could do. What became of that infernal woman? If I'd known she was engaging in that kind of behavior so near my home…"

"It's a moot point now." Max gave a brief account of how he and Linnet had dealt with Nola.

"Have you seen your young friend since then?"

Max felt like cursing Darvell for homing in on that point. Had the mere speaking of her name given him away so blatantly? On the other hand, the doctor's perceptiveness saved Max from bringing up the topic himself. "Actually, that's what I wanted to discuss with you. Valpa suggested it."

"Oh?"

"Valpa has the idiotic notion that I may have fallen in love with the woman."

"Why is it so idiotic?" Darvell's even tone contrasted with the tension Max knew his own voice projected. "Your brother fell in love with a human female, after all."

"He was much younger, and he had a sentimental fondness for ephemerals. I don't have those weaknesses."

"Then you don't think you love her?"

"What the devil is love? It's a word humans use to disguise lust or dependency."

"Do you feel dependent on this woman?" The question hinted at an unspoken "aha."

"I bonded with her, more or less accidentally. It happened in a moment of passion. Once our minds became open to each other, I delved deeper than I intended."

"And you want to repeat that experience, of course. What about her?"

"She rejected me. She doesn't trust me and thinks our attraction is purely physical desire."

"Do you think otherwise?"

"I don't know, confound it!" The memory of her warm flesh, the glow of her aura and the tang of her blood rushed over him. "All I know is that I want her back."

"Do you think you're addicted to her?"

"Possibly. I've never experienced that before, so how can I be sure? I can't stop craving her."

"Have you fed on others since you separated?"

"Of course." No vampire could go more than four or five days without human blood and keep his sanity, much less three weeks.

"Successfully? You've been able to keep it down?"

"Yes. It's not completely satisfying, but it enables me to function."

"Then you aren't physically addicted. You may have to face the possibility that you do love her."

For a second Max considered hanging up with a growl of contempt for the notion. He had asked for advice, though, hadn't he? And Darvell did have experience he lacked. "I don't know what the word means."

"Would you risk your life for her?"

"I've already done that." Max couldn't help smiling at the convoluted arguments Linnet had produced when he'd pointed out that fact. "She doesn't think it counts. She's afraid everything I did was purely opportunistic and selfish. She may be right."

"You're bonded with her. What did you feel when your thoughts merged with hers?"

"Ecstasy. Incredible…" He heard the hunger in his own voice and forced himself to a calmer tone. "I want to repeat that experience. Over and over, indefinitely." Even though it also meant exposing himself to her the way he had in those few unguarded seconds.

"Do you want to be with her for the rest of her life?"

"Her…?"

"Not yours." Darvell's tone hardened. "Understand, you'd be committing yourself to almost certain loss. She will die, and you'll survive. Do you consider the union worth the prospect of eventually losing it?"

"Damn it, I don't know!" He paused to tame his rapid breathing and heartbeat. "Darvell, how do you stand it? Knowing that?"

"Honestly? I try not to think about it. I consider it worth the price, though. We both do."

Striding out the back door, Max stood on his patio, gazing up at the stars in the cloudless mountain sky and wishing he could absorb their remote peace. "I hoped the bond would wear off by now."

"It doesn't. It weakens over time, goes dormant eventually, but it can always be revived with the proper stimulus."

"Then what do you suggest I do?"

"That depends on whether you want to be cured of the obsession or to make her completely yours."

"I want her." The memory of her intoxicating passion made his throat feel parched with thirst. The cilia in his palms bristled with longing to stroke her skin and feel the throb of her pulse.

"Make very sure of that before you start. Once you begin feeding on her regularly, you will become addicted. Very quickly, in fact. There'll be no backing out of the relationship."

"I can live with that." Could physical dependency torment him any worse than the emotional craving that gnawed at him?

"You must also exercise strict control over your appetite. If you overindulge, you'll undermine her health, possibly even endanger her life. And you have to give her fair warning—full disclosure. The potential health risks, the effects of the bond, everything. Love can't flourish with deceit."

"I understand that. I can handle it." He resisted the urge to tack "young upstart" onto the end of that sentence. As much as it grated on him to take lessons from a cub who'd barely passed his first half century, Max had to concede that he'd asked for the lecture.

"Can you care for her the way your brother did for his 'weakness'?"

"Don't taunt me with that," Max snarled. "I was wrong about Anthony. He loved his woman, if the word means putting her welfare above his own. I want to love Linnet. I just don't think I know how. Even the kind of sexuality she expects—"

"Yes, you have to consider quite a few practical matters like that. She doesn't know you aren't cross-fertile with human females."

"We didn't discuss it in detail."

"Before you can fairly expect a lifelong commitment from her, you have to make it clear that you may be able to couple with her, but you'll never be able to impregnate her."

"If she wants children…"

"You have to warn her, just as any infertile man would."

Max shook his head. "It will take some time to get used to the idea of being inferior to an ephemeral male in some ways. That's getting ahead of myself, though. She may not listen to me, much less accept me as a lover. Remember, she doesn't trust me."

"Did she say why?"

Max sighed in frustration. "As far as I could understand, she thinks I regard all human beings as lower animals, her included. I couldn't convince her that she'd changed my mind, at least about her, if not all the others."

"You implied that you saw her as an exception, and she didn't believe you? Can you blame her?"

"Then what do you suggest I do?"

"You have to demonstrate that you value her mind, her selfhood, not merely her blood." Amusement crept into Darvell's voice. "Not unlike a human male, except that with your woman, you also have to convince her that you aren't using mental control to make her desire you."

"And how the hell am I supposed to do that?" Though he knew it didn't make sense to lash out at the doctor, Max couldn't keep the annoyance from his voice.

"That's part of the test, isn't it? If you truly care for the woman, you'll know her well enough to think of some proof that will be meaningful to her."

Since it wouldn't be courteous to dismiss the advice as "voodoo," Max simply thanked Darvell while silently fuming.

"One more thing," said the doctor, before hanging up. "Contrary to the belief and practice of creatures like Nola, your brother had it right. Preying on an endless succession of casual victims is settling for second best. It's far more satisfying to bond with a single donor and merge, body and mind, with that one. If you have a chance at that union, don't throw it away."

Max spent the rest of that night and all of the next mulling over Darvell's advice, sifting the memories of every moment he'd spent with Linnet. On the following day, he caught a flight to Maryland.

Chapter 16

Linnet transferred the last box of Deanna's things from the car to the floor of her own garage. After Robin had accepted her offer to clear out the couple's apartment, Linnet had waited until almost the last minute, mid-July, to undertake the ordeal. She still felt detached from the rest of the family and her own everyday life. Sometimes she felt as if she was talking to people through a pane of glass. Her whole view of the universe had been shattered and reassembled in a bizarre new shape, and she couldn't tell anyone about it.

Thank goodness, she didn't have to return to the apartment again. Sorting Deanna's household possessions had been hard enough, but stumbling across a sketchbook partly filled with self-portraits of Deanna and a few drawings of Linnet herself had almost wrecked what little serenity she could claim. The clothes and nonperishable food had gone to charity, makeup and most other personal supplies into the trash. She'd packed only such items as pictures, books, CDs and jewelry, which had still required several trips with her compact car. She rubbed her dusty hands on her shorts and wiped sweat from her forehead. Grateful to have the job over with, she entered the house through the kitchen. A couple of minutes later, while she hesitated over whether she felt hungry enough to bother fixing a meal, the doorbell rang.

Who would visit her at five in the afternoon without phoning first? Since she wasn't expecting any packages, she marched to the door prepared to confront a salesperson or petition bearer. Squinting through the peephole, she saw the distorted shape of a man's face obscured by sunglasses.

A hand slowly reached into her field of vision and removed the glasses. Max.

To her horror, her first impulse was to throw herself into his arms. *This is insane! I can't possibly be glad to see him.*

Just when she'd rejoiced to think that chapter of her life was closed forever! She considered pretending not to be home. He could probably hear her heartbeat through the door, though. He could catch her if she tried to flee and outwait her if she stonewalled.

Unlocking the door, she opened it a crack. "You aren't here. You're a figment of my imagination."

His eyes swept up and down her body, making her shiver from more than the air conditioner's draft on her damp neck. "What do you mean?"

"I mean I've decided that entire trip never happened. I fantasized you, and now I'm cured. Don't waste your time trying to convince me any different."

"There is no cure for our bond." His voice reverberated through her like the bass notes of an organ.

"What bond? It doesn't exist, because vampires don't exist. You're a figment of my imagination."

"You know that isn't true." With one hand, he blocked the door she tried to shut.

"It's true for me if I want to believe it. Go away."

"I can't leave. I'm withering away with need for you. Give me a chance to show that our bond is not an illusion."

Though his voice lingered over the words like a caress, he made no attempt to invade her thoughts. That restraint weakened her defenses. Maybe she could trust him to carry on a civilized conversation. Rationalizing that if she locked him out, he would lay siege on the stoop, she opened the door.

"I drove straight from the airport in full daylight," he said, as he stepped into the living room. "Doesn't that count for something?"

"Just proves you don't like to lose, which I already knew." She detested the quaver in her voice. "Now that you're here, come in and sit down. Can I get you anything?" Remembering his favored type of refreshment, she blushed.

His eyes locked onto hers, traveled down to her breasts and reversed course to her neck. The blush grew hotter. Finally he said, "I'd appreciate some water."

She snatched at the excuse to flee to the kitchen. Suddenly realizing how grubby she looked, she paused to wash up at the sink. Wiping her face with a paper towel, she waited for her breathing to slow and her hands to stop shaking. So much for her plan to forget him.

When she entered the living room with a glass of ice water, he was waiting on the couch. Slightly calmer now, she noticed that he was holding a small, leather-bound book, which he placed on the coffee table before he took the glass from her. She caught her breath when their fingers touched. "What do you want here?" She sat on a chair out of his reach.

"As I said, you." He drank, watching her over the rim of the glass.

"We've been through this already." After his acceptance of her decision in California, why had he resurfaced to torment her?

"Since then, I've had three weeks to think it over." He gazed at her from violet-silver eyes shadowed by his dark brows. "I've come to the conclusion that I love you. And I can see in your aura that your feelings for me haven't faded."

Speechless at the shock of that word *love,* she had to gulp air before she could answer. "It's not fair. You can skim my emotions at will, but I can't read yours."

"You could if we opened our minds to each other. But you won't allow that, will you?"

Linnet shook her head. "One time was scary enough. I could hardly tell my thoughts from yours."

With a shuddering breath, he said, "Don't you think it was equally hard for me? But I would like to try again."

"Why? You should be glad you escaped falling for an 'ephemeral,' right?"

"Don't hold that prejudice against me. These weeks without you cured me of it, at least as far as you're concerned."

Threatening to melt under the heat of his gaze, she sat up straight and hardened the shell around her mind. "I don't buy that. What's so special about me?"

"You're beautiful."

She couldn't restrain a snort of disbelief. "Coated with dust?" She pulled the smudged T-shirt away from her sticky chest. "And with my hair a mess?" Though she'd tied it back with a scrunchy, loose strands dangled into her face.

"I would like to see your hair unbound, feel the weight of it." He clutched the cold glass like an anchor. "I wasn't referring mainly to your surface charms, dear Linnet. I'm enjoying the glow of your aura, the blood that pulses under your skin, the rhythm of your breath and heartbeat."

"That's another advantage you have over me, X-ray vision."

He sighed. "I would like to tell you in detail how I feel, but I'm not accustomed to framing such things in words.

Among ourselves, we don't have to, with our power to sense each other's emotions. And you won't let me reveal myself to you telepathically. So I decided to borrow some words." He held out the little book.

She automatically took it, hastily sitting down before he could touch her. It turned out to be a nineteenth-century edition of Shakespeare's sonnets with gold edging on the yellowed pages. She opened it to the inside cover.

At the top of the page she saw Max's name in faded ink. Farther down he had written in ballpoint pen, Until I can show you the Globe. Under his signature were the words Sonnet 75.

"Max—" Her breath caught in her throat.

With a tight-lipped nod, he silently mimed turning pages.

Flipping to the seventy-fifth sonnet, she scanned the first line: "So are you to my thoughts as food to life." She read through the poem, conscious of his eyes on her. When she reached the end, she backed up two lines and recited aloud, "'Possessing or pursuing no delight, Save what is had or must from you be took.'"

Max stared at her with what almost looked like anxiety. "You sound dubious."

"I can't help thinking that 'no delight' part is a little bit of an exaggeration." She stroked the leather binding.

"Not at all. I've spent the past few weeks thinking of you constantly. And, yes, it's been a disconcerting experience." His lips quirked in a fleeting smile. "You can't honestly claim you haven't had similar thoughts."

"I've done my best to forget you." Again she read aloud. "'And for the peace of you I hold such strife.'"

"Your poets do have a way with paradoxes."

"Well, I'll take the peace without the strife, thanks."

"Ah, Linnet." His voice softened to a caress. "Have you found peace in these past weeks?"

"What's the use of lying to a man who can read my emotions like some kind of thermometer?" She leaned toward him, hardly aware she was hugging the book to her chest. "Okay, I haven't had peace. I've had weird dreams, and when I wake up, I wonder if I imagined everything that happened on that trip." She flushed at the memory of a few less weird, more pleasurable dreams. "I can't discuss it with anybody. Whenever I talk to my parents and Robin, I have to cut off sentences in the middle to keep from saying things that would make them think I'm crazy."

"You are not. Deep within, you know it's all true."

"Yeah, well, it's not true in the everyday world where I have to live. Robin's seeing a counselor to help her deal. I can't do that, because it would be a waste of money to pay a therapist and then lie to him."

"Another example of your human need to catch experiences in nets of words. As it happens, I know a psychiatrist not far away—in Annapolis—with whom you could discuss these events freely, if that's what you want."

She blinked at him in surprise. She'd expected that offer almost as little as she'd expected a declaration of love. "Don't tell me he's a—he's like you?"

Max smiled at her astonishment. "Yes, why is that so strange? Most of us do hold some sort of job."

"You're kidding." She met his steady gaze, then quickly glanced away. "No, I guess not. You really wouldn't mind having me pour my heart out on a psychiatrist's couch?"

"Given basic safeguards, I'll accept anything that might break down the barriers between us."

Maybe he really had changed his mind about "ephemerals." Recognizing her eagerness to believe him, she knew she needed to exercise caution all the more. "What if I go through all that, just to have you get tired of me a few months or years from now?"

"Since I've waited almost five centuries to find a human

woman I can care about," he said, "I won't let you go once I have you."

"How can you promise what you'll do in the future?"

With unexpected gentleness, he said, "My love, could any human mate guarantee the future, either?"

"You've got a point." The way he sat motionless, speaking softly as if coaxing a wild doe to eat from his hand, made her wonder how he'd developed such patience in so short a time. He was making an honest effort not to pressure her. "But there's one big difference. I'll get sick and old, while you won't. You'll probably have a major change of heart when I develop gray hair, wrinkles and liver spots."

"I told you, we don't focus on superficial standards of beauty. Your heat, your fragrance, your…flavor, physical and emotional, won't fade."

"But eventually I'll die!" Anguish stabbed her at the thought of being only one in a long succession of women whose "flavor" he'd enjoyed. She jabbed a finger at the page that lay open to the sonnet. "'Doubting the filching age will steal his treasure.'" She clapped the book shut. "There's no doubt in this case."

His eyes mirrored her pain. "I'll postpone that moment as long as the 'filching age' will allow. And human lovers also lose each other to death, sooner or later."

"Why me? Because I resisted you? Because I'm a challenge?"

The indignant denial she half expected didn't come. "That was part of it at first. Then I saw your determination and courage demonstrated in other ways. And I touched your mind. I want to plunge into those depths again. I've craved that ever since I saw you last. I'm starved for you."

A hot blush crept over her neck and face. "With you, that's literal. Am I supposed to believe you haven't drunk any other woman's blood in three weeks?"

"No. I need human blood every few days. Once we've renewed our bond, though, I won't be able to feed on anyone else. Literally. I'll have to depend completely on you."

"Is that even possible?" The memory of Nola's attack gave Linnet a chill at the pit of her stomach. Yet the thought of "donating" to Max swept away that image and replaced it with a core of heat.

"Yes, with proper care. I know of couples who've managed an exclusive relationship for years." He stood and took a step toward Linnet. She sprang from the chair and edged away from him. "Please, I have no intention of forcing you, physically or mentally."

"I know. But if you touched me—" She chopped off the sentence, appalled that she'd admitted her weakness aloud.

"I won't do even that without your consent." His smile held a hint of smugness, though. "There are many details we need to discuss, if you decide to accept me. But it's all beside the point if you don't. Since you won't allow me into your mind, all I can do is ask. Linnet, could you love me?"

Light-headed, breathing hard, she clenched her fists at her sides to suppress the urge to rush at him and cling to him like a pillar of rock in a whirlwind. "I think I could."

He held out an open hand. "Shall we go into your bedroom?"

The breath whooshed out of her as if he'd punched her in the diaphragm. "Whoa! I said 'could.' How does that translate into jumping between the sheets?"

His brows arched in clear amusement. "I hope you know that if I planned to seduce you, I'd be more subtle. I have something else in mind, and it requires privacy."

"Why bother asking, when you could hypnotize me into anything you want? I'm not wearing the ankh."

"Surely you realize you don't need it. We've established that you have the strength in yourself, thanks to my brother's influence, reinforced by the exercises we performed. The necklace was only a prop."

"Like the magic feather that made the elephant think he could fly, but when he lost it, he found out it wasn't magic. All he needed was to believe in himself." At Max's puzzled look, she said, "Sorry, pop-culture reference."

Another thought popped into her head as she led the way to her room. "I guess you figure I'll quit my job so you can whisk me away to a life of luxury."

"That depends entirely on your wishes. I can work anywhere. If you don't want to leave your teaching position, we could divide our time between here and Colorado, which has much more pleasant summers."

"Maybe you really aren't looking for a pet, after all."

"If I were," he said with a chuckle, "I wouldn't choose a woman who knows so much about me." The smile vanished. "I want a bond-mate, a companion to nourish me with her passion as well as her blood."

Again the memory of the first time she had "nourished" him flashed across her mind, igniting a flame that nervousness couldn't entirely quench. "All right, what are we doing in the bedroom?" She sat in the chair at the dresser, where he couldn't alight next to her. Though the curtains were closed, blocking the late-afternoon sun, she could see him well enough.

"This." Sitting on the edge of the mattress, he untied his shoes. "You wanted to see me naked." Once divested of shoes and socks, he unbuttoned his shirt. She stared at him in silent shock. "Don't worry, it doesn't have to be reciprocal unless you choose. Although, I won't deny how much I crave the sight and touch of you."

"I'll think about it." "Think" wasn't quite the word for the turmoil in her brain and body. Already she itched to stroke the fine hair on his chest and listen to him purr. She noticed a tremor in his hands. *I don't believe this, he's nervous, too.*

"No other female has ever seen me unclothed." He shrugged out of the shirt and unfastened his belt buckle.

"You mean no human female, don't you?" *Oh, Lord, he's really undressing!*

"No, I meant what I said. I've never been chosen to mate, so I've never had a reason to do this with anyone."

"You're telling me you've never—" It seemed incredible that a man who'd ravished her into oblivion was technically a virgin.

"You needn't look at me in that pitying way," he said with a grin. "I can't miss what I've never had. Besides, according to males of my species who've experienced both, feasting on the passion of a willing donor far surpasses the intensity of simple mating."

"Drinking blood is better than sex?"

"For us, it *is* sex—or rather, our means of erotic satisfaction. And it's more than the blood. The donor's fulfillment feeds us." In his voice she heard a longing that echoed the burning intensity of his gaze. "Yet for the first time I feel I have missed something vital. I want to join with you and fulfill you in every way, with every facet of my body and mind. But only if you desire it."

Her cheeks burned at the thought of how she'd writhed in delirium under his touch. "Just how many other women have you 'feasted' on the way you did me? Hundreds? Thousands?"

"No others, not like that. I've never allowed any others to know the full truth about my nature. I've never before merged my thoughts with a donor's and stripped my own emotions bare." After stepping out of his slacks, he removed his briefs, too, and draped the clothes over the headboard. The triangle of hair ended in a point at his navel, below which a thin line of the same velvety dark hair arrowed downward. He looked like an ordinary man below the waist. Except that few ordinary men had lean, catlike muscles overlaid by skin the paleness of marble. "I'm thirsty for you. Not just for your blood, but for that total union. I've dreamed of it over and over, then awakened feeling hollow."

Hollow. Oh, yes, so have I! She flashed on a fantasy of twining herself around him and drawing him into her to fill that aching emptiness. She sensed his awareness of that image and the way his thoughts mirrored hers, though he said nothing.

Conscious that she was staring, she dragged her gaze up to his face. "I've dreamed, too. Lots of times. About the time you drank—the time we bonded. If that's what you call it."

He nodded. "My kind aren't supposed to dream with such frequency and vividness. It's never happened to me before. As if you had invaded my mind and wouldn't leave."

"I felt that way too, about you. But you were a couple of thousands of miles away, so it wasn't you. It was me." Admitting her desire aloud, with the reassurance that it wasn't one-sided, loosened the tightness in her chest. "What now?"

"Whatever you decide. I'm entirely at your mercy."

"I want to touch you."

He froze, not even visibly breathing. Linnet got up from the chair and stood over him. When she ran her palms down his chest, enjoying the silken-velvet texture of the hair, he tilted his head to look up at her. Determined not to give way to her fears, she met his eyes. A trace of red glinted in their silver.

She picked up his right hand, turned it over, and fingered the tiny hairs in the palm. He shivered as if her touch chilled him. "What's wrong?" she murmured.

"Nothing. It's very…intense."

"This?" She traced a circle on his open hand.

"Yes…" he sighed. "It tingles. Almost as intensely as when I caress you and feel the heat of your blood."

The words set off a tingling in her own body. Her nipples peaked. She trailed her fingers down his chest again. This time she didn't stop at the waist. When she reached the nest of hair at the apex of his thighs, she paused. He encouraged her with a slow nod.

She gently closed her hand around his shaft. Unlike a human male, he hadn't shown any response there so far. When she squeezed, though, the flesh hardened. "You like that?"

He closed his eyes momentarily. "Any touch from you brings pleasure."

"You said that kind of contact wasn't a priority for you."

"It isn't." He opened his eyes and made a sound like a rumbling purr, while she stroked up and down. "That doesn't mean I can't enjoy it. With you."

With her free hand, she lifted his hand to her lips and flicked the fine hairs with her tongue. He convulsed as if she'd bitten him. *Weird,* she thought. *This is more of an erogenous zone than...?* Smiling at his discomfort, she licked his palm again and skimmed her fingernails over his erection.

"Linnet, please," he groaned. "Let me touch you."

"All right," she whispered.

He insinuated one hand into her hair and pulled it free of the scrunchy, rubbing the back of her neck until she wished she could purr, too. His other hand crept under her T-shirt and cupped each breast in turn. She arched her back, impatient with the barrier of her bra.

As if he could read her thoughts even in the absence of mental contact, he said, "I want to savor you without all this."

Past worrying about the wisdom of letting him get that close, she peeled off her shirt, then unhooked the bra and tossed it aside. He fondled both breasts, the hairs in his palms tickling the nipples, making them harden and prickle. "Oh, yes," he hissed.

"That's not all you want, is it?"

"My whole body is ravenous. I want to run my hands over your naked skin, taste you, bathe in the glow of your aura." Abruptly, he stopped caressing her. "Forgive me. I didn't plan to influence you this way."

"Too late," she gasped. "Don't stop now." At his questioning look, she said, "Don't worry, I won't accuse you of seducing me out of my right mind. I want you, too. I admit it. You satisfied now?"

"I haven't begun to be satisfied." With a growl, he returned one hand to her neck, massaging the nape under her hair and teasing the pulse point at the side of her throat, while his other hand attacked the zipper of her shorts.

Trembling, she helped him, wrestling with a tangle of cloth until she stood over him fully exposed. Clasping her derriere, he lowered his mouth to her waist. He nibbled a path over her stomach, down to the triangle of hair and into the cleft below. A bolt of fire lanced through her. Moaning, she grabbed his shoulders, afraid she might collapse. Her nails dug into his flesh. Like a dancing flame, his tongue flickered over the aching nub until she exploded.

"You taste wonderful." He eased her onto the bed. Her head spinning, she let him place her on her back. "It's almost the same flavor as your blood. And you smell delicious."

A hot blush spread over her whole body. "All sweaty, with no perfume?"

"I don't want perfume. It only disguises your irresistible fragrance." To her surprise, he licked her stomach, circling her navel and making her skin tingle. "What a delectably salty appetizer. May I give you pleasure again?"

"You didn't ask permission the first time." She could hardly force herself to meet his crimson-tinged gaze.

"Your body invited it. I felt your need. But I don't want to go any further against your wishes." He turned onto his back. "What do you want of me now?"

She clasped his erection again. "If we made love in the regular way, should I worry about getting pregnant?"

"No, our males are infertile except with females of our own race." His voice wavered, as if he worried about how she might react to this admission. She couldn't focus on side issues now, though.

"But you could still…penetrate?" The firmness of his shaft left her little doubt.

"If that is what you want."

Before she could lose her nerve, pushed him to his back and she climbed astride him. Her hot wetness opened to him. Even if she'd changed her mind at the last second, her body couldn't have stopped. He gasped aloud as she took him in. "Linnet, please, I need—"

"What?" she whispered, already absorbed in the rhythm of rocking on top of him, her nails scoring his chest.

"Let me in—all the way."

Hearing the desperation in his voice, she couldn't deny him. She threw her mind wide-open. He slipped in as smoothly as he'd plunged into her body. Yet just before they completed the merging, she sensed fear in him. He dreaded getting swallowed up as much as she did. The kernel of ice at the center of her own fear dissolved at that realization. *It's all right, Max. Come in.* She dove into the depths of his mind like jumping into a cold pond, which almost instantly heated to a steaming whirlpool.

Their thoughts flowed together like two streams into a lake, yet each current remained itself. *What was I afraid of, anyway?* She felt his delight at the pressure of her internal muscles around him. At the same time, she felt her own climax building and sensed his passion rising to its peak in unison with hers.

Yes, he silently urged. *Again—again—let me soar with you—once more—yes!* She spiraled up over and over, carrying him with her, while his renewed passion ignited hers whenever it began to fade. *Draw my blood, Linnet. Taste me.*

Spurred by the frantic need that strained within him, she scored his chest with her nails. In their aroused condition, neither of them felt the scratch as pain. When the blood trickled, he begged, *Now, taste me. Please!*

She licked the drops and felt him shudder in fresh surges of ecstasy. Unlike the faintly salty taste of her own blood when she'd occasionally sucked on a small cut, Max's vital fluid fizzed like champagne on her tongue. Yet she also felt his sensations, a burning in his throat and the pit of his stomach. *You're thirsty.*

I told you that. But if you don't want your blood sipped, I'm content with the energy you've lavished on me. It's more satisfaction than I've had in—than I've ever had.

Go ahead. Drink! She threw her head back. His teeth nipped the hollow of her throat, and his tongue lapped, goading her to another cycle of climaxes. She tasted the tart sweetness of her blood on his lips. Finally she melted into a blissful daze.

When her head stopped reeling, she snuggled up to the cool, smooth length of his body. "See, there was nothing to be afraid of."

Tightening his arm around her, he nuzzled the top of her head. "Are you reassuring me or yourself?"

"Both, I guess. Taking the plunge into total commitment can be scary whether you're human or not." She drew breath for the final dive. "Max, I love you." While she waited for his response, her heart raced with anxiety, a sound she knew he could hear.

"And I love you." The statement sounded tentative, almost a question. "I love you," he repeated more firmly. "It feels very strange to say that. But it must be true, because I can't bear the thought of losing you. Linnet, could you accept living a large percentage of your future in darkness?"

"Why not? Darkness is just as natural as light."

He cupped her face in his hands. "Will you spend your life with me?"

"No matter how short it is compared to yours?" She couldn't forget the catastrophic end of Anthony and Deanna's love.

Max guided her hand to his chest, so that she felt the pounding of his heart. "Forget about duration. No one can guarantee that. Take each night as it comes. We'll make every one unforgettable."

"Is that a promise?"

"Oh, yes, my beloved. Always."

Joy bubbled up in her. She nudged him onto his back and rolled on top of him. "In that case, want to start with tonight?"

* * * * *

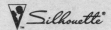
Silhouette®

INTIMATE MOMENTS™

presents the first book in an exciting
new miniseries

FOREVER IN A DAY

A few hours can change your life.

Midnight Hero
(Silhouette Intimate Moments, #1359)

DIANA DUNCAN

New Year's Eve: Beautiful Bailey Chambers breaks up
with SWAT team leader Conall O'Rourke on the very
day he'd planned to propose. She's already lost her
father to his high-stakes job, and she won't lose Con,
too. But when they get caught up in a bank robbery
in progress, Bailey is forced to experience her worst
fears—and witness her lover placing himself in grave
danger as he plots to save the hostages. For Con,
surviving the hours of terror is easy. Winning Bailey's
heart is the true test of his strength. Can he get them
out of this with their lives—and love—intact?

*Don't miss this exciting story—
only from Silhouette Books.*

Available at your favorite retail outlet.

Receive a
FREE copy of
Maggie Shayne's
**THICKER
THAN WATER**
when you
purchase
**BLUE
TWILIGHT.**

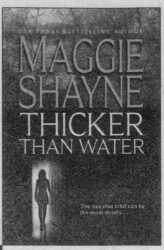

To receive your
FREE copy of
THICKER THAN
WATER, written by
bestselling author
Maggie Shayne,
send us 1 proof
of purchase from
Maggie Shayne's
March 2005 title
BLUE TWILIGHT.

*For full details, look inside
BLUE TWILIGHT.*

www.MIRABooks.com

MSPOPMIRA

If you enjoyed what you just read,
then we've got an offer you can't resist!

Take 2 bestselling
love stories FREE!
Plus get a FREE surprise gift!

Clip this page and mail it to Silhouette Reader Service™

IN U.S.A.	**IN CANADA**
3010 Walden Ave.	P.O. Box 609
P.O. Box 1867	Fort Erie, Ontario
Buffalo, N.Y. 14240-1867	L2A 5X3

YES! Please send me 2 free Silhouette Intimate Moments® novels and my free surprise gift. After receiving them, if I don't wish to receive anymore, I can return the shipping statement marked cancel. If I don't cancel, I will receive 6 brand-new novels every month, before they're available in stores! In the U.S.A., bill me at the bargain price of $4.24 plus 25¢ shipping and handling per book and applicable sales tax, if any*. In Canada, bill me at the bargain price of $4.99 plus 25¢ shipping and handling per book and applicable taxes**. That's the complete price and a savings of at least 10% off the cover prices—what a great deal! I understand that accepting the 2 free books and gift places me under no obligation ever to buy any books. I can always return a shipment and cancel at any time. Even if I never buy another book from Silhouette, the 2 free books and gift are mine to keep forever.

245 SDN DZ9A
345 SDN DZ9C

Name	(PLEASE PRINT)
Address	Apt.#
City	State/Prov.	Zip/Postal Code

Not valid to current Silhouette Intimate Moments® subscribers.

Want to try two free books from another series?
Call 1-800-873-8635 or visit www.morefreebooks.com.

* Terms and prices subject to change without notice. Sales tax applicable in N.Y.
** Canadian residents will be charged applicable provincial taxes and GST.
   All orders subject to approval. Offer limited to one per household].
   ® are registered trademarks owned and used by the trademark owner and or its licensee.

INMOM04R   ©2004 Harlequin Enterprises Limited

eHARLEQUIN.com

The Ultimate Destination for Women's Fiction

For **FREE online reading**, visit
www.eHarlequin.com now and enjoy:

Online Reads
Read **Daily** and **Weekly** chapters from
our Internet-exclusive stories by your
favorite authors.

Interactive Novels
Cast your vote to help decide how these
stories unfold…then stay tuned!

Quick Reads
For shorter romantic reads, try our
collection of Poems, Toasts, & More!

Online Read Library
Miss one of our online reads?
Come here to catch up!

Reading Groups
Discuss, share and rave with other
community members!

For great reading online,
visit www.eHarlequin.com today!

INTONL04R